NEW YORK REVIEW BOOKS
CLASSICS

THE MEMOIRS OF ...
YOUNG WIVES

HONORÉ DE BALZAC (1799–1850), one of the greatest
and most influential of novelists, was born in Tours and
educated at the Collège de Vendôme and the Sorbonne. He
began his career as a pseudonymous writer of sensational
potboilers before achieving success with a historical novel, *The
Chouans*. Balzac then conceived his great work, *La Comédie
humaine*, an ongoing series of novels in which he set out to offer
a complete picture of contemporary society and manners. Always
working under an extraordinary burden of debt, Balzac wrote
some eighty-five novels in the course of his last twenty years,
including such masterpieces as *Père Goriot*, *Eugénie Grandet*,
Lost Illusions, and *Cousin Bette*. In 1850, he married Eveline
Hanska, a rich Polish woman with whom he had long con-
ducted an intimate correspondence. Three months later he died.

JORDAN STUMP is a professor of French at the University
of Nebraska–Lincoln; the author, most recently, of *The Other
Book: Bewilderments of Fiction*; and the translator of some
twenty works of (mostly) contemporary French prose by
authors such as Marie NDiaye, Éric Chevillard, Antoine
Volodine, and Jean-Philippe Toussaint. His translation of
Claude Simon's *The Jardin des Plantes* won the French-
American Foundation's annual translation prize in 2001.

MORRIS DICKSTEIN is a distinguished professor emeritus
at the Graduate Center of the City University of New York and
the author, most recently, of *Dancing in the Dark*, a cultural
history of the Great Depression, and *Why Not Say What
Happened*, a memoir.

THE MEMOIRS OF TWO YOUNG WIVES

HONORÉ DE BALZAC

Translated from the French by
JORDAN STUMP

Introduction by
MORRIS DICKSTEIN

NEW YORK REVIEW BOOKS

nyrb

New York

THIS IS A NEW YORK REVIEW BOOK
PUBLISHED BY THE NEW YORK REVIEW OF BOOKS
435 Hudson Street, New York, NY 10014
www.nyrb.com

This work received support from the French Ministry of Foreign Affairs and
the Cultural Services of the French Embassy in the United States through their
publishing assistance program.

Library of Congress Cataloging-in-Publication Data
Names: Balzac, Honoré de, 1799–1850, author. | Dickstein, Morris, writer of
    introduction. | Stump, Jordan, 1959– translator.
Title: The memoirs of two young wives / by Honore de Balzac ; introduction by
    Morris Dickstein ; translated by Jordan Stump.
Other titles: Mémoires de deux jeunes mariées. English
Description: New York : New York Review Books 2018. | Series: NYRB Classics
Identifiers: LCCN 2017036012 (print) | LCCN 2017036677 (ebook) | ISBN
    9781681371269 (epub) | ISBN 9781681371252 (paperback)
Subjects: | BISAC: FICTION / Psychological. | FICTION / Family Life.
Classification: LCC PQ2165.D4 (ebook) | LCC PQ2165.D4 E5 2018 (print) |
    DDC 843/.7—dc23
LC record available at https://lccn.loc.gov/2017036012

ISBN 978-1-68137-125-2
Available as an electronic book; ISBN 978-1-68137-126-9

Printed in the United States of America on acid-free paper.
10 9 8 7 6 5 4 3 2 1

INTRODUCTION

OUT OF the more than ninety novels that make up the so-called
Human Comedy of Honoré de Balzac, only a handful are still widely
read or assigned in schools, at least in the Anglo-American world:
Père Goriot, *Eugénie Grandet*, *Lost Illusions*, perhaps *Cousin Bette*,
the late novel from which I first learned to read French by dutifully
looking up every other word. Yet Balzac was arguably the creator of
the modern social novel, "the first and foremost member of his craft"
and "the master of us all," according to Henry James, who wrote
about him again and again. His influence was pivotal for writers as
varied as James, Flaubert, Zola, Dostoyevsky, and Dreiser, all of whom
imitated yet rebelled against him. To his successors he was a rough-
hewn genius with an immense appetite for life. "What a man he
would have been had he known how to write," said Flaubert. "But
that was the only thing he lacked. After all, an artist would never
have accomplished so much nor had such breadth." They were awed
by the scope and sheer abundance of his work, as well as his mastery
of scenic detail. So were many social historians and radical writers,
beginning with Marx and Engels. Marx lauded his "profound grasp
of real conditions," despite his self-proclaimed Catholic and monar-
chist views, while Engels felt he had written almost a complete history
of French society from 1816 to 1848, novels from which Engels said
he'd learned more than from any economist. For twentieth-century
critics like Georg Lukács and Erich Auerbach, his work, with its
intricate linkage between characters and their milieu, formed the
very template of literary realism.

Balzac did not at first set out to write a portrait of his age. Always fluent and prolific, in the 1820s he churned out pulp and Gothic novels under pseudonyms before trying his hand as a printer and businessman. But inspired in part by the historical novels of Walter Scott, he became what he called the "secretary" of French society, the observer who cataloged its complex formations. In his 1842 preface to *La Comédie humaine*, the ambitious framework he now conceived for his work, he said he wanted to write "the history which so many historians have neglected, that of *Moeurs* [manners, morals]." On the model of a zoologist classifying animal life, he had become, as he saw it, a "painter of types of humanity, a narrator of the drama of private life, an archaeologist of social furniture, a cataloger of professions, a registrar of good and evil." On this huge, multi-paneled canvas, which ultimately would include more than two thousand characters, many of them reappearing in book after book, he had hoped to "detect the hidden sense of this vast assembly of figures, passions, and incidents."

While complete sets of Balzac's work in English translation were once common, few contemporary readers have sought out many of his lesser-known books. Graham Robb concludes his prodigious 1994 biography of Balzac with the terse suggestion that "Unknown masterpieces are waiting to be rediscovered." *The Memoirs of Two Young Wives*, first published in 1842, is not exactly a masterpiece, but it's a singular work, one of Balzac's Scenes of Private Life, full of arresting detail yet cutting against the grain of his received image as a social realist. James himself wrote a long preface to a 1902 translation, but the novel soon dropped without a trace from the English-speaking world. It's a gem of a book, occasionally florid and schematic yet engrossing, and this new translation by Jordan Stump makes for precisely the kind of rediscovery that Robb invited.

It's not hard to see why the book has attracted little notice even in its own time. A novel like *Père Goriot* is a symphonic work with settings ranging from a faded pension to the great houses of Paris, with a broad spectrum of characters from naive to diabolical, a stark family drama with echoes of *King Lear*, and at its heart a coming-of-age story that exposes the whole fabric of a vicious, amoral society. *The Memoirs of Two Young Wives*, with only two main characters, is a small-scale chamber work, one of the last French epistolary novels, a mode that belongs more to the previous century than to the 1840s. It too is a coming-of-age story, but instead of the young man from the provinces who trades his innocence for vaulting ambition and lays siege to French society, it's made up of the letters exchanged between two young women who leave a Carmelite convent before taking their vows, confronting the limited choices available to them in the wider world. Both spring from the minor aristocracy, their convent life the consequence of their social position, not any religious vocation. Despite the rights granted to women under Napoleon's more egalitarian civil code, still in force after the restoration of the Bourbon monarchy, their inheritances were to be diverted to foster the fortunes of their brothers, the eldest sons who would carry the family title. In the convent they have developed a deep bond, a "secret inner life" that would be played out in their letters. At one level the novel would be a bold exploration of female friendship, surprising from so masculine a writer as Balzac, the titanic figure we know from Rodin's sculpted image. The letters make up a rich tapestry of private life and feeling for women barred from playing any public role. They tell a story of the opposite paths the two of them take in love and marriage, mapping more intimate ground than the social novels for which Balzac has been most appreciated.

That intimacy, with its direct access to the inner life behind the social mask, is a hallmark of the epistolary novels on which Balzac modeled this work, especially Samuel Richardson's *Clarissa* (1747–48), the longest English novel, perhaps the first psychological novel, and its French offshoot, Jean-Jacques Rousseau's *Julie, or the New Heloise* (1761), two celebrated works centered on women, both of them among Balzac's most cherished books. Falling in love with her tutor, an exiled, impoverished Spanish nobleman, one of Balzac's protagonists, Louise, like Rousseau's Julie, actually reenacts some of the medieval Heloise story, her forbidden romance with the philosopher and rising churchman Peter Abelard. Meanwhile, her bosom friend Renée quickly makes a marriage of convenience to the frail son of Provençal gentry, twenty years her elder. Both women embark on discreet missions of redemption, lending their strength to the damaged men they marry. The Spaniard Felipe, heir to a dukedom but deemed an enemy by Spain's Bourbon king, has ceded to a younger brother both his title and the woman he loved. Repeatedly described as physically ugly, "an old young man," he can't imagine attracting another woman until he falls for the witty, vivacious, and passionate Louise. Renée's husband Louis is even more needy, for he's returned a broken man from Russian captivity in Napoleon's wars. With support from her friend Louise, she deftly manages both his family life and his advancement to a title and a parliamentary position.

All this backstory is sketched in only briefly since the men in the book are dim figures, rarely heard from directly, seen almost entirely through the lens of the confiding women. Socially, these women take care to recede into the shadows, especially Renée, who is eager to maintain the appearance of a proper wife and mother. But the letters, free of any third-person narration, highlight their inner strength, their depth of feeling, and their starkly conflicting views of love and marriage. Louise is very much the romantic heroine, determined to live out a grand passion with the men she loves. Felipe himself is a figure out of romance, not only a Spaniard, hence broodingly grave and hot-blooded, but "the last Abencerrage," descended from the fiery Moors who conquered parts of Spain from North Africa until they were expelled or Christianized toward the end of the fifteenth century. (Their legend had only recently been popularized on the stage and in an 1826 tale by Chateaubriand.) Louise's second great love, even more intense and possessive, involves another romantic figure, barely realized, a stereotypical poet. With him she leaves Paris for a bucolic love nest, not far from the city, that excludes society altogether.

Renée, on the other hand, in her own deep provincial life, blends in effortlessly with both nature and society. Pragmatically, she accepts marriage to a man she does not love, a marriage of companionship, social ambition, and common interest. "My life may never be great, but it will be tranquil, smooth, and untroubled," or so she imagines. She takes care to create a beautiful landscape, directs her passion toward motherhood and her busy mind to advancing her weakened husband's position. When children do come, Balzac's physical evocation of pregnancy, childbirth, breastfeeding, and childcare make up some of the most astonishing pages in the book, written completely from a woman's point of view. (Balzac saw himself as an androgynous figure with a "woman's heart.") Renée lives in her body, in her maternal feeling, while leading from behind. Her approach to marriage is thoroughly rational—though far too "calculating," in the view of her friend—but her tormenting anxieties about the children, especially when one of them falls ill, parallel the anxiety Louise has about her lovers. The pangs of jealousy threaten Louise's romantic dream and drive her to a theatrical, almost operatic denouement anticipated from the very first page of the novel.

By the end it has long been clear that the book is less about two women and their stories than a trenchant dialogue about love and marriage by a writer who never hesitated to weave direct commentary and social argument into his story, contrasting these women not by their style or their voices, as Rousseau himself urged (and as a modern writer surely would), but by their clashing ideas. This makes *The Memoirs of Two Young Wives* as much a dialectical as an epistolary novel, built on the contrasts and binaries embodied in the two women's unfolding lives, for all their nourishing friendship. Louise first emerges as a "blithe and worldly girl" in glittering society, witty and sardonic, something of a Jane Austen heroine. As they privately chronicle their hopes and experiences to each other, they highlight the differences between the city and the country, Paris and the provinces, society and domesticity. Once Renée settles quickly on marriage while Louise falls in love with her exiled tutor, their letters turn into a clash between imagination and reason, headlong passion and sober calculation. As Renée invests all in creating a family, Louise pursues an ideal vision of romance, an insufficient word for the kind of "boundless" transcendence she seeks in love. Her marriage is a conflagration, burningly sexual but also beyond the sexual. She longs for a completely transfiguring intimacy of souls, something that would suffer no aging or abatement, no descent into the routine or the familiar, no intrusion from workaday social relations or child-rearing. Hers is a version of the cult of romantic love, the Tristan myth explored by Denis de Rougemont in *Love in the Western World*, a consummation beyond the body that can only be ratified by death, seen as a final perfection, beyond loss or change.

Renée, on the other hand, has "embraced Devotion as a shipwrecked sailor desperately clings to the mast." To her Louise has been "depraving the institution of marriage," living out the "voluptuous excesses that the law unwittingly allows," trying "to be both the wife and the mistress." She warns her friend that "an immense, boundless happiness will destroy you in the end." For Renée, such "devouring" passion—or passion in general—must inevitably decline; permanence in marriage rests instead on a "deep, serene mutual familiarity." She briskly chooses duty over desire, the bond of friendship, companionship over heedless love, yet her call to "devotion" exposes an underlying desperation. One fascinating feature of the book is the reversals that occur as these two women—by now less women than counters in a philosophical debate—live each other's lives vicariously: Louise, otherwise content, cries out in the end for never having had children while Renée unexpectedly laments having missed out on love, being reduced to routine. This is only one of the many doubling effects that gives the novel a classical sense of symmetry.

Baudelaire, in some startlingly incisive remarks about Balzac's work not long after his death, pointed to another feature of this duality. "It often surprises me that Balzac's greatest claim to fame is to pass as an observer; it always seemed to me that his principal merit lay in being a visionary, a passionate visionary. All of his characters are endowed with that life force by which he himself was animated. All of his tales are as vibrantly colorful as dreams." This is why his characters, like those of Dickens, seem so exaggerated, not simply specimens of social types but, as Baudelaire says, the palpable result of Balzac's own visionary intensity. All of them are "more fiercely alive, more active and cunning in their struggles, more patient in their misfortunes, more gluttonous in their pleasures, more angelic in their devotions, than any real-world comedy might reveal to us. . . .

Every soul is a weapon loaded to the muzzle with willpower. Indeed, this is Balzac himself." James, in his introduction, made a similar point about Balzac the historian or reporter and Balzac the "originator," with "his unequalled power of putting people on their feet, planting them before us in their habit as they lived," but doing so "with the inner vision all the while wide-awake." By the "secret of an insistence," says James in his inimitable late style, Balzac "warms his facts into life." Both Baudelaire and James see Balzac's apparent flaws, his heated exaggerations, as secret strengths.

It is not hard to take the argument at the heart of *The Memoirs of Two Young Wives* as a representation of these two sides of Balzac's creative mind, as dramatized in the friction between Louise the visionary, drawn to peak experience, uncompromising and intense in her demands upon life, and Renée the realist, strictly practical, with her iron sense of limits. Together, these two qualities were the source of what commentators have sharply noted: Balzac's visceral *presence* in his work. As one of his best biographers, V. S. Pritchett, put it, "Balzac is always felt as a sanguine presence in his writing, breathless with knowledge, fantasy, and things seen." Describing his "ubiquity" as a novelist, he adds, "There is a spry, pungent, and pervasive sense that in any scene he was *there*, and in the flesh." In the range of his empathy, in the busily peopled world he creates, with characters recurring like real people from book to book, Balzac can be compared not only to Dickens but to Shakespeare. Even as spare a novel as *The Memoirs of Two Young Wives*, with its weighty themes but limited cast, helps explain just how he did it, for its inner drama could well be a reflection of his own divided self.

—MORRIS DICKSTEIN

THE MEMOIRS OF TWO
YOUNG WIVES

To George Sand

Dear George, this dedication will add no luster to your name, which will rather cast its magical glow over my book, but there is neither calculation nor modesty behind it. I seek only to attest to the real friendship that we have kept up through all our travels and separations, in spite of our work and the rigors of our world. That sentiment will doubtless never change. The parade of comradely names that will accompany my works adds a pleasure to the pains caused me by their number, for they are not without their travails, to speak only of the aspersions my threatening fecundity has earned me—as if the world posing before me were not more prolific still! Will it not be a fine thing, George, if one day the archaeologist of long-lost literatures rediscovers in that parade only illustrious names, noble hearts, pure and sacred friendships, and the greatest glories of this century? May I not take more pride in that incontestable happiness than in any ever-disputable success? For those who know you well, is it not a happiness to be able to call oneself, as I do here,

Your friend,
de Balzac
Paris, June 1840

PART ONE

I

FROM MADEMOISELLE LOUISE DE CHAULIEU TO
MADEMOISELLE RENÉE DE MAUCOMBE

Paris, September[1]

My dear doe, I too am now out in the world! And unless you have
written me in Blois, I am also the first to arrive at our charming
rendezvous by correspondence. Unstick your beautiful black eyes
from my first sentence, and save your exclamations for a later letter,
the one in which I tell you of my first love. People always talk about
the first love; is there a second, then? "Hush now!" you must surely
be saying, "and tell me: How did you ever escape from that convent,
where you were meant to take your vows?" My dear, whatever may
go on among the Carmelites, the miracle of my deliverance is the
most natural thing in the world. The protests of a horrified conscience
simply overruled the dictates of a long-settled design. My aunt had
no desire to see me die of consumption; she won out over my mother,
who was still prescribing the novitiate as the only cure for my frailty.
That happy ending was hastened by the bleak melancholy I fell into
after you left. And so now I am in Paris, my angel, and it is to you
that I owe the joy of being here.

My Renée, had you seen me the day I found myself without you,
you would have been proud to inspire such deep emotion in so young
a heart. So much did we dream as one, so often did we spread our
wings together, so long did we live a shared life that I believe our souls
were knit one to the other, like those two Hungarian girls[2] whose
death was recounted to us by Monsieur Beauvisage, who certainly
did not live up to his name—was there ever a man better suited to
be a convent doctor! And did you perhaps suffer right along with
your darling? Listless and despondent, I could only think of the many

bonds that united us, counting them off one by one; I feared they'd
been broken forever by the distance between us, and I conceived a
loathing for existence, like a heartbroken lovebird. Death seemed to
me a sweet relief, and I made my way toward it without complaint.
Oh, the thought of being alone at the Carmelite convent of Blois, the
terror of taking my vows in that place without a prologue like Mademoiselle de la Vallière's,[3] and without my Renée! It was an affliction,
a mortal affliction. That unchanging existence, in which every hour
brings a duty, a prayer, a task so perfectly identical that no matter
where you may be in the world you know just what a Carmelite is
doing at any hour of the day or night; that horrible existence in which
it matters not that the things around us are or are not, had for us
become an existence of the greatest variety: our soaring spirits knew
no boundaries, fantasy had given us the key to its kingdoms. By turns,
we each made a charming hippogriff[4] for the other, the livelier of us
rousing the sleepier, and our souls frolicked in tandem as they laid
claim to the world that had been forbidden us. Even in the *Lives of
the Saints* we could find an aid to the understanding of the most
secret things! The day your sweet company was stolen from me, I
became what a Carmelite is in our eyes, a modern-day Danaïd who
does not seek to fill a bottomless barrel but rather, day after day, hoists
an empty bucket from I know not what well, hoping to find it full.
My aunt had no idea of our secret inner life. She could not understand
my weariness of existence, she who has made a heavenly world for
herself in the two arpents of her convent. If it is to be embraced at
our age, the religious life demands an excessive simplicity that you
and I, my doe, do not have, or the sort of burning devotion that makes
my aunt so sublime. My aunt sacrificed herself for the sake of a cherished brother, but who can sacrifice herself for the sake of strangers,
or of ideas?

For what will soon be two weeks, I have had so many free-spirited
words trapped inside me, so many meditations buried deep in my
heart, so many observations to express and stories to tell that can
only be told to you, that without the stopgap of written confidences
standing in for our precious chats, I would suffocate. How vitally we

require the life of the heart! I begin my chronicle this morning imagining that yours has already been started, that very soon I will live in the heart of your beautiful valley of Gémenos,[5] of which I know only what you have told me, just as you will live in Paris, of which you know only what we dreamt of together.

Well then, my lovely child, on a morning that will remain forever signaled by a pink marker in the book of my life, my grandmother's last valet, Philippe, came from Paris with a lady's maid to take me away. When my aunt summoned me to her room and told me the news, I stood speechless with joy; I could only stare in disbelief.

"My child," she said to me in her hoarse voice, "I can see that you do not regret leaving me, but this is not the final farewell. We shall see each other again. God has marked your brow with the sign of the elect; you have the sort of pride that can lead just as well to hell as to heaven, but you are too noble to descend! I know you better than you know yourself: passion will not be for you what it is for ordinary women."

She gently drew me to her and kissed my brow, stamping it with the flame that devours her, that has dimmed the azure of her pupils, wrinkled her flaxen temples, left her eyelids drooping and her beautiful face sallow. She gave me gooseflesh.

I kissed her hands, then answered, "Dear aunt, if your wonderful kindness has not made me find in your Paraclete[6] a place salubrious to the body and comforting to the heart, I will have to shed so many tears before I return to it that you would never wish to see me again. I will come back to this place only when I have been betrayed by a Louis XIV of my own, and if ever I catch hold of one, only death will tear him from my arms! I fear no Madame de Montespan."

"Go on, then, you mad girl," she said with a smile, "do not leave those silly ideas here, take them away with you, and know that you are more a Montespan than a La Vallière."

I gave her a kiss. That poor, frail woman could not resist seeing me to the carriage, her gaze fixed now on the paternal coat of arms, now on me.

Night came upon me unawares in Beaugency, lost as I was in a bemusement provoked by that singular farewell. What would I find in this world I so longed for? As it turned out, the first thing I found was no one to welcome me. All the preparations I had made in my heart were for naught. My mother was at the Bois de Boulogne, my father at the Council of State; I was told that my brother the Duke de Rhétoré comes home only to dress for dinner. I was shown to my rooms by Miss Griffith (she has claws)[7] and Philippe.

Those rooms once belonged to my beloved grandmother the Princess de Vaurémont, to whom I owe some manner of fortune, of which no one has ever told me. In the lines that follow, you will feel all the sadness that seized me on entering that place hallowed by my memories. Everything was just as she left it! I was to sleep in the bed that she died in. I sat on the edge of her chaise longue and wept, little caring that I was not alone, remembering the many times I had sat at her knees, the better to hear her words, seeing her face swathed in discolored lace, emaciated by age as much as by the torments of her final illness. I thought I could still feel the warmth she imparted to that room. How is it possible that Mademoiselle Armande-Louise-Marie de Chaulieu should be obliged, like a peasant girl, to sleep in her mother's bed, almost on the very day she died? For to me that princess, who died in 1817, might have expired only the day before. I found the room cluttered with things that had no place there, proving how little those occupied with the kingdom's affairs care for their own, and how rarely they thought of that noble woman once she was dead, she who will be remembered as one of the truly great women of the eighteenth century. Philippe seemed to understand the reason for my tears. He told me that the princess had bequeathed her furniture to me in her will, and that my father had still not undertaken to erase the ravages of the Revolution from the house's grand apartments. I rose to my feet, and Philippe opened the door to the little salon that gives on to the reception room. I found it in the dilapidated state I knew so well: no precious paintings set into the walls above the doors but only bare beams; the marble mantels broken; the mirrors pulled down. As a child I was afraid to climb the great staircase and cross through the vast solitude of these high-ceilinged rooms;

when I wanted to visit the princess, I used a little staircase that descends under the vault of the larger one and leads to the hidden door of her boudoir.

Her apartment, made up of a drawing room, a bedroom, and that pretty vermillion-and-gold study I told you of, occupies the wing on the Invalides side. The house is separated from the boulevard only by a vine-covered wall and a magnificent row of trees whose boughs interlace with those of the elms on the boulevard's side street. Were it not for the gray façades and blue-and-gold dome of Les Invalides, one might think oneself in a forest. The style and placement of those three rooms show them to be the former parade apartment of the duchesses of Chaulieu, with the dukes' no doubt in the facing wing, kept at a proper distance by two central buildings and the front pavilion, which holds those huge, dark, echoing rooms Philippe had shown me, still stripped of their splendor, just as I saw them in my childhood. Noting the astonishment on my face, Philippe took on a confidential air. My dear, in this diplomatic house, everyone is discreet and mysterious. He told me that the family was awaiting a law by which those who emigrated during the Revolution would be reimbursed for the value of their property; my father will restore his house only when that restitution comes. The king's architect put the cost at three hundred thousand livres.[8] That revelation fairly threw me to the sofa in my drawing room. So my father was prepared to let me perish in the convent rather than devote that sum to my dowry? There is the thought that greeted me in that doorway. Ah, Renée, how I lay my head on your shoulder, and how I thought back to the days when my grandmother animated these two rooms! She who exists only in my heart, you who are at Maucombe, two hundred leagues away, those are the only creatures in this world who love me, or who once did.

That dear old woman always tried to rouse herself on hearing my voice, her gaze still youthful. How well we got on! That memory immediately brought a change to my mood. I found something holy in what I had a moment before seen as a profanation. I took comfort in the vague lingering odor of wig powder, in the idea of sleeping in the protection of those yellow-and-white damask curtains, on which her gaze and her breath must have left something of her soul. I directed Philippe to restore all these old things to their former beauty, that I might have rooms fit to live in. I told him myself exactly what I wanted, assigning everything a place. I inspected the furnishings one by one, making them mine, advising Philippe how those antiques I so love could be made new again. The white walls have gone a little dull with age, just as the gold of the frolicsome arabesques is tarnished here and there, but those effects harmonize with the faded colors of the Savonnerie rug given to my grandmother by Louis XV, along with his portrait. The clock is a gift from Marshal de Saxe. The porcelains on the mantelpiece come from Marshal de Richelieu. Ringed by an oval frame, my grandmother's portrait, painted when she was twenty-five, faces the king's. The prince is nowhere to be seen. I like that forthright omission, which depicts her delicious character with a single stroke. Once, when my aunt was gravely ill, her confessor insisted that the prince be allowed in from the drawing room where he was waiting. "Along with the doctor and his prescriptions," said the princess. The bed has a canopy and a padded headboard; the drape of the pulled-back curtains is wonderfully sumptuous; the furniture is of gilded wood, upholstered in that same yellow damask with white flowers that also covers the windows, lined with a white silk that resembles moiré. I have no idea who did the paintings over the door, but they depict a sunrise and a moonlit night. The treatment of the fireplace is quite curious. Clearly much of life was lived by the fireside in the last century: great things happened there. The hearth of gilded copper is a sculptural marvel, the mantelpiece is lavishly finished, the shovel and tongs are deliciously worked, the bellows are a thing of beauty. The fire screen's tapestry comes from Les Gobelins, and its frame is exquisite; the most wonderful figures meander along it, on the feet, on the footrest, on the branches; everything is as intricate as a fan. Who gave her that magnificent thing that she so loved? I wish I knew. How many times I saw her sunk deep in her bergère, one foot on that footrest, the hem of her gown hiked up halfway to her knee, picking up, putting down, then once again picking up the snuffbox on the little table between her box of lozenges and her fingerless silk gloves! Was she a coquette? Until the day she died she kept herself up as if that fine portrait had been painted only the day before, as if she were awaiting the cream of the court that forever gravitated around her. Looking at that bergère, I remembered the inimitable movement she gave to her skirts as she sank into it. Those women of bygone days carried off with them certain secrets that paint an entire picture of their age. The princess had a particular way of cocking her head, of casting a glance or tossing out a word, a whole private language that I never saw in my mother. There was a finesse about it, and a congeniality too, full of meaning but never posturing; her conversation was at once garrulous and laconic, she knew how to tell a story, and she could draw a portrait with three words.

Above all, she had an absolute freedom of opinion that must certainly have shaped my own turn of mind. From seven to ten years of age, I lived at her side. She loved having me in her rooms no less than I loved being there. That predilection was the cause of more than one quarrel between her and my mother, but nothing whips up the flames of fondness like the cold wind of persecution. How graciously she used to say "There you are, little mask!" when the serpent of curiosity lent me its undulations so that I might slip through her doors and go to her. She felt she was loved, she loved my naive adoration, which brought a ray of sunlight into her winter. I know not what went on in her rooms in the evening, but she had a great deal of company; tiptoeing into her drawing room the next morning to see if the day had begun there, I saw the furniture out of place, the gaming tables set up, piles of tobacco here and there. The style of that room is the same as the bedroom. The furniture is singularly turned, the wood decorated with concave moldings and hoof feet. Richly sculpted, wonderfully distinctive garlands of flowers wend their way between the mirrors and hang down in festoons. There are fine Chinese vases on the sideboards. All of this is set against walls of white and poppy red. My grandmother was a proud, piquant brunette, and her choice of colors gives an idea of her skin tone. I found in that drawing room a writing table set with tooled silver, whose forms greatly occupied my eye when I was small. It was given to her by a Lomellini of Genoa.[9] The four sides of that table represent the occupations of the four seasons; the characters are in relief, and there are hundreds in each scene. I spent two hours recapturing my memories, all alone in that sanctuary, which saw the last moments of one of the most remarkable women of Louis XV's court, celebrated as much for her mind as for her beauty. You know how abruptly I was snatched away from her, from one day to the next, in 1816. "Go say goodbye to your grandmother," my mother told me. I found the princess unsurprised at my going away, and outwardly impassive. She received me just as she usually did. "You are bound for the convent, my treasure," she told me. "You will be with your aunt, an excellent woman. I shall see to it that you are not sacrificed, you will be independent and in a position to wed whomever you like." She died six months later; she'd entrusted her will to the most faithful of her old friends, Prince de Talleyrand, who, while paying a call on Mademoiselle de Chargeboeuf, had her convey to me that my grandmother forbade me to take my vows. I do hope that sooner or later I will meet that prince, who no doubt will have more to tell me.

And so, my doe, while I found no one to welcome me, I consoled myself with that beloved princess's specter, and I looked forward to honoring one of our pacts, which is, you remember, to tell each other every detail of our new circumstances and surroundings. How comforting it is to know the life of an absent friend! Carefully paint for me every little thing around you, everything, even the light of the setting sun on the tall trees.

October 10

It was three o'clock when I arrived; at around half past five, Rose came to tell me that my mother was at home, and I went down to pay my respects. My mother lives on the ground floor, in rooms laid out like mine, in the same wing. I am above her, and we share a hidden staircase. My father's rooms are in the facing wing, but since on the courtyard side he has the additional space taken up on our side by the great staircase, his rooms are far larger than ours. In spite of the duties of the rank they regained with the return of the Bourbons, my mother and father still live and receive guests on the ground floor alone, so vast are the houses of our forefathers. I found my mother in her drawing room, where nothing has changed. She was dressed as if for company. As I made my way down the stairs, I wondered what to expect from that woman, so little a mother to me that in eight years I received from her only the two letters I showed you. Thinking it unworthy of me to feign an affection I could not feel, I adopted the air of a simpleminded nun and entered the room with some trepidation.

My concerns were soon dispelled. My mother was perfectly gracious: she expressed no false tenderness, but neither was she cold; she neither treated me as a stranger nor clasped me to her bosom like a beloved daughter. She greeted me as if we had seen each other only the day before, like the kindest, most sincere friend; she spoke to me woman to woman, and first of all gave me a kiss on the forehead.

"My dear girl," she said, "if the convent can only be the death of you, then better you should live among us. You are going against your father's plans and my own, but the age of blind obedience to one's parents is long past. Monsieur de Chaulieu agrees with me that we must do all we can to make your life agreeable and to introduce you into society. At your age, I would have felt just as you do, and so I cannot fault you: you cannot understand what we were asking of you. You will not find me absurdly inflexible. If you ever doubted my love, you will soon see your mistake. Although I mean to offer you every freedom, I believe that for the moment you would do well to heed the advice of a mother who will be like a sister to you."

The duchess spoke quietly, all the while straightening my convent-school cloak. She won me over at once. At thirty-eight, she is as beautiful as an angel. She has blue-black eyes with silken lashes, an unwrinkled brow, a natural white-and-pink complexion that might well be mistaken for powder and rouge, stunning shoulders and bosom, a lithe, slender waist like your own, milk-white hands of exceptional beauty: her highly polished nails catch the light, her little finger is always slightly apart from the others, her thumb is like ivory. And her feet match her hands, feet in the Spanish style, like Mademoiselle de Vandenesse. If this is how she is at forty, she will still be a beautiful woman at sixty.

My doe, I answered her in the manner of an obedient daughter. I was as amiable with her as she'd been with me, and even more: conquered by her beauty, I forgave her for abandoning me, I understood that such a woman should be caught up in her role as queen. I told her so openly, just as if I were speaking with you. Perhaps she wasn't expecting to hear affectionate words from her daughter's mouth? My sincere, admiring homages touched her beyond words; her manner changed, became kindlier still, and she no longer called me *vous*.

"You're a good daughter," she said, "and I do hope we shall remain friends."

I found those words adorably naive, though I took care not to show it, for I realized at once that I must let her go on thinking herself far cleverer than her daughter. I played the wide-eyed innocent, and she was enchanted. Several times I kissed her hands, telling her I was overjoyed that she was treating me as she was, that I felt at home here; I even confided to her that I was secretly terrified. She smiled, tenderly put her hand on my neck to draw me to her and kiss my brow.

"Dear child," she said, "we have guests for dinner today; perhaps you will feel as I do that we'd best delay your introduction to society until you have something to wear. Once you have seen your father and brother, you will go up to your rooms."

To this I wholeheartedly acquiesced. My mother's breathtaking gown was the first revelation of the fashionable world we used to glimpse in our dreams, but I felt not the slightest twinge of jealousy.

My father came in. "Monsieur, here is your daughter," the duchess said to him. My father suddenly adopted the most loving demeanor, so perfectly playing the paternal role that I was convinced he had a true father's heart.

"So there you are, you rebellious girl!" he said, taking my hands in his and kissing them in a manner more debonair than fatherly.

And he pulled me to him, took me by the waist, held me close to kiss my cheeks and forehead. "You will heal the sorrow we feel at your change of vocation by our pleasure at your success in society. Do you know, madame, she will be a very pretty young woman, of whom you will one day be proud? But here is your brother Rhétoré."

"Alphonse," he said to a handsome young man who had come in, "here is your sister, the nun who would cast off her habit."

Taking his time, my brother stepped forward, took my hand, and pressed it in his.

"Well, go on, kiss her," said the duke, and he gave me a kiss on each cheek.

"I'm happy to see you, my sister," he said, "and know that I am on your side, against my father."

I thanked him, though I couldn't help thinking he could easily have stopped by Blois sometime on the way to visit our brother the marquis at his garrison in Orléans. I withdrew, fearing that strangers might arrive at any moment. I did some tidying in my rooms, then laid out my pens and paper on the beautiful table's red velvet, all the while thinking over my new place in life.

And there, my fine white doe, without exaggeration or omission, is how a girl of eighteen was greeted on her return to one of the most illustrious families of the realm after nine years away. I was tired from the journey and the emotions aroused by this return to the nest: I thus went to bed as we did in the convent, at eight o'clock, after supper. They've kept even a little Saxony porcelain plate my beloved grandmother used when the fancy took her to dine alone in her rooms.

2

FROM THE SAME TO THE SAME

November 25

The next day I found my rooms straightened and made up by old Philippe, the vases now filled with flowers. I finally made myself at home. But it had occurred to no one that a recent boarder at the Carmelites would be hungry at a very early hour, and Rose had a terrible time with my breakfast.

"Mademoiselle went to bed as we were serving dinner, and she is rising when monseigneur is just coming home," she told me.

I sat down at my table. Toward one o'clock my father knocked at the door of my little drawing room and asked if I would see him; I opened the door, and he came in to find me in the middle of writing to you.

"My dear," he told me, "you will be needing new clothes, and you must get settled here. In this purse you will find twelve hundred francs: one year of the income I have set aside for your upkeep. If Miss Griffith is not to your liking, talk with your mother about engaging a more suitable governess, for during the day Madame de Chaulieu will be unable to stay with you. You will have a carriage at your disposal, and a servant."

"I'd like Philippe," I said.

"Very well," he answered. "But have no fear: your fortune is sizable enough that you will be a burden neither to your mother nor to me."

"Would it be indiscreet to ask the amount of that fortune?"

"Not at all, my child," he said. "Your grandmother left you five hundred thousand francs, her life savings, for she wanted all her lands to remain in the family. That sum was invested in the public debt.

Today the accumulated interest has produced an annual income of some forty thousand francs. My intention was to devote that sum to your second brother's fortune. As you see, you are greatly upsetting my plans, but perhaps one day you will fulfill them; you may decide that for yourself. I find you more reasonable than I expected. I need not tell you how a Mademoiselle de Chaulieu conducts herself; the pride I see in your features is my trusted guarantee. The precautions that ordinary folk take for their daughters are in this house an insult. A malicious rumor concerning you might well cost its impertinent teller his life—or, if heaven is unjust, the life of one of your brothers. Of that I will say no more. Goodbye, my dear."

He kissed my forehead and went off. I cannot understand why that plan was abandoned after nine years' perseverance. My father was admirably to the point. There is no ambiguity in his words: my fortune is meant to go to his son the marquis. Who found it in their heart to take pity on me, then? Was it my mother, my father, could it have been my brother?

I sat there on my grandmother's sofa, gazing on the purse my father had left on the mantelpiece, at once pleased and put out by that act of kindness, which kept my thoughts on money. To be sure, there was no use thinking of it any further; my uncertainties have been dispelled, and there is something noble about sparing me any painful discoveries on that subject.

Philippe spent the day making the rounds of the merchants and artisans who will be charged with my metamorphosis. In my rooms, I received a celebrated dressmaker, a certain Victorine, as well as a woman who will see to my linens and a man for my shoes. I am as impatient as a child to discover what I will look like when I abandon the sack the convent's dress code draped over us, but these artisans will not be hurried: the corsetiere wants a week, so as to do justice to my figure. This is becoming serious—so I have a figure? Janssen, the shoemaker to the Opéra, positively assured me that I have my mother's foot. I spent the entire morning on these weighty concerns. There was even a glover, come to measure my hand. The lingerie maker took my orders. At my lunchtime, which as it happened was their breakfast, my mother told me we would visit the hat shops together, so that I might develop my tastes and learn to order my own. I am dazed by this newfound independence, like a blind woman suddenly recovering her sight. I can now see what a Carmelite is to a young woman of the world: the difference is greater than we ever dreamt.

My father seemed distracted at breakfast, and we left him to his thoughts; he's privy to all the king's secrets. He had entirely forgotten me. He will remember when he has need of me, that I could plainly see. Even at fifty, my father is a most appealing man: his figure is youthful, he is pleasingly built, he is blond, his demeanor and manners are exquisite; he has the face of a diplomat, at once expressive and secretive; his nose is thin and long, his eyes are brown. What a handsome couple! How many curious notions bedeviled me when I realized that those two, equally noble, rich, and superior, do not live together, share only their name, and are united only in the eyes of the world! Yesterday the elite of the court and the diplomatic sphere were here. In a few days I shall go to a ball hosted by the Duchess de Maufrigneuse, where I will be introduced to the society I so long to know. A dancing master will come every morning: I must know how to dance within a month, or I may not go to the ball.

Before dinner, my mother came to see me on the subject of my governess. I chose to keep Miss Griffith, who was given to her by the British ambassador. That *miss* is a government minister's daughter, impeccably bred; her mother was noble; she's thirty-six years old; she'll teach me English. My Griffith is beautiful enough to have aspirations; she is poor and proud, and Scottish, she'll be my chaperone and sleep in Rose's room. Rose will be at Miss Griffith's disposal. I saw at once that I would govern my governess. Over the six days we've been together, she has clearly understood that I alone am allowed to take an interest in her, while I, despite her statue-like reserve, have understood that she will treat me with great indulgence. She seems a good-hearted creature but discreet. Of what was said between her and my mother I could learn nothing.

Another trifling little piece of news! This morning my father refused the ministerial position he had been offered. That explains why he was so preoccupied yesterday. He would prefer an ambassadorship, he said, to the tedium of public deliberations. He has his eye on Spain. I learned this at breakfast, the one time of day when my father, mother, and brother are together more or less in private, for the servants come only when rung for. The rest of the time my brother is away, like my father. My mother goes off to dress, then from two to four she can never be seen. At four she goes out for an hour's walk; from six to seven she receives visitors, when she's not dining in town, and finally the evening is taken up with amusements, the theater, balls, concerts, visits. Her life is so full that I don't believe she has a quarter of an hour to herself. She must devote some considerable time to her toilette every morning, for she is divine at breakfast, which takes place between eleven and noon. I am beginning to understand the sounds I hear from her rooms. She takes an almost cold bath and a cup of cold coffee with cream, and then she dresses. Save in exceptional circumstances, she is never up before nine. In the summer she goes out for an early-morning ride. At two she receives a young man I have yet to catch sight of.

There you have our family life. We meet at breakfast and dinner, though for the latter I am often alone with my mother. Still more often, I suspect, I will be dining with Miss Griffith alone in my rooms, like my grandmother. My mother often dines in town. I am no longer surprised by the little interest my family takes in me. My dear, in Paris there is a certain heroism in loving the people around us, for we are rarely alone with ourselves. How quickly the absent are forgotten here! It's true, of course, that I have yet to set foot outside and know nothing. I prefer to wait until I have lost a bit of my innocence, until my manner and dress are in harmony with the world of society, whose agitations fill me with wonder, though I hear its clamor only from afar. I have yet to venture any farther than the garden. In a few days they'll be singing at the Théâtre des Italiens. My mother has a box there. I am half mad with impatience to hear Italian music and to see a French opera. Little by little, I am shedding the habits of the convent and adopting those of society. I write you in the evening until bedtime, now put back to ten o'clock, the hour when my mother goes out, if she's not at one theater or another. There are twelve the-aters in Paris. I am as ignorant as can be, and I read a good deal, but I read indiscriminately. One book leads me to the next. The cover of the book in my hands lists the titles of several more, but I have no one to guide me, and so many I come across bore me dreadfully.

What I have read of modern literature is centered on love, the subject that so occupied our minds, since our destiny is shaped wholly by men and for men, but those authors are so far below two little girls named the white doe and the darling, Renée and Louise! Ah, dear angel, what dull happenings, what peculiarities, and how palely that emotion is expressed! There are however two books that I have found strangely compelling: one is *Corinne*, the other *Adolphe*.[10] On that subject, I asked my father if I might meet Madame de Staël. My mother, my father, and Alphonse began to laugh. Alphonse said, "Where has this girl been?" My father answered, "Silly us, she's been at the Carmelites." "My daughter, Madame de Staël is dead," the duchess gently informed me.

"How can a woman be deceived?" I asked Miss Griffith on finish-ing *Adolphe*.

"Why, when she's in love," Miss Griffith answered.

Tell me, Renée, will any man ever be able to deceive us?

Miss Griffith soon realized that I am only half innocent, that I've had a secret education, the one we gave each other with our endless cogitations and speculations. She saw that I am ignorant only of external matters. The poor creature opened her heart to me. The la-conic answer she gave me, seen against the backdrop of all the many sorrows one might imagine, sent a small shiver down my spine. La Griffith told me once again that I must not be dazzled by anything I find in the world and must be wary of everything, especially what pleases me most. She knows nothing more and can tell me nothing more. Her lectures are too much of a piece. She has this in common with a bird that knows only one song.

3

FROM THE SAME TO THE SAME

December

My dear, I am ready to make my entrance into society; I have done my best to be very free before settling down for its sake. This morning, after countless fittings, I found myself well and properly corseted, shod, cinched, coiffed, dressed, adorned. I did as a duelist does before facing his foe: I practiced behind closed doors. I wanted to see how I looked fully armed, and I was gratified to find a triumphant, conquering air before which there will be no choice but surrender. I studied and judged my reflection. I reviewed my forces, putting into practice that great maxim of antiquity: Know thyself! I was infinitely pleased to make my acquaintance. Griffith alone was allowed to be present and watch me play doll—I was the doll and the child at once. You think you know me? You do not!

Here, Renée, is the portrait of your sister, once disguised as a Carmelite, now resuscitated as a blithe and worldly girl. I am one of the most beautiful young women of France, Provence excepted. There, I think, is an accurate summary of this whole pleasant chapter. I have flaws, but if I were a man I would love them, for they are the sign of a promise yet to be fulfilled. When for two weeks straight one has admired the exquisite curve of one's mother's arms, and when that mother is the Duchess de Chaulieu, my dear, one is none too pleased to discover that one's own arms are skinny, but one consoles oneself with one's dainty wrists, with the elegant lines sketched out by those hollows, soon to be full, plump, and shapely, with soft, satin flesh. The faint angularity of the arm can also be seen in the shoulders. In truth, I have no shoulders, only hard shoulder blades forming two jagged planes. My waist is equally unsupple, and there is no litheness in my hips.

There, I've told you all. But those forms are delicate and firm, the bright, pure flame of good health burns in those sinewy limbs, life and blue blood pulse in abundance beneath a transparent skin. But next to me blond Eve's blondest daughter is a Negress! But I have a foot like a gazelle! But every curve is delicate, and I have the regular features of a Greek portrait. My skin tones are not perfectly even, it's true, mademoiselle, but they glow: I am a very pretty green fruit, with the same green freshness. In short, I resemble the figure emerging from a violet-tinged lily in my aunt's missal. My blue eyes are not mindless but proud, in two settings of living nacre shaded by pretty little fibrils; my long, close-set lashes are like silken fringe. My brow gleams, my hair's roots are perfectly sown, creating little waves of pale gold, browner in the middle, with an occasional rebellious lock slipping free to assert with some eloquence that I am not an insipid, fainting blond but a southern, hot-blooded blond, a blond who strikes before she can be struck. The coiffeur even wanted to part it in the middle, smooth it down, and adorn my brow with a pearl on a golden chain, telling me I would seem something straight from the Middle Ages. "Allow me to inform you that I am too young to be in the middle of any age, or to require an ornament to make me seem younger!" My nose is thin, the nostrils neatly cut out and separated by a charming pink partition: a haughty and superior nose, its tip too fine to ever grow fat or red. My doe, if that's not enough to have a girl snatched up with no dowry, then I don't know what's what. My ears make teasing twists and turns, a pearl would look yellow against the lobe. I have a long neck, endowed with the kind of serpentine motion that confers such majesty on a woman. In the shadow, the white turns to gold. Ah! my mouth might be just a bit wide, but it's so expressive, the color of my lips is so lovely, my teeth are so quick to laugh! And, my dear, all the rest is in harmony: there's a walk, there's a voice! One remembers the miraculous oscillations of one's ancestor's skirt, unaided by her hand; in brief, I am beautiful and full of grace. Depending on my mood, I can laugh as we so often laughed, and I will be respected:

there will be something commanding in the dimples put into my white cheeks by Amusement's deft fingers. I can lower my eyes and give myself a heart of ice beneath my snowy brow. I can display a swan's melancholy neck as I strike a Madonnaesque pose, and the painters' Virgins will be left far behind; I will be above them in the heavens. Any man who would speak to me will have to put music in his voice.

And so I am armed from head to toe, and I can play the full keyboard of coquetry, from the gravest tones to the most fluting. It's an enormous advantage not to be uniform. My mother is neither frolicsome nor virginal: she is nothing other than dignified and grand. She cannot break out and turn leonine; when she wounds, she has no gift for healing. I will be able to wound and to heal both. I could not be less like my mother—and so no rivalry is possible between us, unless we were to quarrel over the relative perfections of our limbs, which are similar. I am far more like my quick-witted, astute father. I have my grandmother's manners and charming voice, a head voice when it's forced, a mellifluous chest voice in the medium of the tête-à-tête. I feel as if I had only today left the convent behind. I do not yet exist for society, I am an unknown. What a delicious moment! I still belong to myself, like a new-bloomed flower, as yet unseen. My angel, as I glided through my drawing room, looking at myself, seeing the ingenue defrock the convent-school girl, I can't say what I felt in my heart: regrets of the past, concerns for the future, fears of the wide world, farewells to the pale daisies we so gaily gathered, so innocently plucked, there was all of that, but also a few of those wild fancies I force back down into the depths of my soul, where I do not dare go, and whence they come.

My Renée, I have a trousseau! Everything is very tidily put away and perfumed in the lacquer-fronted cedar drawers of my delicious dressing room. I have ribbons, shoes, gloves, everything in profusion. My father has generously given me a young lady's most precious jewels: a makeup case, a toiletry kit, a vinaigrette, a fan, a parasol, a book of prayers, a golden chain, a cashmere shawl. He promised that I would learn to ride. And finally, I know how to dance! Tomorrow, yes, tomorrow evening, I will be introduced to society. I will be dressed in white chiffon. In my hair will be a garland of white roses in the Greek style. I will put on my Madonna look: I want to be quite unworldly and have all the women on my side.

My mother knows nothing of what I write you here; she thinks me incapable of reflection. Were she to read my letter, she would be struck dumb with surprise. My brother honors me with a deep disregard and never fails to give me the gift of his indifference. He is a fine-looking young man, but gloomy and irascible. I know his secret, which neither the duke nor the duchess have guessed. Although young and a duke, he is jealous of his father, he has no place in the state, no duties at court, no call to say "I'm off to the chamber." I alone in this house have sixteen hours a day to devote to reflection: my father is occupied with matters of state and his own pleasures, and my mother is busy as well. No one ever examines themselves in this house, everyone is always out and about, there is no time for life. I am exceedingly curious to know what invincible attraction society holds, that it can detain you each evening from nine o'clock to two or three in the morning, that it can make you spend such vast sums and endure such exhaustion. In the days when I longed to come to this place, I never imagined such distances, such intoxications, but I am forgetting that this is Paris, and in Paris people can live together as a family and never know each other. Then an almost-nun arrives, and in two weeks she sees what a man of state does not see in his own house. Or perhaps he does, and perhaps there is a fatherly benevolence in his willful blindness. I will explore that dark corner.

4

FROM THE SAME TO THE SAME

December 15

Yesterday, at two o'clock, I went out for a drive down the Champs-Élysées and through the Bois de Boulogne, on one of those autumn days we so admired by the banks of the Loire. At long last, I have seen Paris! The Place Louis XV[11] is truly beautiful, but only with the beauty that men create. I was elegantly dressed, pensive but ready to laugh, my face serene beneath a charming hat, my arms crossed. I did not arouse the slightest smile, I did not leave one poor little young man standing stock-still in wonderment, no one turned around to look at me, despite the carriage's leisurely pace, in harmony with my pose. No, I'm wrong, there was one charming duke who abruptly turned around as he passed by. That man who rescued my vanity in the eyes of the passing crowd was my father, whose pride, he told me, had just been pleasantly tickled. I came across my mother, who gave me a little greeting with one fingertip, like a kiss. My Griffith was peering about every which way, little caring who was watching. I believe a young lady must always know where she is aiming her gaze. I was furious. One man very meticulously studied my carriage and never once glanced my way. That flatterer was very likely a coach maker. Clearly I was overrating my forces: beauty, that rare privilege given by God alone, is more widespread in Paris than I believed. Simperers were graciously saluted. Men said to themselves "There she is!" on catching sight of a mottled, flushed face. My mother was greatly admired. There is an answer to this mystery, and I will seek it out.

The men, my dear, seemed to me generally very ugly. The handsome ones resemble us, in a less comely form. I know not what misguided mind invented their garb, which is surprisingly graceless compared to centuries past. It has no style, no color or poetry; it speaks neither to the senses nor to the mind nor to the eye, and it must be impractical: it's too tight and too short. I was especially struck by the hat they all wear, a truncated column, entirely unsuited to the shape of the head, but I have been told it is easier to bring about a revolution than to make a hat elegant. In France, the most valiant heart quails at the idea of wearing a round-topped felt hat, and lacking the courage for one day, men go their whole lives ridiculously coiffed. And to think the French are said to be carefree! But then, whatever their hats, they are perfectly horrible. I saw only hard, tired faces, with nothing serene or tranquil about them: the lines are angular, and the wrinkles bespeak disappointed ambitions and defeated vanities. Fine brows are rare.

"So these are the Parisians I've heard so much about," I said more than once to Miss Griffith.

"Very amiable gentlemen, very amusing," she answered.

I said nothing. There is a great deal of indulgence in the heart of an unmarried thirty-six-year-old woman.

In the evening I went to the ball. I stayed close by my mother, who gave me her arm with well-rewarded devotion. All the homages were for her, I was a pretext for the most pleasant flatteries. She showed a rare gift for pairing me with imbecilic dance partners who spoke to me of the warmth as if I were freezing and of the beauty of the ball as if I were blind. Not one failed to fall into ecstasies over a strange, incredible, extraordinary, singular, bizarre thing, which was seeing me at the ball for the first time. My dress, which so thrilled me as I paraded alone through my white-and-gold drawing room, was scarcely noticeable among the splendid gowns on most of the women. They all had their faithful admirers, they all watched one another out of the corners of their eyes, several of them stood out by their triumphant beauty, my mother among them. A young woman counts for nothing at the ball: she is a dancing machine. With a few rare exceptions, the men are no better than on the Champs-Élysées. They are worn, their faces have no character, or rather they all have the same character. The proud, vigorous faces we see in our ancestors' portraits, wedding physical vitality to force of mind, those faces no longer exist. But there was one man of great talent in that assembly, a man who stood out in the crowd by the fineness of his face; nonetheless, he did not move me in the least. I know nothing of his work, and he is not of the true nobility. However brilliant or fine a commoner or newly minted noble[12] may be, I do not have a single drop of blood in my veins for him. Not to mention that I found him so deeply occupied with himself and so little with others that I concluded that we women must be mere things, and not people, for such great adventurers of the mind. When a man of talent is in love, he must no longer write, or else he is not in love. There is something in his mind that comes before his mistress. I thought I could see all that in this man's demeanor, he who is, I am told, a teacher, a talker, an author, whose ambition makes him a servant of any power. I made my decision then and there: I thought it most unworthy of me to blame the world around me for my lack of success, and I began to dance without troubling myself about such things. I very much liked dancing, as it happens. I heard a great deal of dull gossip about people I didn't know, but perhaps I simply still have much to learn, for I saw most of the men and women taking a very keen pleasure in saying or hearing one thing or another. Society offers a host of enigmas whose solution seems very difficult to find. The mysteries proliferate. My eyes are keen enough, and my ear sharp; as for the quickness of my mind, you know it well, Mademoiselle de Maucombe!

I came home tired, and glad of that tiredness. I very naively told my mother of my state, and she advised me to say such things only to her. "My dear girl," she added, "good taste means knowing what mustn't be said as much as what may be."

On hearing that counsel, I conceived an idea of all the feelings we must tell no one of, perhaps not even our own mother. With one glance I surveyed the whole vast realm of feminine dissimulations. I can assure you, my dear doe, that with the effrontery of our innocence we would seem two very bold little misses here. How much there is to learn from a finger pressed to the lips, from a word, from a glance! All at once I was greatly intimated. So I must say nothing of the very natural happiness caused by the movements of the dance? What, then, I wondered, of our sentiments? I went to bed dispirited. I am still reeling from the shock of my open, lighthearted nature's first collision with society's hard laws. A bit of my white wool has already been snagged on the brambles by the roadside. Farewell, my angel!

5

October

How moved I was by your letter, and above all by the differences in
our two destinies! What a glittering world will be yours! In what a
quiet repair I will live out my little life! Two weeks after I arrived at
the Château de Maucombe—of which I have already told you too
much to say anything more, and where I found my bedroom much
as before, though I was now able to appreciate the sublime landscape
of the valley of Gémenos, which as a child I looked at and never
saw—my father and mother, accompanied by my two brothers, took
me to dine at the home of a neighbor, an aged Monsieur de l'Estorade,
a nobleman who has grown very rich in the time-honored provincial
fashion: by the good graces of avarice. That old man had not succeeded
in protecting his only son from Bonaparte's clutches; he saved him
from conscription but was obliged to surrender him to the army in
1813 for the Honor Guard—and then, after the Battle of Leipzig,
Baron de l'Estorade heard nothing more from him. In 1814 he went
to see Monsieur de Montriveau, who claimed he had seen his son
captured by the Russians. Madame de l'Estorade died of grief as the
fruitless search she had ordered in Russia was still going on. The
baron, a very Christian old man, practiced that beautiful theological
virtue we cultivated in Blois: Hope! With Hope's aid, he saw his son
in his dreams; for that son, he saved up his income and set aside a
share of the inheritances that came to him from the late Madame de
l'Estorade's family. No one ever made so bold as to mock the old man
for it. I soon came to realize that this son's unexpected return was
the cause of my own. If someone had told us that while our thoughts

were racing wildly hither and yon my future husband was trudging homeward through Russia, Poland, and Germany! His ordeal came to an end only in Berlin, where the French minister helped him make his way back to France. Being a minor nobleman of Provence with an annual income of ten thousand livres, Monsieur de l'Estorade père lacks the Europe-wide renown that might have inspired someone to take an interest in the Chevalier de l'Estorade, whose name sounds so oddly like an adventurer's alias.

With an annual interest income of twelve thousand livres from Madame de l'Estorade's assets, and his father's savings on top of that, the poor Honor Guard has what is considered in Provence a sizable fortune, something like two hundred and fifty thousand livres, not counting his land. The day before he was to be reunited with the chevalier, l'Estorade bought a neglected but very fine estate, where he plans to plant the ten thousand mulberry trees he had been culti-vating in his nursery to that end, having long foreseen this purchase. Once he was reunited with his son, the baron could think of only one thing: finding him a wife, and not just any wife but a young woman of the nobility. My father and mother fell in with their neighbor's plans for me as soon as he announced his intention to take Renée de Maucombe with no dowry, and to claim receipt of the sum due the aforementioned Renée in their wills. On attaining the age of majority, my younger brother, Jean de Maucombe, was accorded an advance on his parental inheritance equal to one third of their legacy. This is how the noble families of Provence evade Monsieur de Bonaparte's shameful civil code, which will put as many noble girls in the convent as it has caused to be married.[13] From what little I have heard on the subject, French nobility is deeply divided on these very serious matters. That dinner, my dear darling, was a business meeting between your doe and the exile. Let us begin at the beginning. Count de Maucombe's servants dressed in their old corded livery and rib-boned hats; the coachman donned his big flared boots. We fit five people into the old coach and majestically arrived toward two o'clock for a three o'clock dinner at the *bastide*[14] that is Baron de l'Estorade's home. The father-in-law has no château, only a simple country house at the foot of one of our hills, at the end of our beautiful valley, whose glory is certainly the old de Maucombe *castel*. That *bastide* is a true *bastide*: four rubble-stone walls faced with dull yellow mortar, topped with curved tiles of a beautiful red. The roof sags under the weight of that brickyard. Set into those walls without the slightest regard for symmetry the windows are flanked by enormous yellow-painted shutters. The garden is a typical Provençal garden, enclosed by low walls built of big round stones stacked in layers, the mason's genius being expressed in his manner of arranging them alternatively lying flat or standing on end; here and there the layer of mud that covers them is falling away. What gives that *bastide* the air of a true estate is a tall metal gate at the entrance to the grounds, just by the road. It took a great deal of begging to have that gate built; it is so frail that it made me think of Sister Angélique. The house has a stone staircase in front, and the doorway is decorated with an awning that no peasant of the Loire would ever want for his elegant house of white stone, its blue slate roof glinting in the sunlight. The garden and grounds are horribly dusty, the trees scalded by the sun. Clearly the baron's life has long consisted in rising, retiring, and rising again the next day with no thought in mind but saving up his sous. He eats the same meals as his two domestics, a Provençal boy and his late wife's aged chambermaid. The rooms are sparsely furnished. Nonetheless, the house of l'Estorade went all out for the occasion. They emptied their cupboards and enlisted every last one of their serfs for this dinner, which was served to us on tarnished, dented silver.

The exile, my beloved darling, is like the gate, very frail! He is pale, he has suffered, he says little. At thirty-seven, he might pass for fifty. The ebony of his ex-beautiful hair is streaked with white, like the wing of a lark. His fine blue eyes are sunken, he is slightly deaf, and all told he seems a little like the Knight of the Sad Countenance; nonetheless, I have graciously consented to become Madame de l'Estorade, to allow myself to be endowed with two hundred and fifty thousand livres, but only on the condition that I be given authority to oversee the furnishing and decoration of the *bastide* and to create a park on the grounds. I formally demanded that my father grant me a small supply of water, which will flow here from Maucombe. In a month I shall be Madame de l'Estorade, for I proved to his liking, my dear. After the snows of Siberia, a man may well find merit in these black eyes of mine, which, as you used to say, ripened any fruit that I gazed upon. Louis de l'Estorade seems exceedingly happy to be marrying *the beautiful Renée de Maucombe*, for such is your friend's glorious cognomen. While you are preparing to reap the joys of the grandest existence, that of a young de Chaulieu lady in Paris, which you will have kneeling at your feet, your poor doe Renée, that girl of the desert, has fallen from the Empyrean realm into which we once launched ourselves and landed in the everyday realities of a life as humble as a daisy's. Yes, I have sworn to console that young man who never had a youth, who went from his mother's arms to the war's, from the joys of his *bastide* to the snows and privations of Siberia. The sameness of my days will be varied by the modest pleasures of the countryside. I will bring the oasis that is the valley of Gémenos to my very house, which will be majestically shaded by beautiful trees. I will have perpetually green lawns in Provence; my park will climb to the very top of the hill, where I will place some pretty belvedere from which I might perhaps gaze on the shining Mediterranean. Orange trees, lemon trees, all of botany's most sumptuous creations will beautify my retreat, and there I will be mother to a family. A natural, indestructible poetry will surround us. So long as I remain true to my duties, there is no sadness to fear. My father-in-law and the Chevalier de l'Estorade share my Christian sentiments. Ah! my darling, I see my life to come as one of those great highways of France, flat and smooth, shaded by age-old trees. There will not be two Bonapartes in this century; should I have children, I will be allowed to keep them, to raise them, to make men of them, and through them I will enjoy the pleasures of life. Assuming you do not fail your destiny, you who will be the wife of some great and important man, your Renée's children will have a tireless protector.

Adieu, then, for me at least, to the novels and dramas of which we once made ourselves the heroines. I already know my life's story line. It will be marked by such momentous events as the young de l'Estorade masters' teething, by their feeding, by the ravages they will wreak on my flower beds and my person; embroidering their bonnets, being loved and admired by a poor sickly young man at the entry to the valley of Gémenos, those will be my enchantments. Perhaps one day that countrywoman will take to spending her winters in Marseille, but even then she would only be appearing on the narrow stage of the provinces, where there is little peril lurking in the wings. I will have nothing to fear, not even one of those admirations in which we women take such pride. We will have an abiding interest in silkworms, for which we will have mulberry leaves to sell. We will know the strange vicissitudes of Provençal life and the storms of a household where no quarrel is possible: Monsieur de l'Estorade has announced his definitive intention to let his wife lead him where she will. And since I will do nothing to ensure that he keeps to this wise course, he will very likely never stray from it. You, my dear Louise, will be the glamorous part of my existence, so tell me all your adventures, paint me pictures of the parties you go to, the balls, carefully describe your dress, the flowers crowning your beautiful blond hair, the words and ways of the menfolk. There will be two of you listening, dancing, having your fingertips squeezed. It would make me very happy to be amusing myself in Paris while you are mother to a family at La Crampade, for such is the name of our *bastide*. Poor man, who thinks he is marrying only one woman! Will he ever realize they are two? I am beginning to say foolish things. And as I can no longer do foolish things but vicariously, I will stop here. I hereby give you a kiss on both cheeks; my lips are still those of a girl (he has dared take only my hand). Oh! we are rather distressingly respectful and respectable. Ah, there I go again. Farewell, my dear!

P.S. I have just opened your third letter. My dear, I have some thousand livres at my disposal: use them, then, for pretty things that cannot be found around here, nor even in Marseille. As you shop for yourself, think of your recluse in La Crampade. Remember that neither my intended nor I have grandparents with tasteful friends in Paris to make their purchases. I will answer that letter another time.

6

FROM DON FELIPE HÉNAREZ TO DON FERNAND

Paris, September

The date of this letter will tell you, my brother, that the head of your house is out of danger.[15] Although the massacre of our ancestors in the Court of the Lions made of us Spaniards and Christians in spite of ourselves, it also instilled in us the prudence of the Arabs; perhaps I owe my salvation to the Abencerrage blood still flowing in my veins. Terror made of King Ferdinand such a convincing actor that Valdez believed his protestations. Were it not for me, that poor admiral was a dead man. No Liberal will ever understand the nature of a king. I myself long ago grasped that Bourbon's character; the more His Majesty assured us of his protection, the deeper my mistrust. A true Spaniard has no need to repeat his promises. He who speaks too much seeks to deceive. Valdez boarded a ship bound for England. As for myself, as soon as the sad fate of my beloved Spain was sealed in Andalusia, I wrote to the steward of my holdings in Sardinia with orders to provide for my safety. Skilled coral fishermen were awaiting me with a boat on a coastal point. As Ferdinand was ordering the French to take me into custody, I was in my own barony of Macumer, amid bandits who scoff at all laws and all threats of reprisal. Grenada's last Hispano-Moorish house rediscovered the deserts of Africa, and even the Saracen horse, on lands passed down from the Saracens. Those bandits' eyes glowed with savage joy and pride on learning that they were protecting their master, the Duke de Soria, from the King of Spain's vendetta, that they had among them a Hénarez, the first to have visited them since the island belonged to the Moors, they who only the day before feared my justice! Twenty-two rifles offered to take aim at Ferdinand de Bourbon, that son of a race unknown on the day the Abencerrages arrived in triumph on the banks of the Loire. I thought I might live on the revenues brought in by those lands, to which we have unfortunately given so little thought; my stay there showed me my mistake and the truthfulness of Queverdo's accounts. The poor man had twenty-two human lives at my service and not a real, twenty thousand arpents of open land and no house, virgin forests and no furniture. It would take a million piastres and half a century of the master's attention to fully develop those magnificent lands; I will consider that. As they flee, the defeated turn their thoughts to themselves and their losses. With tears in my eyes, I imagined that noble corpse insulted by the monks, and I saw the sad future of Spain herself. It was in Marseille that I learned of Riego's fate. I sadly mused that my life too would end in martyrdom, but of a long and obscure sort. Is a man truly alive when he can neither devote himself to a country nor live for a woman? Love and conquest, those two aspects of one single idea, were the law engraved on our sabers, written in letters of gold on the vaults of our palaces, endlessly repeated by the sprays of water shooting heavenward in our marble fountains. But in vain does that law rule my heart: the saber is broken, the palace lies in ruins, the rushing spring has been swallowed by the sterile sands.

Here, then, is my testament.

Don Fernand, you will soon understand why I reined in your fervor with the command to remain faithful to the *rey netto*.[16] As your brother and friend, I implore you to obey; as your master, I order it. You will go to the king, you will ask him for my *grandezas* and my holdings, my position and my titles; he may well hesitate, he will put on a few royal scowls, but you will tell him that you are loved by Maria Hérédia, and that Maria can only marry the Duke de Soria. You will then see him all atremble with joy: the Hérédia family's vast fortune barred him from consummating my destruction, and now he will think it complete. He will immediately give you everything that was mine. You will marry Maria, for I have discovered the secret of your covert love, and I have prepared the old count for that substitution. Maria and I always respected the rules of good conduct, just as we respected our fathers' wishes. You are as handsome as a child of love, and I as ugly as a Spanish grandee; you are loved, and I the object of an unspoken repugnance. You will soon overcome any resistance my misfortunes might inspire in her noble Spanish soul. Duke de Soria, your predecessor will exact from you not one single regret, will not deprive you of one single maravedi. With Maria's jewels, you will have no need for my mother's diamonds in your house; those diamonds will assure me an independent existence, and so you will send them to me along with my old nursemaid, Urraca, the only one of my former domestics I wish to keep, for she alone knows how to make my hot chocolate.

During our short-lived revolution, my constant labors reduced my life to its barest essentials, and I lived solely on my ministerial salary. You will find the revenues of those last two years in your steward's hands. That sum belongs to me: the wedding of a Duke de Soria will cost a great deal, and so we shall half it. You will not refuse this wedding present from your brother the bandit. In any case, such is my will. The barony of Macumer not being under the thumb of the King of Spain, it remains mine alone, and so I still have a fatherland and a name, should I ever wish to make something of myself.

God be praised, it is over, the house of Soria is saved!

At this moment, when I am nothing more than Baron de Macumer, the French cannons are announcing the Duke d'Angoulême's entry into Madrid. You will understand, monsieur, why I interrupt my letter here. . . .

October

I had not ten quadruples to my name when I arrived in this place. Is there any smaller man than a man of state who, amid the catastrophes he failed to prevent, proves to have planned ahead for his preservation? For defeated Moors, only a horse and the desert; for disappointed Christians, the monastery and a handful of coins. Nonetheless, my resignation is for the moment nothing more than weariness. I am not so near the monastery as to give up all thoughts of living. Believing they might prove useful, Ozalga provided me with letters of introduction, among them one written to a bookdealer, who is for our compatriots here what Galignani[17] is for the English. That man has found me eight students, at three francs a lesson. I visit my students every other day; each day, then, I teach four lessons and earn twelve francs, far more than I need. When Urraca comes, I will pass my clients on to some lucky Spanish exile. I have found lodging in a poor widow's boardinghouse on the rue Hillerin-Bertin.[18] My bedroom faces south and overlooks a small garden. I hear none of the sounds of the city, I see only greenery, and all told I spend no more than one piaster per day; I am quite astonished at the pure, tranquil pleasures I find in this life, like Dionysius the Younger in Corinth.[19] From sunup to ten, I smoke and drink my chocolate, sitting at my window, gazing out at two Spanish plants, a broom plant standing tall amid clumps of jasmine: gold on a white background, an image that will always cheer a descendant of the Moors. At ten I set off for my lessons, returning home at four; I dine, then smoke and read until it comes time to retire. I can go on for some time leading this life, divided between labor and meditation, solitude and society. Be happy, then, Fernand: my abdication comes with no misgivings, none of the regrets felt by Charles V, no urge to leap back into the fray like Napoleon. It has been five nights and five days since I wrote my testament; my thoughts have moved on by five centuries. For me, it is as if those *grandezas*, those titles, that property never existed.

Now that the respectful barrier that separated us has fallen, I can allow you to read into my heart, dear child. Clad by my gravity in impregnable armor, that heart is brimming with untapped tenderness and devotion, but no woman has ever seen it, not even she who, from my cradle, was destined to be mine. That is the secret behind my passion for matters of state. Lacking a mistress, I adored Spain. And Spain too has escaped me! Now that I am nothing, I can contemplate my ruined *I*, wonder why life came to me and when it will leave me; why the most chivalrous race there ever was should instill in its last offspring its prime virtues, its African ardor, its fiery poetry; whether the seed must forever be sealed away in its coarse envelope, never to send out a shoot, never to release its Oriental perfumes from a radiant flower. What crime did I commit in some previous existence that I have never inspired love in a woman? Was I born a mere piece of wreckage, destined to wash up on an arid shore? In my soul I find the deserts of my fathers, condemned to sterility by a blazing sun. The proud remnant of a fallen race, my strength useless, my love lost, an old young man, I will thus wait here, better than anywhere else, for the final favor that will be my death. Alas! beneath these gray skies, no spark will revive the flame amid all these ashes. And so, as my last words, I might well say, like Jesus Christ, *My God, you have abandoned me!* Fearsome words that no one has yet dared to examine.

Consider, Fernand, how happy I am for the chance to live anew through you and Maria! I will contemplate you with the pride of a creator pleased at his handiwork. Love each other well and forever, cause me no sorrows: one tempest between you would hurt me more than it would you. Our mother foresaw that events would one day fulfill her hopes. Perhaps a mother's wish is a compact between her and God. Was she not one of those mysterious beings who can communicate with heaven and bring back a vision of the future? How often I read in the wrinkles of her brow that she wished Felipe's properties and honors on Fernand! I used to tell her just that, and she answered with two tears, showing me the wounds of a heart owed to us both, but which an invincible love gave to you alone. Her joyful shade will hover over your heads when you kneel at the altar. Will you finally come and caress your Felipe, Dona Clara? As you see, he has abandoned to your beloved even the girl you reluctantly placed on his knees. What I do here is pleasing to women, to the dead, to the king; it was God's will, so do not resist it, Fernand: only obey, and hold your tongue.

P.S. Tell Urraca she must never call me by any name other than Monsieur Hénarez. Say nothing of me to Maria. You must be the only living creature who knows the secrets of the last Christianized Moor, in whose veins the blood of a great desert-born family will die, and who will live out his days alone. Farewell.

7

FROM LOUISE DE CHAULIEU TO RENÉE DE MAUCOMBE

January 1824

Soon married? Can it be? But does one hire even a servant like that? You promise yourself to a man after only a month, knowing nothing of him, never having made his acquaintance! That man might be deaf—there are so many ways!—or feeble, or dull, or intolerable. Renée, do you not see what they want to make of you? They need you to perpetuate the glorious house of l'Estorade, nothing more. You will become a provincial. Is that what we promised each other? In your place, I would sooner make for the Hyères Islands in a skiff, waiting for some Algerian corsair to kidnap me and sell me to the grand vizier; I would become a sultana, and then one day a valide sultan[20]; young and old alike, I would sow havoc in the seraglio. You're simply leaving one convent for another! I know you, you're weak, you will enter into married life with the submissiveness of a lamb. Let me advise you, you'll come up to Paris, we'll drive all the men mad, we will be queens! Within three years, my beautiful doe, your husband could be a *député*.[21] I now know what a *député* is, I'll explain everything; you will master this machine beautifully, you can live in Paris and become what my mother calls a woman of fashion. Oh! one thing is certain, I will not leave you there in your *bastide*.

Monday

For two weeks now, my dear, I have been living the life of high society: one evening at the Théâtre des Italiens, another at the Grand Opéra, and from there, always, to the ball. Ah! this world is a magical place.

The music at the Italiens thrills me, and as my soul swoons in divine rapture I am ogled and admired from all sides—but with a single glance I can make the boldest young man lower his eyes. I have seen charming young men there; not one of them pleases me, none has ever caused me the emotion I feel when I hear Garcia sing his magnificent duo with Pellegrini in *Otello*. My God! what a jealous man this Rossini must be, to have expressed jealousy with such eloquence! *Il mio cor si divide*, what a devastating cry! I'm speaking Greek to you, you've never heard Garcia, but you do know how jealous I am! What a dreary dramatist Shakespeare is! Othello triumphs, he conquers, he commands, he struts, he comes and goes, leaving Desdemona to languish all alone, and Desdemona sees him preferring the trivialities of public life to her, but she never explodes? That sheep deserves to die. Just let the man I will one day deign to love take it into his head to do anything other than love me! I strongly approve of the endless trials required by the old chivalric code. I see only impertinence and stupidity in that delicate young lord who complained when his lady dispatched him to retrieve her glove from among a pack of lions:[22] very likely she had in store for him some beautiful flower of love, and he lost it after having earned it, the insolent dolt! But listen to me babbling on, as if I did not have great news! My father will very likely serve as our master the king's representative in Madrid; I say *our* master because I will be a part of the embassy as well. My mother wishes to stay here in Paris, and so my father will take me with him, to have a woman at his side.

My dear, to you this may all seem perfectly simple, but there are enormities behind it. In the past two weeks I have discovered all the secrets of my house. My mother would follow my father to Madrid if he were willing to engage Monsieur de Canalis as ambassadorial secretary, but secretaries are named by the king, and the duke dares not vex that king, who is quite absolute, nor upset my mother. My father the brilliant politician believes he has adroitly solved the problem by leaving the duchess behind. Monsieur de Canalis, the great poet of the day, is the young man cultivating my mother's company, who I suppose is studying diplomacy with her each afternoon from three to five. Diplomacy must be a wonderful thing, because he is as punctual and regular as a speculator in the stock market. The good Duke de Rhétoré, our elder brother, solemn, cold, and peculiar, would be utterly outshone by my father in Madrid; he too will stay in Paris. Not to mention that Miss Griffith has it on good authority that Alphonse is in love with a dancer at the Opéra. How can one possibly fall in love with legs and pirouettes? We have observed that my brother never misses a performance when Tullia is dancing; he applauds that creature's turns and then leaves at once. I do believe that two unmarried women can do more damage in a house than the plague ever could. As for my other brother, he is off with his regiment, I have yet to see him. And so I am destined to be the Antigone of an ambassador of His Majesty. Perhaps I will marry in Spain; perhaps my father's plan is to marry me off there with no dowry, exactly as you are being married to that wreck of the Honor Guard. It was my father's suggestion that I come with him, and he offered me the services of his Spanish teacher. "Do you hope many men will come seeking my hand in Spain?" I asked him. A sly look was his only answer. For several days now he's been annoying me at breakfast, studying me as I pretend not to notice, so *in petto* I played a good trick on him, both as a father and an ambassador. Did he not take me for a naive little fool? He asked what I thought of some young man and several young ladies I'd run into at various parties. I answered with the most mindless discussion of the color of their hair, the differences between their figures, the young men's appearance. My father seemed disappointed to find me so shallow; he was secretly sorry he'd asked.

"That said, Father," I added, "I am not telling you my true thoughts: the other day my mother made me fear I might come across as a boor if I spoke of my impressions."

"Among family, you may speak freely," my mother interjected.

"Well then," said I, "so far I find the young men far more ambitious than attractive, more preoccupied with themselves than with us, but in truth they have little talent for display: they put on a fine face to talk to us, then immediately let it slip when they turn away, no doubt convinced we don't know how to use our own eyes. The man speaking to us is the lover; the man no longer speaking to us is the husband. As for the young ladies, they are so artificial that their true character comes out only in their dance: their physiques and their movements alone do not lie. Above all, I am shocked by the coarseness of the beau monde. Things happen at supper—on a different scale, to be sure— that give me an inkling of what a popular uprising must be like. Politesse does a very imperfect job of hiding the universal egoism. I imagined society differently. Women count for very little; perhaps that is a lingering effect of Bonaparte's doctrines."

"Armande has made remarkable progress," my mother said.

"Mother, do you believe I will go on asking you forever if Madame de Staël is dead?"

My father smiled and rose.

Saturday

My dear, I have not told you all; here are some observations I have been saving for you. The love we used to imagine must be very deeply hidden away, for I've seen no trace of it anywhere. To be sure, I have caught an occasional quick exchange of glances in the salons, but how pale it all seems! Our notion of love, that universe of marvels, of beautiful daydreams, of delicious realities, of interlaced torments and joys, those smiles that light up the whole world, those words that enrapture, that happiness ever given, ever taken, those sorrows provoked by a lover's distance, those joys set off by his presence ... no such thing have I found. Where are all those splendid flowers of the soul born? Who is lying? Is it us, or is it the world? I have seen boys and men by the hundreds, and not one of them stirred me in the slightest; they could have sworn their undying love and devotion, they could have fought duels over me, I would have looked on unmoved. Love, my dear, is a phenomenon so rare that one can live an entire lifetime and not meet the one person endowed by nature with the ability to make us happy. A chilling notion, for suppose that meeting comes too late—do you have any thoughts on that?

Over the past few days, I have begun to look with horror on our destiny, to understand why so many women have such downcast faces beneath the layer of vermillion applied to them by the false festiveness of a party. They marry by chance, just as you will. A hurricane of reflections has blown through my soul. Oh, to be loved every day just the same but in ever new ways, to be loved no less after ten happy years than on the first day! Such a love takes time: one must let oneself be desired for a good while, one must awaken and satisfy many curiosities, one must arouse and return many sympathies. Are there laws, then, governing the creations of the heart, as there are governing the visible creations of nature? Can joy endure? In what proportion must love combine pleasures and tears? The cold routine of the convent's dreary, unchanging, interminable existence then seemed to me possible, whereas the richness, the splendor, the tears, rapture, rejoicing, bliss, and pleasures of a mutual, equal, licit love seemed inconceivable. I see no place in this city for love's tender sweetness, its sacred strolls beneath a bower by the light of the full moon, the waters glimmering, the maiden resisting her lover's urgent entreaties. Rich, young, and beautiful, I have nothing to do but love, love can become my whole life, my sole occupation, but for three months I have been curiously casting about, and in all those shiny, eager, alert gazes I have found nothing. No voice has moved me, no glance has lit up the world. Music alone enchants my soul, it alone has filled the void left by our separation. I have sometimes sat at my window for an hour, deep in the night, looking out at the garden, wishing something would happen, begging for some event from the unknown source whence they spring. I have sometimes taken the carriage out for a drive, alighting on the Champs-Élysées and telling myself that a man was about to appear, he who would awaken my insensible soul, that he would follow me, look at me, but I saw only hucksters, gingerbread sellers, and conjurers, passersby hurrying about their business, or lovers fleeing all eyes, whom I was tempted to stop and ask, "You who are happy, tell me, what is love?" I fought back those ridiculous notions, climbed into my carriage, and vowed to remain unmarried forever. Love is an incarnation, and how many conditions must be met for it to occur! We are never entirely in agreement with ourselves, how hard must it be when there are two! God alone can answer that. I am beginning to think I may return to the convent. If I remain out in the world, I will do things that people think foolish, for I cannot accept what I see. Everything offends my sensibilities, the mores of my soul, or my secret thoughts. Ah! my mother is the happiest woman in the world, she is adored by her great little Canalis. My angel, I am sometimes overcome by a horrible fancy to know what goes on between that young man and my mother. Griffith has had all these same thoughts, she says, she has wanted to lash out at the women she saw to be happy, she has scorned them, she has savaged them. According to her, virtue consists in burying that hatefulness at the bottom of one's heart. What, then, is the bottom of one's heart? A storehouse of all that is wicked within us. I am quite humiliated not to have met one man who adores me. I am a girl of marriageable age, but I have brothers, I have a family, I have difficult parents. Ah! if that's why the men have proven so reserved, they must be very great cowards. I marvel at Chimène, in *Le Cid*, and at Le Cid himself. What a grand play that is! Enough of this, farewell.

8

FROM THE SAME TO THE SAME

January

Our Spanish teacher is a poor refugee, forced into hiding by his involvement in the revolution quelled not long ago by the Duke d'Angoulême—a success that was the occasion of some wonderful parties. Liberal though he be, and very likely a commoner, this man interests me: I imagined he had been condemned to die. I drew him out to discover his secret, but he is as taciturn as any Castilian, proud as Gonzalo de Córdoba,[23] though gentle and patient as an angel. He does not make a show of his pride, as Miss Griffith does; he keeps it entirely to himself. He exacts his due as he pays his respects to us, and he holds us at a distance with his courtliness. My father claims there is more than a little of the nobleman about this Monsieur Hénarez, and as a joke calls him Don Hénarez in private. When, a few days ago, I took the liberty of addressing him by that name, he raised his usually lowered eyes and threw out two bolts of lightning that left me without words; my dear, he truly has the most beautiful eyes in the world. I asked if I'd done something to anger him, and in his sublime, grandiose Spanish tongue he answered, "Mademoiselle, I am here to teach you Spanish, nothing more."

I was humiliated, I blushed; I was about to lash back with some cutting impertinence when I remembered what our dear mother superior used to tell us, and so answered, "If I have wronged you in any way, then I am in your debt."

He started, the blood rushed to his olive face, and in a gently moved voice he said, "Religion must have taught you, better than I ever could, to be respectful of deep sorrows. Were I a don in Spain who had lost everything with King Ferdinand's triumph, there would be cruelty in your little jest, but if I am only a poor language teacher, is there not stinging mockery? Neither is worthy of a highborn young woman."

I took his hand and said, "Let me invoke religion in turn, and beseech you to forgive me my trespass." He bowed his head, opened my *Don Quixote*, and sat down.

That little incident caused me more emotion than all the compliments, stares, and fine words I ever reaped at my most successful evening party. As the lesson went on, I closely studied that man, who let himself be examined without knowing it: he never looks up at me. I discovered that our teacher, whom we thought to be forty, is in fact a young of man of perhaps twenty-six or twenty-eight. My governess, with whom I had left him alone for a moment, remarked to me on his beautiful black hair, his pearl-white teeth. As for his eyes, they are at once velvet and fire. And that's all: apart from that, he is short and ugly. We have heard the Spanish described as a slovenly people, but he is impeccably groomed, his hands whiter than his face. His back is slightly stooped, his head huge and oddly shaped. His rather dashing ugliness is aggravated by the smallpox scars that pepper his face. His brow is very prominent, his eyebrows meet and are exceedingly thick, and give him a hard and daunting air. He has the sullen, drawn face of a child destined to die young, who owes his life only to constant care, like Sister Marthe. As my father said, he has the wizened face of Cardinal Jimenez.[24] My father is not fond of him; he makes him uncomfortable. Our teacher has a natural dignity that seems to disturb the dear duke; he cannot tolerate any sort of greatness around him. We will leave for Madrid as soon as my father has learned Spanish. Two days after the lesson he'd taught me, when Hénarez returned, I said to him, marking a sort of gratitude, "I do not doubt that you left Spain because of the events; if my father is sent there, as they say he shall be, we will be in a position to help you, to obtain your pardon, perhaps, should you have a sentence hanging over you."

"No one can help me," he answered.

"Do you mean, monsieur," I asked, "that you will not accept it or that it cannot be done?"

"Both," he said, with a little bow, and in a tone that ordered me to be silent. My father's blood growled in my veins. Vexed by that haughtiness, I left Monsieur Hénarez there. Nonetheless, my dear, there is something beautiful about this refusal to want anything from others. He would never accept even our friendship, I told myself as I conjugated a verb. I broke off and told him what I was thinking, but in Spanish. This Hénarez very courteously answered that no sentiment is possible without an equality that would be absent here, and so the question was moot.

"Do you mean equality of sentiment or equality of rank?" I asked, trying to drag him out of that seriousness I find so trying. He raised his formidable eyes once again, and I lowered mine.

My dear, this man is an impenetrable enigma. He seemed to be asking if my words were a declaration: in his gaze I saw a happiness, a pride, an agonizing uncertainty that tugged at my heart. I realized that such coquetries, which in France are seen as nothing more than they are, can become dangerously meaningful with a Spaniard, and I retreated into my shell, feeling rather foolish. When the lesson was over, he bade me goodbye with a glance full of humble prayers, a glance that said, "Do not toy with an unhappy man." That sudden contrast with his grave, dignified manner made a powerful impression. This is a dreadful thing to think and to say, but I believe there are vast reserves of affection in that man.

9

FROM MADAME DE L'ESTORADE TO MADEMOISELLE
DE CHAULIEU

December

Everything has been said, my dear child, and everything has been done: it is Madame de l'Estorade who writes you now, but nothing has changed between us, there is simply one maiden the less. Have no fear: I devoted great thought to my consent and did not give it lightly. The course of my life is now set. The certainty that comes with following a well-blazed trail suits my mind as it does my nature. A great inner strength has smoothed forever what are known as the ups and downs of life. We have land to cultivate, a home to decorate and improve; I have a household to run and make pleasant, a man who must be reconciled with life. I will no doubt have a family to look after, children to raise. There is no way around it: everyday existence has no room for grandeur and excess. The extravagant desires that exalt the soul and the mind have no place in these matters, or so at least it seems. What stops me from letting the boats that we launched onto the seas of the infinite sail ever onward? But do not believe that the humble things to which I intend to devote myself are devoid of passion. It is a very fine undertaking to make a poor man who has been the plaything of life's tempests believe in happiness again, and that is enough to vary the sameness of my existence. I believe I have left no hold for sadness, and I have seen good to be done.

Between you and me, I do not love Louis de l'Estorade with the love that makes the heart beat faster at the sound of a footstep, that sends a thrill through the soul on hearing a single word or feeling the embrace of an ardent gaze, but neither does he displease me. What will I do, you may ask, with the instinct for the sublime, with the gift for powerful thought that you and I share, that binds us, inhabits us? That has indeed been much on my mind, but is it not a grand thing to conceal it, to secretly use it for the happiness of the family, to make of it a means for the felicity of those entrusted to us, to whom we owe ourselves? The season in which those faculties shine is a short one among women and will soon have passed; my life may never be great, but it will be tranquil, smooth, and untroubled. We women have an inborn advantage: we can choose between love and motherhood. I have made my choice. I will make of my children my gods, and of this patch of land my Eldorado. That is all I can tell you today. I thank you for the things you sent me. Have a look at my orders, the list of which accompanies this letter. I want to live in an atmosphere of luxury and elegance, and to have about me nothing of the provinces but the pleasures they offer. A woman who protects her solitude can never be provincial, she will forever remain herself. I am counting on your devotion to keep me apprised of the latest fashions. In his enthusiasm, my father-in-law refuses me nothing and is remaking his house from top to bottom. We have workmen out from Paris, and we are making everything modern.

10

January

O Renée! You made me sad for several days. So that delicious body, that fine, proud face, those naturally elegant ways, that soul laden with rare gifts, those eyes in which the spirit drinks deep as at a fresh spring of love, that heart bursting with exquisite sensibilities, that broad mind, all those rare talents, those effects of nature and of our mutual education, those treasures that should have offered up price-less riches for passion and desire, poems, hours fuller than years, delights to make a man a slave with one elegant gesture, so all that will be wasted on the tedium of a vulgar, common marriage, all that will vanish into the emptiness of a life you will soon tire of! I already hate your future children; they will be ill-begotten. Everything is planned out in your life: you will have no cause for hope, for fear, for suffering. Suppose that one glorious day you meet a man who wakes you from the sleep to which you are about to abandon yourself? . . . Ah! that thought sent a chill down my spine. But all the same, you have a friend in me. No doubt you will be the living spirit of that valley, you will discover its beauties, you will live amid that nature, you will fill yourself with the grandeur of it all, the slow growth of the greenery, the speed of racing thoughts; and when you look at your cheerful flowers, you will question yourself. And when you are out walking, with your husband ahead of you and your children behind, the children shrieking, whining, capering, the man silent and self-satisfied, I know already what you will write me. Your perfumed valley, its hills, whether barren or adorned with fine trees, your meadow, so unlikely in Provence, with the little rivulets of its limpid stream, the changing hues of the light, all that infinity around you, varied by God, will call to your mind the infinite monotony of your heart. But I will be here, my Renée, and in me you will find a friend whose heart is untouched by social pettiness, a heart wholly devoted to you.

Monday

My dear, my Spaniard is wonderfully melancholic: he has a calmness about him, an austerity, a dignity, a depth that interests me to the highest degree. There is something provocative for the soul in that constant solemnity, in the silence enshrouding that man. He is as silent and superb as a fallen king. We dwell on him, Griffith and I, as on an enigma. How very odd it all is! A language teacher captures my attention as no man ever has, I who have now reviewed the entire parade of well-born sons, attachés to the embassy, ambassadors, generals, sublieutenants, peers of France, their sons and their nephews, the court and the city. The coldness of that man is beguiling. The most profound pride fills the desert that he tries to and does put between us, for he wraps himself in darkness. He is the demure one, and I the bold. This oddity amuses me all the more in that it is of no consequence at all. What is a man to me, a Spaniard, a language teacher? I feel no respect for any man alive, were he even a king. I believe we are worth more than any of them, even the most justly celebrated. Oh! how I would have dominated Napoleon! How I would have made him feel, had he loved me, that he was at my command!

Yesterday I threw out a jape that must have cut Hénarez to the quick, for he made no reply; he finished the lesson, put on his hat, and took his leave, giving me a look that convinces me he will not come again. That suits me very nicely: there would be something sinister about reliving Jean-Jacques Rousseau's *La nouvelle Héloïse*, which I have just read and which has inspired in me a great hatred of love. I can't bear a love that's all philosophizing and fine words. Clarissa Harlowe is also entirely too happy when she writes her long little letter, but at the same time, my father tells me, Richardson's novel explains the soul of the Englishwoman admirably. Rousseau's strikes me as a philosophical sermon in letters.

I see love as an entirely private poem. No writer says anything of it that is not true and false at the same time. In truth, my dear beauty, since the only love you can now tell me of is a conjugal love, I believe—in the interest, of course, of our double existence—that I must never marry but must rather experience some wonderful passion, so that together we might know life to the fullest. Give me a detailed account of everything that happens to you, especially in the first days, with that animal I call a husband. I promise to be no less precise, should I ever be loved. Farewell, my poor swallowed-up love.

11

La Crampade

You and your Spaniard make me shiver, dear beauty. I write these few lines to beseech you to send him away. Everything you tell me of him bespeaks the dangerous nature of those who have nothing to lose and so risk everything. That man must not be your lover, and he cannot be your husband. I will write you more fully of the secret events of my marriage, but only when my heart is free of the anxiety your last letter has created in it.

12

February

My beautiful doe, this morning at nine o'clock my father had himself announced in my rooms; I was up and dressed. I found him sitting gravely by the fire in my salon, more pensive than usual. He nodded at the armchair facing his; I understood his meaning and sank into it with a gravity so perfectly imitating his own that he broke into a smile, but a smile stamped with solemn sadness.

"You are at least as sharp-witted as your grandmother," he said.

"Come now, Father," I answered. "Don't play the courtier with me: you have something to say!"

He rose to his feet, greatly agitated, and spoke to me for a full half hour. This conversation deserves to be recorded, my dear. As soon as he went on his way I sat down at my table and endeavored to capture his words. Never before have I heard my father truly speak his mind. He began by flattering me, and he did not go about it at all badly; I was grateful to him for so well understanding and appreciating me.

"Armande," he said, "you have curiously misled me and agreeably surprised me. On your arrival from the convent, I took you for a young girl like all the rest, of limited intelligence, uninformed, the sort who can be won over at little expense with baubles, a pretty gem, and who do not think overmuch."

"On behalf of youth, Father, I thank you."

"Oh! there's no such thing as youth anymore," he said, reflexively making an orator's gesture. "You have a mind of astonishing breadth, you judge all things at their true value, you are farsighted and shrewd: you seem to have seen nothing, when in fact you have already discovered the causes while others are still examining the effects. You are a minister in skirts; you are the only one here who can understand me. Should anyone seek some sacrifice from you, you are the only one who will successfully argue against you, so let me frankly lay out certain plans I made some time ago, which I have not abandoned. If I am to make you concur with them, I must convince you that they are rooted in fine and elevated sentiments, and so I must delve with you into political considerations of the highest importance for the kingdom, which would bore anyone else. Once you have heard me out, I would ask you to carefully think over my words: I am prepared to give you six months, if need be. You are your own mistress, without question. Should you refuse the sacrifices I ask of you, I will accept your refusal and torment you no further."

Hearing that preamble, my doe, I grew genuinely serious, and I said to him, "Speak, Father." And here is the speech that statesman then made:

"My child, France is in a precarious position known only to the king and a handful of great thinkers, but the king is a head without arms, and the great thinkers privy to this danger have no authority over those who must be used to arrive at a favorable outcome. Those men, vomited up by popular election, do not wish to be tools. However worthy they may be, they continue the work of society's demolition, rather than help us to shore up the edifice. In a word, there are only two parties left: the party of Marius and the party of Sulla. I am for Sulla and against Marius.[25] There, in a nutshell, is the matter at hand. To explain all this more fully: the Revolution has not come to an end. It is implanted in our laws, it is written on our soil, it is in every mind, it is all the more formidable in that most of those counselors to the throne believe it has been defeated, seeing no soldiers or fortunes now serving it. The king is a man of great perception and sees all this clearly, but with each passing day he is increasingly won over by his brother's people, who want to go too quickly; he has not two years to live, and is preparing his deathbed so that he might die in peace.[26] Child, do you know the Revolution's most destructive effect? You would never guess. When it decapitated Louis XVI, the

Revolution decapitated fathers everywhere. There is no family today, only individuals. Wanting to become a nation, the French gave up on being an empire. By proclaiming that every child has an equal right to the father's legacies, they killed the family spirit, they created the Tax Office! But in this they have foreordained the weakening of the elite and the rise of the masses' blind force, the ruination of the arts, the reign of personal interest, and they have paved the way for conquest. We find ourselves between two systems: a state founded on the family or a state founded on personal interest. Democracy or aristocracy, argument or obedience, Catholicism or religious indifference, there is the question in a few words. I belong to the small number who would resist what is known as the people, in the people's own interest, of course. This has nothing to do with feudal rights, as fools are often told, nor with the ruling class; this is a matter of the state, it is a matter of France's survival. Any country not founded in paternal authority has no guarantee of existence, for with that authority begins the ladder of responsibilities and subordinations, which runs straight up to the king. The king is us all! To die for the king is to die for oneself, for one's family, which does not die, anymore than the kingdom dies. Every animal has its own instinct; man's is the family spirit. A country is strong when it is composed of rich families, with every member engaged in the defense of the common treasure, a treasure of money, of glory, of privileges, of enjoyments; it is weak when it is composed of individuals without solidarity, who little care if they are obeying seven men or one, a Russian or a Corsican, so long as each individual still owns his own plot of land, and that wretched egoist cannot foresee the day when it will be taken from him. We are headed toward a terrible debacle, should we fail. There will be nothing left but penal or fiscal laws, your money or your life. The most generous country on earth will no longer be guided by sentiment. Incurable wounds will have been inflicted and treated. Universal jealousy, to begin with: the superior classes will be confounded, equality of desires will be mistaken for equality of abilities, and the true elite, recognized and acknowledged, will be invaded by the onrush of the bourgeoisie. Once we could choose one man out of a thousand; now we can find nothing among three million similar ambitions, all dressed in the same livery, the livery of mediocrity. This triumphant horde will not realize that it is opposed by another fearsome horde, that of the landowning peasants: twenty million arpents of land living, walking, arguing, understanding nothing, always wanting more, throwing up barricades everywhere, brute force at its service—"

"But," I said, interrupting my father, "what can I do for the state? I have no inclination to become the Joan of Arc of the Family and to perish over a slow fire tied to some convent's stake."

"You are a little pest," said my father. "If I speak reasonably to you, you answer with jokes; when I joke, you speak like an ambassador."

"Variety is the spice of life," I told him. And he laughed until tears rolled down his cheeks.

"I want you to think about what I have just explained to you; you will realize how much trust and forthrightness there is in speaking to you as I just have, and perhaps events will serve to further my plans. From your point of view, I realize, those plans are hurtful and unjust; I seek the approval, then, not so much of your heart and imagination as of your reason, for I have found in you more reason and good sense than I have seen in anyone. . . ."

"You flatter yourself," I answered with a smile. "I am your daughter, after all!"

"I believe I am no fool, at least," he said. "He who desires a certain end must desire the necessary means, and we must serve as an example to all. For that reason, you will have no fortune so long as your younger brother's is not guaranteed; I would like to use all your capital to establish a *majorat* for him."[27]

"But," I replied, "you do not forbid me to live as I please, and to be happy, even as I relinquish my fortune?"

"Ah!" he answered, "so long as the life you intend to lead does no harm to the honor, the reputation—and, may I add, the glory—of our family."

"Well now," I cried, "you're very quick to discount my superior reason."

"In all of France," he said bitterly, "we will not find one man willing to take as his wife a girl of the highest nobility with no dowry, who gives him only a promissory note. Should such a husband be found, he would necessarily be a bourgeois social climber. In such matters I come straight from the eleventh century."

"As do I," I told him. "But why should I despair? Are there no elderly peers of France?"

"You are making admirable progress, Louise!" he cried. And on that he took his leave, smiling and kissing my hand.

I had received your letter that very morning, and it made me carefully consider the abyss into which you claim I might fall. I thought I could hear a voice crying out from inside me: "Fall you will!" I thus took my precautions. Hénarez dares to look at me, my dear, and his eyes trouble me, they produce a sensation I can only compare to deep terror. One mustn't look at that man, anymore than at a toad: he is ugly and fascinating. I have been debating with myself for two days, wondering if I should inform my father that I am tired of studying Spanish and have that Hénarez sent away, but no sooner have I bravely resolved to do just that than I feel a need for the horrible sensation the sight of him causes me, and I tell myself: Just one more lesson, and then I will speak. My dear, there is a penetrating sweetness to his voice, he speaks like La Fodor sings. His manners are simple, entirely unaffected. And such beautiful teeth! Just now, as he was leaving, he thought he had seen how deeply he interests me, and he very respectfully reached out to take my hand and kiss it, but then he held back, as if terrified by his boldness and the great leap he was about to make. Little of this could be seen, but I sensed it; I smiled, for there is nothing more endearing than seeing an inferior's surge of emotion retreat in this way. There is such audacity in a commoner's love for a noble girl! My smile emboldened him, the poor man looked around for his hat, seeing it nowhere, not wanting to find it; I gravely brought it to him. His eyes were damp with ill-repressed tears. There was a world of things and thoughts in that very brief moment. We understood each other so well that I abruptly held out my hand for him to kiss. Perhaps that was a way of saying that love could fill the gap separating us. Now I cannot say what made me take that step: Griffith turned her back, I proudly extended my white paw, and I felt the fire of his lips tempered by two swollen teardrops. Ah! my angel, I sat drained in my armchair, pensive, I was happy, and I cannot explain how or why. What I felt was pure poetry. I had lowered myself, and at this hour I am ashamed of it, but at the time I thought it a beautiful and elevated thing. I had fallen under his spell: there is my excuse.

Friday

He truly is a beautiful man. His words are elegant, his mind remarkably fine. My dear, he shows the confidence and logic of Bossuet as he explains the mechanics not only of Spanish but of all languages and all human thought. French might almost be his mother tongue. When I expressed my surprise at this, he answered that he had come to France at a very young age, to Valençay, with the King of Spain.[28] What has happened in the depths of that soul? He is not the same as before: he appeared at our house dressed very simply, but in every way like a true gentleman out for a morning walk. His mind shone as bright as a lighthouse in that lesson: he deployed all his eloquence. Like an exhausted man regaining his strength, he revealed a vast soul, heretofore carefully hidden. He told me the story of a poor devil of a valet who went to his death for a single glance from a Queen of Spain. "Death was his only choice!" I told him. That answer filled his heart with joy, and his gaze left me genuinely terrified.

That evening I went to a ball at the Duchess de Lenoncourt's, where I spied the Prince de Talleyrand. By way of Monsieur Vandenesse, a charming young man, I inquired if he might have had a guest by the name of Hénarez at his château in 1809.

"Hénarez is the Moorish name of the de Soria family, who are said to be Abencerrages converted to Christianity. The aged duke and his two sons accompanied the king. The elder son, become Duke de Soria in his turn, has just been stripped of his assets, honors, and titles by King Ferdinand, thereby avenging an old enmity. The duke made an enormous mistake by accepting a constitutional ministry with Valdez. Happily, he escaped Cadiz before the arrival of Monseigneur the Duke d'Angoulême, for despite his best efforts, the duke could never have protected him from the king's wrath."

That answer, relayed word for word by the Viscount de Vandenesse, gave me much food for thought. I cannot tell you how anxiously I awaited my next lesson, which took place this morning. For the first quarter of an hour I studied him, trying to determine if he was a duke or a commoner, and unable to arrive at an answer. He seemed to read my thoughts as they came and to take pleasure in frustrating them. Finally I could bear it no longer. I brusquely put down the book I was translating aloud and said to him in Spanish, "You are deceiving us, monsieur. You are not a poor liberal commoner, you are the Duke de Soria, are you not?"

"Mademoiselle," he answered with a dispirited gesture, "I am, sadly, not the Duke de Soria."

I clearly perceived all the despair in that *sadly*. Ah! my dear, no man will ever be able to put so much meaning and passion into one single word. He had lowered his eyes, no longer daring to look at me.

"Monsieur de Talleyrand," I said, "at whose château you spent the king's years of exile, believes a Hénarez can only be either a disgraced Duke de Soria or a servant."

He looked up, showing two dark, glowing embers, two eyes at once fiery and humiliated. He seemed to be in torment.

"My father was indeed a servant of the King of Spain," he said.

Griffith was finding all this a very curious way of studying. With every question, every answer, we fell into worrisome silences.

"Are you a noble or a commoner, then?" I asked him.

"You know, mademoiselle, in Spain everyone is noble, even the beggars."

My patience had had more than its fill of these evasions. After the last lesson, I'd prepared one of those amusements that so tease the imagination: I wrote a letter describing the ideal man I would like to be loved by, telling myself I would give it to him as an exercise in translation. I have so far translated only from Spanish to French, never from French to Spanish; I observed as much, and asked Griffith to go and fetch the latest letter I had received from one of my girl-friends. I told myself that the effect produced in him by this statement of purpose would show me what manner of blood he has in his veins. I took the page from Griffith with the words "I do hope I've copied this out properly," for it was written in my own hand. I gave him the paper—the bait, if you prefer—and studied him as he read the following:

The man who will win me, my dear, must be brusque and haughty with other men, but gentle with women. His eagle-like stare will have the power to instantly silence anything resembling ridicule. He will have a pitying smile for those who want to make light of sacred things, especially those underlying the poetry of the heart, those without which life would be no more than a drab reality. I have only deep scorn for any man who would deprive us of the source of religious ideas, so rich in consolations. His beliefs must thus be as simple as a child's, with the unshakable conviction of a thoughtful man who has carefully considered his own reasons for believing. His mind, inventive and original, will be free of artifice or ostentation: he can say nothing excessive or out of place, will no more bore others than be bored himself, for he will have a rich treasury in his soul. All his thoughts must be of a noble, elevated, chivalrous sort, with no trace of selfishness. His every act will reveal an absolute absence of calculation or self-interest. His faults will spring from the very breadth of his ideas, which will be above those of his fellows. In all things, I must find him ahead of his time. Full of the delicate attentions owed to the weak, he will be kindly with all women, but very slow to love: he will see that as a thing too serious to be trifled with. He may well, then, go his entire life and never truly know love, even as he displays all the qualities that can inspire profound passion. But should he one day find his ideal woman, she whom he has glimpsed in those dreams one dreams with eyes open, should he meet a creature who understands him, who fills up his soul and casts a ray of happiness over his entire life, who to his eyes shines like a star through the clouds of this dark, cold, glacial world, who lends a wholly new charm to his existence and sets once-mute strings vibrating inside him, I believe there is no need to say that he will recognize and appreciate his happiness, and so he will make her perfectly happy. Never, by word or glance, will he hurt the loving heart entrusted to his hands with the blind love of a child asleep in a mother's arms, for were she to wake from that sweet dream, her heart and soul would be forever blighted: he would never set sail on that ocean without engaging his entire future.

That man will necessarily have the face, the manner, the walk, the way of doing both the greatest and the humblest of things that bespeaks a superior being, simple and natural. He may be ugly, but his hands will be beautiful. His upper lip will be slightly drawn back into an ironic and disdainful smile for people of no consequence; only those he loves will see the celestial, shining ray of his soulful gaze.

"Would mademoiselle permit me," he asked in Spanish, deep emotion in his voice, "to keep this as a memento? This is the last lesson I will have the honor of giving her, and the teachings I find in these lines may well rule my conduct forever. I left Spain an impoverished fugitive, but today I have received from my family a sum of money sufficient to my needs. I will have the honor of sending you some poor Spaniard to replace me." With those words he seemed to be telling me, "This game has gone on long enough." He stood up with incredible dignity, leaving me awed at the extraordinary delicacy of men of his class. He went downstairs and asked for a word with my father.

At dinner my father said to me with a smile, "Louise, you have been given Spanish lessons by an ex-minister of the King of Spain, and a man with a death sentence on his head."

"The Duke de Soria," I said.

"The duke!" my father answered. "No longer: his title now is Baron de Macumer, named for a fiefdom he still holds in Sardinia. He seems a rather unusual man."

"On your lips, Father, there is always something ironic and contemptuous in that word," I told him. "Do not use it to speak of a man who is every bit your equal, and who I believe has a very beautiful soul."

"Baroness de Macumer, I presume?" my father shot back at me with a teasing look. I proudly lowered my eyes.

"But," said my mother, "Hénarez must have run into the Spanish ambassador on the front step?"

"Yes," my father answered, "the ambassador even asked if I was conspiring against his master the king, but he greeted the former grandee with great deference, declaring himself at his service."

This, my dear Madame de l'Estorade, happened two weeks ago, and two weeks have gone by without my once seeing that man who loves me, for love me he does. What he is doing? I wish I were a fly, a mouse, a sparrow. I wish I could see him alone in his rooms, without his knowing. We now have a man to whom I can say, "Go and die for me!" And it would be in his nature to do it, or so at least I believe. In short, there is a man in Paris I am thinking of, one whose gaze floods my innermost self with light. Oh! he is an enemy I must trample underfoot. Can there truly exist on this earth a man I cannot live without, a man I need! You will soon be married, and I am in love! After four months, those two doves who once flew so high have fallen into the swamp of reality.

Sunday

Yesterday at the Italiens, I could feel myself being looked at; my eyes were magically drawn to two fiery eyes glowing like hot coals in a dark corner of the parterre. Hénarez never once looked away. The monster had sought out the only seat from which he could see me, and there he sits. I know nothing of his political gifts, but he has a genius for love. *And that, dear Renée, is where we now stand*, in the words of the great Corneille.[29]

13

La Crampade, February

My dear Louise, I had to wait some time before writing you, but now I know—or, more precisely, I have learned—a great many things that I must impart to you for your future happiness. So great is the difference between a girl and a married woman that the girl can no more imagine it than the married woman can become a girl again. I found marriage to Louis de l'Estorade preferable to the convent. That much is clear. Realizing that I would find myself back in the convent if I did not marry Louis, I had no choice but to resign myself, to use a girl's language. Thus resigned, I sat down to consider my situation, with a view to making the most of it.

The gravity of the marriage vows first filled me with terror. Marriage is for life, where love is only for pleasure, but marriage goes on after pleasure has faded and gives birth to interests far more precious than those of the man and woman it unites. Perhaps, then, a happy marriage requires only the kind of friendship that overlooks many human failings for harmony's sake. There is nothing to stop me from feeling friendship for Louis de l'Estorade. Thoroughly resolved not to seek in marriage the amorous ecstasies we so often dreamt of, with such dangerous exaltation, I felt the sweetest tranquillity within me. "If I do not have love, why not seek happiness?" I asked myself. And indeed, I am loved and will allow myself to be loved. My marriage will not be a servitude, but it will be a perpetual commandment. What difficulties might that present for a woman who wishes to retain an absolute mastery over her person?

This very serious question—that of my having a marriage but not a husband—was settled in a conversation between Louis and me, in which he revealed both the fineness of his character and the gentleness of his soul. My darling, I wanted nothing so much as to remain in that beautiful season when love is but an anticipation, a season that yields no pleasure and leaves the soul its virginity. To concede nothing to duty, to the law, to depend only on oneself, and retain one's free will—what a noble and delicious thing! Such a compact, contradicting the law and the sacrament itself, could only be made between Louis and myself. That point of contention, the first to arise, was the sole impediment to the resolution of my marriage. In the beginning, I was prepared to do whatever was necessary to stay out of the convent, but it is in our nature to ask for more when we have been granted a little, and we, my dear angel, are the type of young women who must have it all. I studied my Louis from the corner of my eye, asking myself, "Have his miseries made him kindly or cruel?" Eventually my scrutiny convinced me that his love was in fact a true passion. Having attained the rank of idol, seeing him pale and tremble at even the slightest cool glance, I realized I could dare anything. I took him out for a casual stroll, far from his family's ears, and carefully sounded his heart. I asked him to speak of his thoughts, of his plans, of our future. My questions implied so many carefully considered ideas, and so skillfully touched on the weaker spots of that dreaded shared life, that Louis has since confessed he was dismayed by so worldly a virginity. As for me, I listened closely to his answers; he tripped himself up like those who lose all their assurance in the face of fear. I soon realized that chance had given me an adversary all the feebler in that he could see what you so grandly call my great soul.

Ravaged by sorrow and poverty, he considered himself a broken man, and he was consumed by three terrible fears. First, he is thirty-seven years old, and I seventeen; not without terror did he measure that twenty-year gulf. Second, it is generally agreed that I am very beautiful, and Louis, who shares our opinion on that score, was all too painfully aware of the youthfulness his sufferings had cost him. And third, he found me greatly superior as a woman to himself as a man. His confidence shaken by these three visible inferiorities, he feared he might not make me happy and believed he had been taken only as a last resort. Were it not for the convent, I would never be marrying him, he timidly told me one evening. "That is true," I answered gravely. My dear friend, he then caused me the first great emotion of the sort men inspire in us. The two swelling tears in his eyes touched me deep in my heart. "Louis," I reassured him, "it is entirely in your power to make this marriage of convenience a marriage to which I can wholly consent. What I intend to ask of you will require a sacrifice far greater than the apparent servitude of your love, however sincere. Can you rise to the level of friendship as I understand it? We have only one friend in our lives, and I want to be yours. Friendship is the coming together of two kindred souls, united in their strength and yet independent. Let us be friends and partners, and so endure this life together. Allow me to retain my complete independence. I do not forbid you to make me love you as you claim to love me, but I want to be your wife only of my own free will. Make me long to abandon that free will to you, and I will give it at once. Understand, then, that I do not forbid you to inject passion into this friendship, to trouble it with the voice of love; for my part, I will see to it that our affection remains unbroken. Above all, spare me the trials that our somewhat unusual arrangement might cause me outside these walls. I would not want to seem capricious or prudish, because I am not, and I think you a fine enough man to assure you that I will keep up the appearances of marriage."

My dear, I have never seen a man so happy as Louis was on hearing that proposition; his eyes were shining, the fire of happiness had dried his tears. "You must realize," I told him, by way of conclusion, "that there is nothing perverse in what I am asking of you. The condition I make stems from my immense desire for your esteem. If you owed me only to marriage, would you one day be deeply grateful that your love had been consecrated by legal or religious formalities, but not by me? Suppose I had a child before I am drawn to you, passively fulfilling your wishes as my esteemed mother recommends: do you believe I would love that child as much as one born of a shared will? No doubt two people need not be as drawn to each other in the way lovers are, but you must concede, monsieur, that they must not displease each other. And we are about to find ourselves in a perilous situation: we are to live in the country. Must we not then consider the instability of the passions? May two thoughtful people not forearm themselves against the sorrows that come with changes of heart?" He was strangely surprised to find me both so reasonable and so reflective, but he gave me his solemn word, whereupon I took his hand and pressed it affectionately.

We were married at the end of the week. Certain that I would not lose my liberty, I merrily made my way through the tedious details of the many ceremonies: I was free to be myself, and perhaps seemed a bold little miss, as we used to say back in Blois. I was taken for a headstrong woman, when I was simply a girl charmed by the new situation, full of possibilities, into which I had managed to place myself. My dear, I had seen all the difficulties of my life, as if in a vision, and I sincerely wanted to make that man happy. But in the solitude that is ours, marriage soon becomes intolerable if a woman does not take charge. A wife must have the charms of a mistress and the qualities of a spouse. By depriving pleasure of its certainties, does a woman not prolong her husband's illusions and safeguard the joy of self-respect to which we all so rightly cling? Marital love, as I conceive it, cloaks a woman in anticipation, endows her with mastery, and gives her an inexhaustible force, a vital warmth that makes everything around her flourish and thrive. The more she is her own mistress, the more certain she is to make love and happiness last. Nonetheless, I demanded that our domestic arrangement be veiled by the most profound secrecy. Ridicule is rightly heaped on a man who is dominated by his wife. A woman's influence must remain perfectly hidden: mystery is our greatest grace. If I undertake to rehabilitate that broken soul, to restore the luster to the qualities I have glimpsed in him, I want Louis to think it is all happening on its own. Such is the beautiful task I have set myself, more than enough to seal a woman's glory. I am almost proud to have a secret to animate my life, a project to which I will devote all my efforts, known only to you and to God.

Now I am almost happy, and perhaps I would be less so if I could not announce it to a beloved soul, for how could I ever tell him? He would be hurt by my happiness; I have had to keep it from him. He is as sensitive as a woman, my dear, like all men who have suffered terribly. For three months we lived just as we did before the wedding. As you will surely imagine, I carefully considered a host of little personal questions, on which love depends more than people think. In spite of my coolness, that emboldened soul came to life; I saw a changed look on that face, a newly youthful air. The elegance I was introducing into the house cast its glow onto his person. Little by little I grew accustomed to him, I made of him another me. I discovered the correspondence between his soul and his outward appearance. The animal we call a husband, as you put it, was no more to be seen. Eventually, one lovely evening, I saw before me a lover, one whose words went straight to my soul, on whose arm I walked with a pleasure beyond words. At long last, to speak true to you, as I would to God who cannot be deceived, Curiosity rose up in my heart, perhaps roused by the admirable devotion with which he had kept his word. I resisted, ashamed of myself. But alas! when one resists only out of dignity, the mind soon comes up with concessions. And so the moment was celebrated—in secret, as two lovers would, and our secret it must remain. When you marry, you will see the sense in my discretion. Know, however, that nothing the most exacting love might demand was missing, nor the element of surprise, which is in a sense the glory of that moment: the mysterious beauties our fancy asks of it, the irresistibility that excuses it, the surrender, the long-imagined delights that overpower our soul before we abandon ourselves to the reality, all the charms were there in their most rapturous forms.

All these wonderful things notwithstanding, I must confess that I have once again asserted my free will, and I prefer not to explain all the reasons. You are most assuredly the only soul to whom I will entrust that semi-secret. Even as we belong to our husbands, beloved or otherwise, I believe we have much to lose from not concealing our emotions and our judgment of our marriage. The only joy I felt, which was heavenly, derived from the certainty that I had given life back to that poor man, before giving it to his children. Louis has recovered his youth, his strength, his good cheer. He is not the same man. Like a good fairy, I have erased the very memory of his sorrows. I have transformed Louis: he has become charming. Sure that he appeals to me, he gives free rein to his wit and reveals ever new qualities. To know that one is the perpetual source of a man's happiness, when that man realizes it and mingles his gratitude with love, oh! my dear, that certainty fuels a force in the soul far mightier than the most wholehearted love. That fearless, enduring force, single and varied, finally gives birth to the family, that magnificent creation of womankind, which I now see in all its fertile beauty. The aged father is a miser no more, he blindly provides whatever I wish. The servants are cheerful; Louis's felicity seems to have radiated all through the house, which I rule by love. The old man has remade himself to harmonize with the improvements we have undertaken, not wanting to be a blot on my luxury; to please me, he has adopted the garb, and with it the manners, of the present day. We have English horses, a coupé, a calèche, and a tilbury. Our servants are simply but elegantly dressed, and so we are widely thought of as spendthrifts. I make use of my intelligence (I do not mean that as a joke) to run my house in an economical way, to create the greatest pleasure at the smallest possible cost. I have already shown Louis the need to make an effort to earn the reputation of a man concerned with the good of his province. I am forcing him to complete his education. I hope to see him soon on the Regional Council, relying on the influence of my family and his mother's. I told him outright that I am a woman with ambitions, that I did not think it a bad thing for his father to go on overseeing our assets, looking for savings, because I wanted him wholly devoted to politics; were we to have children, I wanted to see them happy, with a comfortable place in the state. Lest he lose my esteem and affection, he must be named *député* in the next election; my family would offer their support for his candidacy, and we would have the pleasure of spending our winters in Paris. Ah! my angel, from the ardor with which he obeyed me, I could see how deeply I was loved. And then yesterday he wrote me this letter from Marseille, where he had gone for a few hours:

When you gave me permission to love you, my sweet Renée, I believed happiness might be possible, but today I see happiness without end. The past is no more than a dim memory, a shadow to bring out the dazzling light of my joy. When I am near you, love so transports me that I cannot begin to express the depth of my affection: I can only admire you, adore you. Words return to me only when I am far away. You are perfectly beautiful, with a beauty so serious, so majestic, that time will have difficulty altering it, and, although love between spouses cares less for beauty than for the sentiments, which in you are exquisite, allow me to say that this certainty of seeing you forever beautiful gives me a gladness that grows each time I look at you. Your sublime soul shines forth from your face; behind the hearty, robust cast of your skin there is a kind of purity, created by your serene and harmonious features. The gleam of your black eyes and the bold curve of your brow express the loftiness of your virtues, the steadiness of your company, the resilience of your heart in the face of life's tempests, should they ever arise. Nobility is your distinctive trait; I do not claim to reveal that to you, but I write these lines that you might understand how well I know the worth of the treasure that is mine. Whatever you may grant me will always be pure happiness, years from now as today, for I see all that is elevated in our mutual vow to hold fast to our absolute freedom. We will never owe a manifestation of tenderness to anything other than our own desire to offer it. In spite of the tight bonds that unite us, we will always be free. Knowing the value you place on it, I will be all the prouder to make your conquest anew. Never will you speak or breathe, act or think, without my admiring ever the more the grace of your body and soul. There is something divine in you, something wise, something captivating, that brings together thought, honor, pleasure, and hope, something that gives love an expansiveness greater than life. Oh! my angel, may the genius of love remain ever faithful to me, and may the future be full of those raptures with whose aid you have brought beauty to everything around me! When will you become a mother, that I might see you laud the vitality that is in you, that I might hear you, with your musical voice and your subtle ideas, so fresh and so curiously well-turned, bless the love that has renewed my soul, that has restored my faculties, that has filled me with pride, and from which I have drawn a new life, as from some magical spring? Yes, I will be everything you would have me be: I will become a man useful to my homeland, and I will reflect that glory onto you, for your satisfaction will be its only aim.

As you see, my dear, I am teaching him well. That style is of recent vintage; in a year it will be better. Louis is still in the throes of his first transports, while I wait for him to join me in the steady, untroubled contentment that a happy marriage cannot help but offer when, sure of each other, truly knowing each other, a man and a woman have found the secret of varying the infinite, of making life's simplest things magical. I can half glimpse that beautiful secret, and I want to possess it. As you see, he thinks himself loved as if he were not my husband, the smug simpleton! But in fact I have progressed no further than the kind of material attachment that gives us the strength to endure many things. Nonetheless, Louis is lovable, there is a great steadiness in his character. Things that most men would boast of he does very simply. Even if I do not love him, I believe I could grow fond of him.

Here, then, is my black hair, here are my black eyes, whose lashes, you used to say, part like the slats of a jalousie, here is my imperious air and my person elevated to the rank of a sovereign power. We shall see if in ten years we are not both of us very happy and gay in that Paris of yours, from which I will sometimes take you away to my beautiful Provençal oasis. Oh, Louise, do not compromise the fine future that awaits us! Do not fall into the follies you threaten. I am marrying an old young man; you must marry some young old man of the peerage. On that point at least, you are entirely right.

14

Madrid

My dear brother, you have made me the Duke de Soria, and I intend to act like a Duke de Soria. If I knew you to be drifting from town to town with none of the comforts money provides us wherever we go, I would curse my own happiness. Neither Maria nor I will consent to be married until we hear that you have accepted the funds sent you by way of Urraca. Those two million come from your own savings, and Maria's. We have both knelt at the same altar and prayed—oh! God knows with what fervor!—for your happiness. Oh my brother! Our prayers will surely be granted. The love you seek will descend from the heavens and console you for your exile. Maria wept as she read your letter; she admires you with all her heart. For my part, I accept your generous gesture for the sake of our house and not for my own. The king did just as you supposed. Ah! You so scornfully flung his pleasure in his face, as one flings a tiger its prey; I long to tell him how small he seemed next to you at that moment. The one thing I took for myself, dear brother, is my joy, is Maria. And so before you I will always be what a mere man is before his Creator. In my life and Maria's, there will be one day as beautiful as the day of our happy marriage: the day we learn that your heart has been understood, that a woman loves you as you should and want to be loved. Do not forget that, if you live through us, we live no less through you. You may write us in all confidence by way of the papal nuncio; address all your future letters to Rome. The French ambassador in Rome will forward them to the secretariat of state, Monsignore Bemboni, who has been alerted to this arrangement by our legate. Any other method would be a grave mistake. Farewell, dear despoiled one, dear exile. If you cannot be happy yourself, be proud, at least, of the happiness you have given us. God will surely hear our prayers, which are full of you.

Fernand

15

March

Oh! my angel, I see marriage has made you philosophical?...Your dear face must have been grim and gray as you penned those somber thoughts on the subject of human existence and duty. Do you believe you will convert me to the cause of marriage with these subterranean labors you're planning? Alas! is this where our overworldly daydreams have led you? We left Blois armored in our innocence and armed with the daggers of thought: the sharp point of that purely abstract experience of the world has turned back on you! If I did not know you to be the purest, most angelic creature in this world, I would tell you that there is something depraved in your calculations. Can it be, my dear? For the sake of your life in the country, you order your pleasures in regular parcels, you do with love as you'll do with your forests! Oh! Better to die in the violence of my heart's whirlwinds than to live in the draft of your tidy arithmetic. Like me, you were the best-taught of all girls, since we devoted such deep thought to few things, but, my child, philosophy without love, or disguised by a feigned love, is the most horrible conjugal hypocrisy I can imagine. I am not convinced that even the greatest imbecile on earth would not sometimes glimpse the owl of wisdom hiding beneath your pile of roses, an unenticing discovery, capable of routing the most ardent passion. You are shaping your destiny, rather than submit to its whims. We are undergoing a curious change, you and I: much philosophy and little love, that's your system; much love and little philosophy, that's mine. To think that I took Jean-Jacques's Julie for a teacher! She is a mere student next to you. O feminine virtue! Have you ever once taken the measure of life?

Alas! here I am mocking you, and you may well be right. You have thrown away your youth in one day and made yourself a miser before your time. Your Louis will no doubt be happy. If he loves you, and I have no doubt he does, then he will never see that you're acting in the interest of your family exactly as a courtesan acts in the interest of her fortune; and surely courtesans do make men happy, if we are to believe the mad dissipations they inspire. No doubt a husband who knew all would not lose his passion for you, but would he not in the end absolve himself of the duty to be grateful to a woman who makes of dishonesty a sort of spiritual corset, as necessary to her life as the other kind is to her body? Now, as I see it, my dear, love is the guiding principle of all the virtues we associate with the divine! Like all principles, love is beyond calculation; it is the infinity of our soul. Are you not seeking some way to justify the terrible lot of a girl married to a man for whom she can feel only esteem? Duty, that is your rule and your yardstick, but is acting out of necessity not the morality of an atheistic society? And is acting out of love and sentiment not womankind's secret law? You have made yourself a man, and your Louis will find that he is the woman! Oh my dear, your letter has plunged me into endless meditations. I have seen that the convent can never replace a mother for girls. I beg you, my noble, dark-eyed angel, so pure and so proud, so grave and so elegant, think of these first cries ripped from my breast by your letter! I consoled myself with the thought that, even as I lamented, love was perhaps toppling the scaffolding of your reason. I will perhaps do worse without reasoning, without calculating; passion is a way of life that must have a logic every bit as implacable as yours.

Monday

Yesterday evening, just before bed, I stood at my window to gaze at the sky, which was sublimely pure. The stars were like silver nails holding up a blue veil. I heard breathing in the silence of the night, and by the half-light of the stars I saw my Spaniard perched like a squirrel in the branches of a tree on the little side street by the boulevard; no doubt he was gazing admiringly at my windows. The first effect of that discovery was to send me scurrying back into my room, my feet and hands numb with fright, but deep beneath that terror I felt a delicious joy. I was shocked and happy. Not one of those fine Frenchmen who want to marry me was ever so fine as to spend his nights in an elm tree, at the risk of being dragged away by the night watch. My Spaniard must have been there for some time. Ah! he is done giving me lessons, he wants me to teach him, and so I shall. If he knew all I've said to myself about his outward ugliness! I too, Renée, have philosophized. I have reflected that there is something ignoble about loving a handsome man. Is that not an admission that love is three-quarters sensual, when it should be divine? Recovering from my first rush of fear, I put my head out the window to see him again, and how glad I am that I did! Using a hollow cane, he blew a letter to me, artistically rolled around a lead pellet. "My God! Will he think I left my window open on purpose?" I asked myself. "And if I now slam it shut, that will make me his accomplice." I did better: I came back to my window as if I hadn't heard the sound of his note landing, as if I'd seen nothing, and I said very audibly, "Griffith, come and look at the stars!" Griffith was sleeping like an old maid. Hearing me, the Moor slithered down the tree as fast as a shadow. He must have been half dead with fear, and so was I, not having heard him walk off; he must still have been close by the elm's trunk. After a good fifteen minutes, during which I plunged into the blue of the sky and swam in the ocean of curiosity, I closed my window and lay down to unroll the fine paper, cautious as any scholar of ancient volumes in Naples. I felt fire beneath my fingers. What a horrible power that man has over me! I told myself. I immediately held the paper to my lamp, intending to burn it without reading it.... A thought stayed my hand. What is he writing me, that he must write me in secret? Well, my dear, I burned the letter, thinking that if every other girl on earth would have devoured it, I, Armande-Louise-Marie de Chaulieu, mustn't read it.

The next day, at Les Italiens, he was at his post, but, first constitutional minister though he once was, I do not believe he could see the slightest agitation in my soul from my manner: I behaved exactly as if I'd seen nothing and received nothing the evening before. I felt more than a little pleased with myself, but he was very sad. Poor man, it's so natural in Spain for love to come in through the window! At intermission he came up to stroll through the corridors. The first secretary of the Spanish embassy informed me of that as he was telling me of a sublime thing he had done. Being the Duke de Soria, he was to marry one of the wealthiest heiresses in Spain, the young Princess Maria Hérédia, whose fortune would have eased the sorrows of his exile, but it would seem that, contrary to the wishes of their fathers, who had settled their marriage when they were but children, Maria loved his young brother, and my Felipe forswore all claim to Princess Maria, allowing the King of Spain to deprive him of his titles.

"I imagine he did that noble deed as if it were the most natural thing in the world," I said to the young man.

"You know him, then?" he answered, naively. My mother smiled.

"What will become of him?" I asked. "After all, he is condemned to die."

"Though he be a dead man in Spain, he has the right to live in Sardinia."

"Ah! so there are also tombs in Spain?" I said, to suggest I was taking all this as a joke.[30]

"There is a bit of everything in Spain, even old-fashioned Spaniards," my mother answered.

"He required some convincing, but the King of Sardinia granted Baron de Macumer a passport," the young diplomat continued. "In the end, he became a Sardinian subject; he owns a magnificent fiefdom, with the right to deliver justice both high and low. He has a palace in Sassari. If Ferdinand VII were to die, Macumer would very possibly enter the diplomacy and the royal court of Turin would make of him an ambassador. Although still young, he—"

"Ah! so he's young!"

"Yes, mademoiselle, although young, he is one of the most distinguished men of Spain!"

I was looking all around the theater as I listened to the secretary, and seemed to be only half paying attention, but, between us, I was distraught at having burned that letter. How does a man such as this speak when he is in love? And he is indeed in love. What a thing it is to be loved, to be secretly adored, to have in this theater, where all of Paris's finest are gathered, a man of one's own, unknown to all! Oh! Renée, at that moment I understood life in Paris, its balls and festivities. All at once everything made perfect sense to me. You need other people around you when you're in love, if only to sacrifice them to your beloved. I felt another, happy self inside me. How flattering all this was for my vanity, my pride, my self-regard! God knows what a gaze I cast upon the world! "Clever little vixen!" the duchess smilingly whispered in my ear. Yes, my very shrewd mother had glimpsed some secret joy in my manner, and I surrendered to that most astute woman. Those few words taught me more about the world than all I had gleaned in the previous year, for it's now March. Alas! In a month we will no longer have the Italiens. What can one do with oneself without that adorable music when one's heart is full of love?

My dear, on my return, with a resolve worthy of a Chaulieu, I opened my window to admire a rain shower. Oh! If men only knew the power of seduction exerted on us by heroic acts, they would do great things indeed; the greatest cowards would be heroes. What I'd learned of my Spaniard had fired my blood. I thought he must be outside, ready to send a new letter my way. And this time I burned nothing: I read it. Here, then, is the first love letter I have ever received, my very well-reasoned madame: to each our own.

> Louise, I do not love you for your sublime beauty; I do not love you for the breadth of your mind, the nobility of your sentiments, the infinite grace you impart to all things, nor for your

pride, your regal disdain for all that is not of your world, which does not make you unkind, for you have the charity of the angels. Louise, I love you because you relaxed that sovereign superiority for the sake of a poor exile; because, with one gesture, one glance, you consoled a man so far beneath you that he deserved only your pity, generous though that pity be. You are the only woman in the world who has tempered the hardness in her eyes for my sake, and because you allowed that beneficent gaze to land on me when I was nothing more than a grain of dust among all the others, something never granted me when I had all the power a subject may have, I must tell you, Louise, that you have found a place in my heart, that I love you for yourself alone and with no other thought, far beyond your requirements for a perfect love. Know, then, O idol whom I have placed in the highest reaches of heaven, that there is in this world an offspring of the Saracen race whose life belongs to you, of whom you may ask anything, as you would a slave, and who will be honored to carry out your orders. I have given myself to you forever and solely for the pleasure of giving myself, for one single glance from you, for the hand you extended one day to your Spanish teacher. You have a servant, Louise, and nothing else. No, I dare not suppose I will ever be loved, but perhaps I will be tolerated, and only for my devotion. Ever since that morning when you smiled like a noble girl on discovering the misery of my lonely, wronged heart, I placed you on a throne: you are the absolute ruler of my life, the queen of my thoughts, the divinity of my heart, the light that shines in my rooms, the flower of my flowers, the perfume of the air I breathe, the richness of my blood, the glow in which I sleep. That happiness was troubled by one single thought. You did not know you had a boundless devotion to serve you, a loyal arm, a blind slave, a mute agent, a treasury, for I am now only the caretaker of all that is mine; you did not realize, in other words, that you owned a heart in which you may always confide. The heart of an aged ancestress of whom you may ask whatever you please, the heart of a father from whom you may demand any protection, the heart of a friend, of a brother: I know you have no such sentiments around you. I have discovered your secret solitude! My boldness was born only of my desire to show you all that you owned. Accept everything, Louise, and you will give me the only life there can be for me in this world, a life of complete devotion. You commit yourself to nothing by placing the yoke of servitude over my neck: never will I ask anything more than the pleasure of knowing I am yours. Do not even tell me that you will never love me. That is how it must be, I know; I must love from afar, with no hope, and for myself alone. I long to know if you will accept me as your servant, and I have struggled to find some way to prove that your dignity will not be compromised by telling me that you do, for I became yours many days ago, and you had no idea. I will understand that your answer is yes if, some night at the Italiens, you hold in your hand a bouquet of one white and one red camellia—the image of all a man's blood at the beck and call of a beloved purity. With that everything will be said: at any time, in ten years or tomorrow, whatever you would it were possible for a man to do will be done, the moment you ask it of your happy servant,

Felipe Hénarez

P.S. You must admit, my dear, highborn men truly know how to love! What a leap, worthy of an African lion! What repressed ardor! What faith! What sincerity! What greatness of the soul in that humility! Reading those lines, I felt small, and I wondered, lost: What must I do?... It is in the nature of a great man to upset all our little plans. He is sublime and endearing, naive and titanic. With one single letter he goes beyond all of Lovelace's hundred letters, beyond even Saint-Preux.[31] Oh! Here is true love, without half measures: it is or it is not, but when it is, it must exist in all its immensity. My wiles are of no use to me now. Decline or accept! I must do one or the other, with no pretext behind which to hide my indecision. All discussion is silenced in advance. This is no longer Paris, it's Spain, it's the Orient; there is the voice of the Abencerrage, kneeling before the Catholic Eve and offering her his scimitar, his horse, and his head. Will I accept this survivor of the Moors? Reread that Hispano-Saracen letter over and over, my Renée; you will see that love sweeps away all the Judaic provisos of your philosophy. See there, Renée, I cannot drive your letter from my mind, you have bourgeoisified my life. Is there any need to dither? Am I not the eternal mistress of that lion, its roars now become meek, lovestruck sighs? Oh! How he must have roared in his lair on the rue Hillerin-Bertin! I know where he lives, I have his card: F., BARON DE MACUMER. He has left me no occasion for an answer, I can only throw two camellias in his face. What infernal talent pure, true, naive love possesses! Here is everything that is most momentous for a woman's heart reduced to one plain, simple act. O, Asia! I have read the *Thousand and One Nights*, and here is its spirit: with two flowers all is said. We race through the fourteen volumes of *Clarissa* with one single bouquet. That letter makes me squirm like a rope in the fire. Take your two camellias, or do not. Yes or no, kill or give life! In the end, a voice cries out to me: "Test him!" And so I shall!

16

FROM THE SAME TO THE SAME

March

I am dressed in white; I have white camellias in my hair and a white camellia in my hand. My mother's are red; I will take one from her if I choose. I feel a curious urge to make *him* pay dearly for his red camellia by hesitating a moment and making my decision only then and there. I am very beautiful! Griffith asked for a moment to look at me. The solemnity of this evening and the drama of this secret consent have colored my face: on each cheek I have a red camellia blooming against a white one!

One o'clock in the morning

Everyone admired me; only one was capable of adoring me. His face fell when he saw me with a white camellia in my hand, and I saw him turn white as that flower when I took a red one from my mother. I might have brought those two flowers purely by chance; by picking one before his eyes, I gave him an answer and so made of my confession an event! The opera that evening was *Roméo et Juliette*, and as you know nothing of the two lovers' duet, you cannot understand the happiness that divine expression of tenderness inspires in two newcomers to love. I went to bed hearing footfalls on the resonant stones of the side street. Oh! Now, my angel, my heart is on fire, and my mind. What is he doing? What is he thinking? Does he have one thought in his mind that does not involve me? Is he the ever-willing slave that he claims? How to be sure? Does he have in his soul the slightest suspicion that my acceptance sweeps away any rebuke, any return, any gratitude? I am lost in the labyrinthine ruminations of the women in *Cyrus* and *L'Astrée*, in the subtleties of the Courts of Love.[32] Does he know that in love a woman's slightest act is the conclusion of a world of reflections, inner battles, lost victories? What is he thinking at this moment? How may I order him to write me a detailed account of his day every evening? He is my slave, I must keep him busy, and I intend to drown him in work.

Sunday morning

I slept only a little, after dawn. It is now noon. I have just dictated the following letter to Griffith.

> To Monsieur le Baron de Macumer,
> Mademoiselle de Chaulieu has directed me, Monsieur le Baron, to ask for the return of a letter written her by one of her friends and copied out in her hand, which you took away with you.
>
> Yours, etc.
> Griffith

My dear, Griffith went off to the rue Hillerin-Bertin and had that love note delivered to my slave, who returned my statement of purpose, damp with tears, in an envelope. He obeyed me. Oh! My dear, how much that page must have meant to him! Any other man would have refused in a letter overstuffed with flattery, but that Saracen did just as he promised: he obeyed. I am moved to tears.

17
FROM THE SAME TO THE SAME

April 2

The weather yesterday was magnificent. I dressed in the manner of a girl who is loved and eager to please. At my request, my father gave me the finest conveyance to be seen in all of Paris: two dappled gray horses and a calèche of the greatest elegance. I wanted to try out my finery. I was like a flower beneath a parasol lined with white silk. As I drove up the Champs-Élysées, I saw my Abencerrage coming toward me on a magnificent stallion: people stopped in their tracks to examine it, for most men are amateur horse traders nowadays. He saluted me with one hand, and I gave him a friendly sign of encouragement; he slowed his horse, which gave me a moment to tell him, "Do not take it amiss that I asked for my letter back, Monsieur le Baron; it was of no further use to you." To which, in a low voice, I added, "You have already exceeded those requirements."

I paused for a moment, then went on: "Your horse seems to attract a good deal of attention."

"My steward in Sardinia sent it to me as a point of pride, for this Arabian stallion was born in my maquis."

This morning, my dear, Hénarez was riding an English sorrel horse, again very beautiful, but causing no stir: the very slight mocking criticism in my words had sufficed. He saluted me, and I answered with a faint nod. Macumer's horse had been bought by the Duke d'Angoulême. My slave understood that he was straying from the requisite simplicity by attracting the passing crowd's gaze. A man must be noticed for himself alone, not for his horse nor for any mere thing. Riding too fine a horse seems to me as ridiculous as wearing an oversize diamond on one's breast. I was enchanted to be taking him to task, and perhaps there was a touch of arrogance in his choice, forgivable in one who has been banished. That childishness pleases me. Oh my old reasoning friend! Are you finding as much pleasure in my love as I find grimness in your stern philosophy? Dear Philip II in a skirt, are you beside me here, riding in my calèche? Do you see the velvety gaze, humble and fulsome, proud of its servitude, briefly sent my way by that truly great man, who now wears my livery, since he always has a red camellia in his buttonhole, just as I hold a white one in my hand? What clarity love imparts! How well I understand Paris! Now everything here seems full of refinement. Yes, love here is prettier, grander, more charming than anywhere else in the world. I have realized that I could never torment or trouble a fool, nor have the slightest hold over him. Only superior men can fully understand us, and only on them can we exert our influence. Oh! poor friend, forgive me, I was forgetting about our l'Estorade, but did you not tell me that you planned to make of him a genius? Oh, I believe I understand why: you are carefully cultivating him so that one day you will be understood. Farewell, I'm feeling a bit giddy, and I prefer not to go on.

18

April

Dear angel, or should I say dear demon, you have saddened me without meaning to; were we not one single soul, I would say you have
hurt me—but can one not also hurt oneself? How obvious it is that
you have not yet let your thoughts linger on that word *indissoluble*
as it applies to the contract binding a woman to a man! I have no
wish to contradict the philosophers or the legislators—they are entirely
capable of contradicting themselves—but, my dear, by making marriage irrevocable and imposing on it one single form, universal and
unbending, they have made of each union an entirely unique thing,
as distinct as one individual from the next. Every marriage has its
own internal laws: those of a marriage in the country, where two
people will constantly be in each other's presence, are not those of a
household in the city, where life is variegated by more numerous
distractions, and those of a household in Paris, where life goes by like
a rushing torrent, will not be those of a marriage in the provinces,
where life is not so hectic. If the conditions vary with the location,
they vary still more with the two natures involved. The wife of a man
of genius has only to let herself be carried along; the wife of a fool,
assuming she is more intelligent than he, must seize the controls lest
still greater misfortunes befall her. Perhaps, taken to an extreme,
reflection and reason can become what is known as depravity. For
our purposes, by depravity do we not mean the presence of calculation
in the sentiments? A passion that reasons is depraved; it is beautiful
only when it is involuntary, only in those sublime surges of emotion
untouched by self-interest. Ah! Sooner or later, my dear, you will say

to yourself, "Yes! A woman requires artifice no less than her corset," if by artifice we mean the silence of a woman who has the courage to hold her tongue, if by artifice we mean the calculations required for future security. Every married woman learns the laws of society at her own expense, laws that are in many ways incompatible with nature's. A woman who marries at our age can have a dozen children in her marriage; if she did, she would be committing twelve crimes, she would be creating twelve miseries. Would she not be delivering charming creatures into the hands of misery and despair? Whereas two children are two joys, two good deeds, two creations in harmony with today's laws and ways. Natural and civil law are enemies, and we are the field on which they do battle. Do you, then, call depravity the wisdom of a wife who sees to it that her family is not ruined by its own existence? With one calculation or a thousand, all is lost in the heart. You will find yourself engaging in that dreaded calculation, my beautiful Baroness de Macumer, when you are the proud, happy wife of the man who loves you—or rather, that fine man will spare you the trouble, for he will undertake it himself. As you see, dear free spirit, I have carefully studied the civil code as it applies to conjugal love. You will learn that we are responsible only to ourselves and to God for the means we employ to ensure happiness in our homes; better a calculation that achieves that end than an unreflecting love that brings sorrow, strife, or distance. I have unflinchingly studied the role of the wife and the mother. Yes, dear angel, we have sublime lies to tell in order to be the noble creatures we are when we accomplish our duties. You accuse me of artifice because I want to mete out Louis's knowledge of me from day to day, but is distance not caused precisely by too intimate a knowledge? I want to keep him busy so as to keep him distracted from me, in the name of his own happiness, and that has nothing to do with calculation in the passions. Affection may well be inexhaustible, but love is not, so it is an entirely worthwhile occupation for a woman to distribute it judiciously over her lifetime. You may well think me abominable, but I have not abandoned my principles, and I think myself very great and very generous for it. Virtue, my darling, is an abstract idea whose manifestations vary

from one setting to the next: the virtues of Provence, of Constanti-
nople, of London and Paris are perfectly disparate in their outward
forms, but they are all virtue nonetheless. The tissue of every human
life is woven of the most idiosyncratic combinations, but from a
certain height they all look the same. If I wanted to make Louis
unhappy and bring about an estrangement, I would have only to put
myself on his leash. I have not had the happiness of meeting a superior
man, as you have, but perhaps I will have the pleasure of making my
man superior, and I hereby set a date with you in five years in Paris.
You yourself will be taken in; you will tell me I was mistaken, that
Monsieur de l'Estorade was born an exceptional person. As for the
wonders of love, as for those emotions I feel only through you, as for
those nightly lingerings on the balcony by the light of the stars, those
adorations, those deifications, of those, I have learned, I must abandon
all hope. Your glittering success in life radiates all around you, as far
as you please; mine is confined, its walls are those of La Crampade,
and you rebuke me for the precautions a poor, fragile, secret happiness
requires to become durable, rich, and mysterious! I thought I had
discovered the graces of a mistress in my wifely position, and you have
almost made me blush at myself. Between the two of us, who is right,
who is wrong? Perhaps we are both equally right and wrong, and
perhaps society sells us our lace, our titles, and our children at a very
dear price! I have red camellias of my own, I wear them on my lips,
in the form of smiles that bloom for those two souls, father and son,
to whom I am devoted, at once slave and mistress. But, my dear! your
last letters have given me a sense of all I have lost. You have shown
me the full extent of the sacrifices a married woman must make. I
have scarcely so much as glimpsed those beautiful, wild steppes you
are now bounding over, and I will say nothing to you of the tears I
wiped away on reading your words—but regret is not remorse, even
if it is a close cousin. "Marriage has made you philosophical!" you
wrote me, but alas no, as I realized when I wept on learning you had
been swept away on that surging wave of love. But some time ago my
father advised me to read one of the most profound writers of our
lands, an heir to Bossuet, one of those cruel manipulators who never

fails to convince. While you were reading *Corinne*, I was reading Bonald,[33] and here is the whole secret of my philosophy: I came to see the Family as a powerful, holy thing. By Bonald, your father said only the truth in his little speech. Farewell, my dear imagination, my friend, you who are my only folly!

19

Well, you are a wonderful wife, my Renée, and I now quite agree that it is an honorable thing to deceive: there, are you happy? Besides, the man who loves us belongs to us; we have the right to make of him a fool or a man of genius, though, between us, they are most often our fools. You will make a man of genius out of yours, and you will keep it a secret: two glorious deeds! Ah! It would be a good joke on you if there were no heaven, for you have abandoned yourself to voluntary martyrdom. You want to make him ambitious and keep him in love with you! But, child that you are, simply keeping him in love with you is endeavor enough. To what degree is calculation virtue or virtue calculation? Hmm? We won't quarrel over that question, since Bonald is here. We are and we want to be virtuous, but at this moment I believe that, for all your charming little games, you are a better woman than I. Yes, I am a horribly duplicitous girl: I love Felipe, and I hide it from him with an appalling dissimulation. I would like to see him leap from his tree to the top of the wall, from the top of the wall to my balcony, and if he did as I wish I would wither him with my disdain. As you see, I am brutally honest. Who is stopping me? What power prevents me from telling that dear Felipe of all the happiness his pure, whole, great, secret love sends flooding through me? Madame de Mirbel is painting my portrait; I intend to give it to him. I am each day more astonished at the vitality love brings to life. How interesting each hour becomes, every act, down to the tiniest things! And what a wonderful mingling of the past and the future in the present! One lives in three tenses at once. Oh! Answer me, tell me about happiness—does it calm, or does it excite? I am sick with anxiety, I have no idea what to do: there is a force in my heart that draws me to him, against all reason and convention. I finally understand your curiosity about Louis, are you happy? Felipe's joy in being mine, his love from afar, his obedience, all that goads me no less than his deep respect needled me when he was only my Spanish teacher. Seeing him pass by, I am tempted to cry out, "Idiot, if you love me in a painting, what would it be to truly know me?"

Oh! Renée, you do burn my letters, don't you? And I will burn yours. If any eyes but ours were to read these thoughts spilled out heart to heart, I would order Felipe to go and gouge them out, and then kill their owners while he's about it, just to be sure.

Monday

Ah! Renée, how to sound the heart of a man? My father must introduce your Monsieur Bonald to me, and then, since he's so wise, I'll ask him. God is lucky indeed to be able to plumb the depths of the human heart. Am I still an angel for that man? That is the great question.

If ever I were to glimpse, in a gesture, a glance, a tone of voice, any waning of the respect he showed me as my Spanish teacher, I believe I would find the strength to forget everything! Why these grand words, these grand resolutions, you will ask? Ah! I shall tell you, my dear. As I say, my charming father, who behaves with me like an old consort with a woman of Italy, has been having my portrait done by Madame de Mirbel. I succeeded in having a rather skillful copy made; that copy was for the duke, the original for Felipe. I sent it off yesterday, accompanied by these few lines:

Don Felipe, your wholehearted devotion is answered by an implicit trust. Does any man merit this blind faith? Only time will tell.

It's a generous reward, it sounds like a promise and, horrors, an invitation, but what you will find more awful still is that I wanted the reward to express both a promise and an invitation, without going so far as an offer. If in his answer I see the words *my Louise*, or even simply *Louise*, he is lost.

Tuesday

No! he is not lost. That constitutional minister is a glorious lover. Here is his reply:

I have not gone one moment away from you without thinking of you, my eyes closed to everything around me and riveted through my meditations on your image, which could never appear promptly enough in that dark palace where dreams are set, a palace that you filled with light. Henceforth my gaze will find repose in that marvelous miniature—or that talisman, I should say, for I see your blue eyes come to life, and all at once the painting becomes a reality. My delay in writing you this letter comes from my insistent, imperious need to luxuriate in that contemplation, and that opportunity to tell you all the things I must never say. Yes, since yesterday, closeted away alone with you, I abandoned myself to a whole, unmingled, infinite happiness for the first time in my life. If you could see yourself where I have placed you, between God and the Virgin, you would understand the terrors that filled my night, but I hope I will not offend you by speaking of them, for I find so many torments in one single glance unlit by the angelic goodness I live for that I can only beg your pardon in advance. Oh queen of my life and soul, if only you would consent to grant me one one-thousandth of the love I feel for you!

The if only in that endlessly repeated prayer ravaged my soul. I found myself between belief and error, between life and death, darkness and light. A criminal awaiting his verdict is no more petrified than I as I plead guilty to this boldness before you. The smile on your lips, to which my eyes returned again and again, calmed those tempests aroused by the fear of displeasing you. In all my life, no one has ever smiled at me, not even my mother. The beautiful girl who was meant to be my wife spurned my heart and fell in love with my brother. My political efforts met only with defeat. In the eyes of my king I saw only a desire for vengeance; we have been such great enemies since our earliest days that he took my elevation to power by the Cortes[34] as a personal affront. For less than this, even the hardiest soul could lose all hope. Not to mention that I am under no illusion: I am fully aware of my external homeliness, and I know how difficult it is to gauge the value of my heart through such a vessel. When I first saw you, love was nothing more than a dream for me. Finding myself growing fond of you, I realized that devotion alone could inspire you to forgive me my affection. I looked at that portrait, I heard the divine promises expressed by that smile, and a hope I had never allowed myself to feel cast a glow through my soul. That dawn-like gleam must continually do battle with the gloom of doubt, with the fear that I might offend you should I let it shine out. No, you cannot love me yet, I understand that, but once you have felt the power, the deathlessness, the depth of my inexhaustible affection, you will offer it a small place in your heart. If my ambition is an insult, you need only tell me so without anger, and I will go back to my role, but should you be willing to try to love me, do not, without the most careful precautions, make it known to one who has made serving you the whole of his happiness in life.

My dear, I believed I could see him as I read those last few words, just as pale as he was that evening I displayed the camellia to tell him I accepted the treasures of his devotion. I saw in those submissive sentences something very different from a mere flight of amorous rhetoric, and I felt a sort of great stirring inside me . . . the fresh wind of happiness.

The weather has been dreadful, I've had no chance to go to the Bois de Boulogne, lest I arouse curious suspicions; for my mother, who often goes out even in the rain, has stayed at home alone.

Wednesday evening

I've just seen *him*, at the Opéra. My dear, he is no longer the same man; he came to our box, introduced by the Sardinian ambassador. Seeing in my eyes that I was not displeased by his boldness, he suddenly seemed awkward and shy, and then he called the Marquise d'Espard "mademoiselle." The fire in his eyes outshone the lamps. Finally he went out, as if terrified he might commit some irreparable gaffe.

"Baron de Macumer is in love!" Madame de Maufrigneuse said to my mother.

"An extraordinary sight—and him a deposed minister!" my mother answered.

I found the strength to look at Madame d'Espard, Madame de Maufrigneuse, and my mother with the curiosity of one unversed in some foreign language, trying to guess the things being said, but inside I felt an exquisite joy submerging my soul. There is only one word by which to explain what I now feel, and that word is "bliss." Felipe loves so deeply that I find him worthy of love. I am the very principle of his life, and I hold in my hand the string that guides his thoughts. If you and I must tell each other all, then I will say that I long most ardently to see him beat down every obstacle, to see him come and ask me for myself, so that I might learn if I can still make that raging love quiet and meek with one single glance.

Ah! my dear, I interrupted my letter there, and now I am all atremble. I heard a faint sound outside as I was writing. I rose to my feet, and through the window I saw him walking along the top of the wall, at great risk to his life. I hurried to the bedroom window and gave him nothing more than a sign; he leapt from the wall, which is ten feet high, and then ran down the road until I could see him, to show me he was unhurt. That thoughtfulness at a time when he was very likely dazed by his fall so moved me that I now find myself weeping without knowing why. Poor toad! Why did he come here, what did he want to tell me?

I dare not write what I am thinking; I will now go to bed in my joy and reflect on all we would say if we were together. Farewell, my mute beauty. I have no time to chide you for your silence, but a month has gone by with no word from you. Have you perhaps become a happy wife? Have you perhaps surrendered the free will that made you so proud, and which nearly deserted me this evening?

20

May

If love is the life of the world, why do austere philosophers allow it
no place in marriage? Why does Society take Woman's sacrifice to
the family as its highest law, inevitably sparking a silent battle in the
very heart of every marriage? A battle that Society has in fact foreseen,
so dangerous that Society has invented powers with which to arm
men against us, realizing that we could undo everything by the magic
of romance or the power of a secret hatred. I now see in marriage two
opposed forces that the lawmakers should have united; when will
they come together? So I say to myself as I read your words. Oh! my
dear, just one of your letters makes a ruin of the edifice built by the
great writer of the Aveyron, an edifice into which I had settled with
some satisfaction. Old men make the laws, as any woman can plainly
see; they have most sagaciously decreed that conjugal love without
passion is no indignity for a woman, that she must give herself without love once the law has authorized a man to claim her as his. In
their preoccupation with the family, they imitate nature, concerned
solely with the perpetuation of the species. Once I was a living being,
and now I am a thing! I have choked back more than one tear, far
away and alone, which I wished I could exchange for a consoling
smile. Why must our two fates be so different? Thanks to a shared
love, your soul is growing and flourishing. You will find virtue in
pleasure. You will suffer only by your own will. Your duty, if you
marry your Felipe, will become the sweetest and most exalted of all
sentiments. Our future is pregnant with the answer to that question,
and I await it with anxious curiosity.

You love, you are adored. Oh! my dear, you must give yourself over entirely to that beautiful poem that once so filled our minds. Feminine beauty, so refined and so sparkling in you, was created by God to charm and to please; He has His reasons. Yes, my angel, keep your ardor a closely held secret, and subject Felipe to all the subtle tests we invented to learn if the lover we dreamt of would be worthy of us. Above all, determine less if he loves you than if you love him: nothing is more deceptive than the mirage created in our soul by curiosity, by desire, by the anticipation of happiness. You who, unlike me, are still wholly your own, do not enter into the dangerous bargain of an irrevocable marriage without demanding the proper guarantees, I beg of you! A single gesture, a word, a glance, in a conversation without witnesses, the two souls stripped of their worldly masks, can illuminate many dark corners. You are noble enough, self-assured enough to venture boldly down paths where others would lose their way. You cannot imagine how anxiously I follow after you. In spite of the distance between us, I see you, I feel your emotions. Do not fail to write me, then, and omit nothing! Your letters offer me a life rich with passion here in my very simple, very sedate household, plain as a highway on a sunless day. What is happening here, my angel, is a series of quarrels with myself, which I prefer to keep secret for today; I will tell you more later. I give myself and then stubbornly take myself back, going from discouragement to hope and hope to discouragement. Perhaps I am asking life for more happiness than it owes us. When we are young, we always expect the ideal and the real to be one! My reflections, to which I must now devote myself alone, sitting at the foot of a high bluff in my grounds, have led me to conclude that love in marriage is a matter of chance on which no law can be founded, for law must be founded in universals. My Aveyron philosopher is right to see the family as the only source of social cohesion, and to submit woman to it as she has always been. The solution to that great question, that almost fearsome question for us, is in the first child we bear, and so I am eager to be a mother, if only to give fodder to the ravenous energy of my soul.

Louis is as always wonderfully kind, his love is concrete and my tenderness is abstract; he is happy, he gathers the rosebuds all alone, little caring what the soil has given up to produce them. Happy egoism! Whatever it might cost me, I maintain his illusions, just as a mother—such, at least, as I conceive of a mother—must exhaust herself for the sake of her child's contentment. His joy is so deep that it closes his eyes, and it casts its glow even onto me. I fool him with my smile, or with the satisfied gaze given me by the knowledge that I am making him happy. My pet name for him in our private moments is thus "my child"! I await the fruit of all these sacrifices, which will be a secret between God, you, and me. Maternity is an enterprise in which I have invested a ruinous sum. Today it owes me too much, and I fear I may never be fully repaid: its task is to make use of my energy and enlarge my heart, to compensate me with unlimited joys. Oh! please God, may I not be deceived! For there lies my entire future, and, a terrifying thing to think, my virtue's as well.

21

June

Dear married doe, your letter came just when it was needed; it let me justify to myself a bold act I have been thinking of night and day. I have a kind of hunger for the unknown—or, if you like, the forbidden—which worries me and portends a battle inside me between society's laws and nature's. I don't know if nature is stronger in me than society, but I find myself seeking concessions from each of those two powers. To say all this more clearly, I wanted to speak with Felipe alone, by night, under the linden trees at the far end of our garden. That is most certainly the desire of a girl who deserves the title of bold little vixen, as the duchess laughingly calls me, echoed by my father. Nonetheless, I find that scandalous project both prudent and wise. For one thing, I would be repaying him for so many nights spent at the foot of my wall; for another, I want to know what Monsieur Felipe would think of this escapade, and to judge him in such circumstances—to make of him my beloved spouse should he transform that indiscretion into a beautiful moment, or to never see him again if he is not more respectful and tremulous than when he greets me from his horse on the Champs-Élysées. As for the opinion of society, there is less risk in seeing my suitor this way than in smiling at him in the drawing room of Madame de Maufrigneuse or the aged Marquise de Beauséant, where we are now surrounded by spies, for, God knows, when a girl is suspected of taking an interest in a monster like Macumer, every eye is upon her! Oh, if you only knew how I've stirred myself up with dreams of that project, how the search for a way to bring it about has occupied my thoughts! I missed your company: we would have talked it all over for several sweet little hours, lost in the labyrinths of uncertainty, reveling in all the good or bad things that might come with a first nocturnal rendezvous, in the shadows and silence, beneath the Chaulieu mansion's magnificent, moon-dappled lindens. Instead, I trembled all alone, thinking, "Ah! Renée, where are you?" Your letter was the spark in the powder keg, and my last scruples were blown to kingdom come. From my window, I dropped into my lover's hands a very precise drawing of the key to the little garden door, along with this note:

> You must be stopped from making a grave misstep. Should you fall and break your neck, you would ruin the honor of the one you claim to love. Are you worthy of a new proof of esteem, and do you deserve a private conversation at the hour when the moon leaves the lindens at the end of the garden in darkness?

Last night, at one o'clock, as Griffith was preparing for bed, I said to her, "Take your shawl and come with me, my dear, I want to go to the end of the garden without anyone knowing!" She followed me without a word. What feelings I had inside me, my Renée! for, after a rather long wait in the grips of a delightful little terror, I caught sight of him, gliding along like a shadow. Once safely arrived in the garden, I said to Griffith, "Don't be surprised. Baron de Macumer is here; that's precisely why I've brought you along." She said nothing.

"What do you want with me?" said Felipe, in a voice whose emotion showed that the sound of our rustling dresses in the silence of the night and our footfalls in the sand, however discreet, had had a marked effect on him.

"I want to say to you what I would never be able to write," I answered.

Griffith walked off some six paces. It was one of those warm, flower-scented nights, and I was dizzy with pleasure to find myself virtually alone with him in the soft darkness of the lindens, with the garden beyond all the brighter in that the moonlight shone white off the façade of our house. That contrast vaguely created an image of the mystery of our love, destined to end in the dazzling public display that is marriage. After wondering together for a moment at the thrill of this situation, equally new to us both, as full of surprise for us both, I recovered my voice.

"I have no fear of slander, but I would like you never to climb that tree again," I said, pointing to the elm, "nor this wall. We have played the schoolboy and the boarding-school girl long enough: let us elevate our sentiments to the level of our destinies. Should you die from a fall, I would die dishonored...." I looked at him; he was ashen. "And were you caught, my mother or I would be suspected...."

"Forgive me," he said weakly.

"Simply walk along the boulevard, and I will hear your footsteps. Should I want to see you, I will open my window, but I will make you run that risk, and I will run it myself, only in the gravest of circumstances. Why have you forced me, by your imprudence, to commit an imprudence of my own, and to lower your opinion of me?" I thought the tears I saw in his eyes the most beautiful answer in the world. "You must find what I've done tonight exceedingly dangerous," I said with a smile.

We silently walked one or two circles beneath the trees before he spoke again. "You must think me very dull; I am so drunk with happiness that I find myself without strength or wit, but know at least that to me your every act is sacred simply because you allow yourself to undertake it. My respect for you can be compared only to my respect for God. And of course, Miss Griffith is here."

"She's here for the others, Felipe, not for us," I answered sharply. My dear, he understood me.

"I know full well," he went on, giving me the humblest of looks, "that were she not here everything would be just as if she were watching us: even when we do not stand before men, we stand before God, and we require our own esteem no less than the world's."

"Thank you, Felipe," I answered, extending my hand in a gesture you can surely imagine. "A woman—and take me for a woman—is inclined to love a man who understands her. Oh! inclined, nothing more," I added, putting a finger to my lips. "I would not have you feel more hope than I mean to give you. My heart will belong only to him who can read it and truly know it. Our sentiments need not be identical, but they must have the same breadth and the same elevation. I do not wish to overestimate myself, for no doubt there are many flaws in what I see as my qualities, but I would be very sorry if I did not have them."

"First you accepted me as your servant, and then you allowed me to love you," he said, trembling and looking at me with each word. "I already have more than I ever desired."

"But," I hurried to answer, "I find your lot preferable to mine; I would not be sorry to change it, and that change depends on you."

"And now it is my turn to thank you," he answered. "I know the duties of a loyal lover. I must prove that I am worthy, and you have the right to test me for as long as you please. You may send me away, my God! should I disappoint your hopes."

"I know you love me," I told him. "So far"—and I cruelly emphasized those words—"you are the favorite, which is why you are here."

We began walking in circles again, talking, and I must confess that, once placed at his ease, it was with the most heartfelt eloquence that my Spaniard told me not of his passion but of his tender sentiments, explaining his feelings by way of an adorable comparison with divine love. His penetrating voice lent a particular force to his already refined ideas; it called to mind the tones of the nightingale. He spoke softly, in his rich middle register, and his sentences came one upon the next, quick as the bubbles in boiling water. His heart overflowed in each one.

"Stop," I said, "or I will be here longer than I should." And with a gesture I sent him away.

"Well, here you are promised to a man, mademoiselle," said Griffith.

"In England, perhaps, but not in France," I answered airily. "I want to marry for love and not be deceived, nothing more." As you see, my dear, love was not coming to me, so I did as Muhammad did with his mountain.

Friday

I saw my slave again; he grew timid, he put on a mysterious, reverent air that I like, for it seems imbued with my glory and power. But nothing in his gaze or demeanor might suggest to society's sibyls that he feels the boundless love I can see plain as day. Nonetheless, my dear, I am not overcome, dominated, tamed; on the contrary, it is I who tame, who dominate, who overcome.... I am finally reasoning for myself. Ah! I would so like to feel once more the fear caused me by the fascination of the great man or commoner to whom I refused myself. There are two sorts of love: there is one love that commands and another that obeys. They are not the same, and they give birth to two very different passions; in order to have a full measure of life, perhaps a woman must know both. Can those two passions intermingle? Can a man in whom we inspire love, inspire love in us? Will Felipe one day be my master? Will I tremble as he does? Those questions send a shiver down my spine. How blind he is! In his place, I would have thought Mademoiselle de Chaulieu very coquettishly cold, stiff, and calculating beneath those linden trees. No, that's not loving, it's playing with fire. Felipe continues to please me, but I now feel calm and at ease. No more obstacles! What a terrible thought. Everything is settling down and relaxing inside me, and I am loath to study myself too closely. He was wrong to hide the violence of his love, for he left me my own mistress. In other words, I am not enjoying the benefits of that semi-scandalous behavior. Yes, my dear, however sweet I find the memory of that half hour beneath the trees, the pleasure it brought me seems far fainter than the emotions I felt as I wondered, "Shall I go? Shall I not? Shall I write him? Shall I not?" Is the same perhaps true of all our pleasures? Are they better deferred than enjoyed? Is anticipation better than possession? Are the rich poor? Did you and I overdevelop our emotions by too vigorous an exercise of our imaginations? There are times when that thought makes my blood run cold. Do you know why? I imagine returning to the end of the garden, this time without Griffith. How far would I go then? Imagination has no limits, and pleasures do. Tell me, my dear professor in a corset, how to reconcile those two terms of a woman's existence?

22

I am not happy with you. If you did not weep as you read Racine's *Berenice*, if you did not see in it the most devastating of all tragedies, then you will never understand me, and we will never be one: we must break it off at once, we must never see each other again, you must forget me, for if you do not give me the answer I wish, I will forget you. You will become Monsieur le Baron de Macumer to me, or rather you will become nothing at all: in my eyes you will be like a man who never existed. Yesterday at Madame d'Espard's I saw on your face a self-satisfied look that deeply displeased me. You seemed certain that you were loved. I was horrified by that complacency; at that moment I did not see in you the servant you claimed to be in your first letter. Far from being lost in meditation as a man who loves must be, you were finding witty words to say. This is not the behavior of a true believer, who perpetually prostrates himself before the divinity. If I am not a creature superior to all other women, if you do not see in me the source of your life, then I am less than a woman, for then I am only a woman. You roused my mistrust, Felipe: it growled loudly enough to drown out the voice of tenderness, and when I consider our past, I believe I have a right to be wary. Know this, my fine monsieur constitutional minister of Spain, I have deeply reflected on the sad lot of my sex. My innocence has held a torch in each hand, and it has never been burned. Listen well to what my youthful experience has taught me, which I here repeat. In every other domain, duplicity, faithlessness, and unfulfilled promises come up before judges, and those judges inflict punishments, but no such thing is true of love, which must be at once the victim, the accuser, the lawyer, the judge, and the executioner, for the most appalling betrayals and the most horrible crimes remain unknown, committed as they are between one soul and another, unwitnessed, and it is of course in the victim's interest to say nothing. Love has its own legal code, its own vengeance; society has no part in it. I myself have resolved never to pardon a crime, and no crime is ever minor in matters of the heart. Yesterday you seemed a man confident of being loved. You would be wrong not to feel that confidence, but I would find your conduct criminal if that rid you of the innocent grace once given you by the anguish of uncertainty. I would have you neither timid nor self-assured. I would not have you fear you might lose my affection, for that would be an insult, but neither do I want you so secure that you take love for granted. Your mind must never be easier than my own. If you do not know the torment that a single doubt inflicts on the soul, be afraid that I might teach you. I delivered my soul up to you with one glance, and you read its meaning. You hold in your hands the purest sentiments ever born in a girl's soul. Those studies and meditations I told you of enriched only my mind, but when one day my troubled heart seeks counsel from my intelligence, believe me, the girl will have something of the angel who knows all and can do all. I swear to you, Felipe, if you love me as I believe, and if you give me grounds to suspect the slightest weakening in the fear, obedience, respectful patience, and docile desire you told me of, if I one day see the slightest waning in the fine, first love that entered my soul from yours, then I will say nothing, I will not bore you with a letter, however dignified, proud, or angry, or simply scolding, like this one. I would say nothing, Felipe: you would simply find me sad, in the manner of those who feel death growing near, but I would not die without having left a horrible mark on you, without dishonoring in the most shameful way the one you once loved, without having planted eternal regrets in your heart, for you would see me become a creature lost in the eyes of men on this earth and forever cursed in the next life.

Do not make me jealous, then, of another Louise, a Louise who was happy, a Louise devoutly loved, whose soul bloomed in a love without shadow, who, in Dante's sublime words, enjoyed *Senza brama, sicura richezza!*[35] Know that I have dug deep into his *Inferno* to un-earth the most painful of tortures, a fearsome emotional punishment to which I will add the eternal vengeance of God.

By your conduct yesterday, then, you thrust the cold, cruel blade of suspicion into my heart. Do you understand? I doubted you, and it so tormented me that I never want to doubt again. If you find fealty to me too onerous, then abandon it: I will not be angry. Do I not know already that you are a man of great wit? Save all the flowers of your soul for me, let your eyes be dull in society, never hold yourself up for flattery, praise, or compliments. Come and see me burdened by hatred, withered by disregard, the object of a thousand slanders, come and tell me that women do not understand you, that they walk past you without even seeing you, that none could ever love you; you will then learn what the heart and the love of Louise hold for you. Our treasure must be so carefully buried that the entire world treads over it and suspects nothing. If you were handsome, no doubt I would never have accorded you a second glance, I would never have discov-ered in you the world of forces that make love bloom; and although we understand them no more than we know how the sun causes a flower to blossom or a fruit to ripen, there is nonetheless, among all those forces, one I know well, which enchants me. Your sublime face has its character, its language, its physiognomy for me alone. I alone have the power to transform you, to make of you the most adorable of all men, and so I do not want your mind to slip free of my posses-sion: it must no more reveal itself to others than your eyes, your charming mouth, and your features must speak to them. It is my place alone to light the fires of your intelligence, just as I inflame your gaze. You must remain the somber, cold, gloomy, disdainful grandee that you were before. You were a wild, broken eminence, into whose ruins no one ventured; people contemplated you from a distance, and now here you are clearing easy little trails so that everyone can get in, and you are on your way to becoming an affable Parisian! Have you then forgotten my statement of purpose? Your high spirits expressed a little too clearly that you were in love. It took a glance from me to stop you revealing to the shrewdest, the most derisive, the wittiest

salon of Paris that Armande-Louise-Marie de Chaulieu had transformed you into an amusing young man. I think you too great to
introduce the slightest ruse into your love, but were you not as innocent with me as a child, I would pity you; and despite this first
misstep, you remain an object of deep admiration for

Louise de Chaulieu

23

FROM FELIPE TO LOUISE

When God sees our misdeeds, he also sees our remorse: you are right, my dear mistress. I sensed that I had displeased you, but I could not discern the cause; now you have explained it, and you have given me new reasons to adore you. Your jealousy, a jealousy in the manner of the God of Israel, has filled me with happiness. There is nothing more holy nor more sacred than jealousy. Oh my beautiful guardian angel, jealousy is the sentinel that never sleeps; it is to love what pain is to man, a warning that must be heeded. Be jealous of your servant, Louise: the more you strike him, the more he will humbly, obediently, happily lick the stick whose every blow shows him how much he means to you. But alas, my love, if you have not seen them, will it be God who rewards me for my attempts to overcome my timidity, to master the talents you thought I lacked? Yes, I did indeed seek to show you myself as I was before I fell in love. In Madrid there were those who took a certain pleasure in my conversation, and I wanted you too to see my true worth. Is that vanity? You have punished it well. Your last glance left me trembling as I never trembled before, not even when I saw the French forces advancing on Cadiz, my life endangered by one treacherous sentence on my master's lips. I searched for the cause of your unhappiness, and I found nothing; I despaired of that disharmony in our souls, for I must act according to your will, think through your thoughts, see by your eyes, revel in your pleasure and feel your pain as plainly as I feel cold and heat. To me, the very soul of wrongness and anguish was that lack of concurrence in the life of our hearts, which you have made so beautiful. "I have displeased her!" I said to myself a thousand times, like a madman. My beautiful, noble Louise, if anything could heighten my absolute devotion for you, and my unshakable faith in your holy conscience, it would be the philosophy laid out in your letter, which has entered my heart like a new light. You have told me my own sentiments, you have explained things once tangled and confused in my mind. Oh! if this is how you punish, what must it be when you reward? But once you accepted me as your servant, I had nothing more to wish for. You have given me a life I never dared think might be mine: I have a cause, my breath is not pointless, my strength has some purpose, if only to suffer for you. I have said it before, and I repeat it now: You will forever find me just what I was when I offered myself to you as a humble, lowly servant! Yes, even were you lost and dishonored as you say you might be, my tenderness would only grow the greater from your voluntary sorrows! I would clean your wounds, I would heal them, my prayers would convince God that you are innocent, that your wrongs are the crimes of others.... Have I not said that I bear for you in my heart the diverse sentiments of a father, a mother, a sister, and a brother? That I am above all else a family for you, everything and nothing, as you wish? But was it not you who imprisoned so many hearts in a lover's heart? Forgive me, then, if I am sometimes more a lover than a father or brother, and know that behind the lover there is still a brother and a father. If you could read what I have in my heart when I see you beautiful and glowing, serene and admired in your coach on the Champs-Élysées or in your box and the theater! ... Ah! if you only knew how selfless is my pride when I hear words of acclaim summoned forth by your beauty, your bearing, how I love the strangers admiring you! When you chance to give me a nod, and so bring a bloom to my soul, I am at once humble and proud, I go on my way as if blessed by God Himself, I joyously return to my rooms, and my joy leaves a long, shining trail inside me; it shimmers in the clouds of smoke from my cigarette, and shows me that the blood simmering in my veins is entirely yours. Do you not understand how deeply you are loved? Once I have seen you I go back to my study, whose Saracen splendor is eclipsed by your portrait the moment I press the latch that conceals it from the world's prying eyes; I lose myself in an unstoppable contemplation of that image, and I write poems of joy. From the height of the heavens I spy the course of an entire life I dare hope might be mine! Have you, in the silence of the nights or through the tumult of the world around you, sometimes heard a voice in your dear, beloved little ear? Are you not aware of the thousand prayers addressed to you? I have so long contemplated you in silence that I have discovered why your every feature is as it is, its correspondence with the perfections of your soul, and I write you sonnets in Spanish inspired by that unity, sonnets you have never seen, for my verse is too unworthy of the subject, and I dare not send them to you. My heart is so wholly absorbed in yours that I cannot go one moment without thinking of you, and if ever you ceased to animate my life as you do, there would be torment inside me. Do you now understand, Louise, how I suffer to find myself, most unintentionally, a cause of displeasure for you, and to have no idea why? That beautiful double life had come to an end, and I felt an icy cold in my heart. Finding no explanation for that discord, I concluded that I was no longer loved; very sadly, though still happy, I became once more a mere servant—but then your letter arrived and filled me with joy. Oh! always scold me exactly like that.

A child who has tripped and fallen says to his mother "Forgive me!" as he stands up, concealing his pain. Yes, he seeks her pardon for having upset her. I am that child. I have not changed, I offer you the key to my character with the submission of a slave, but, dear Louise, I will never lose my footing again. Take care that the chain binding me to you, which you hold in your hand, is always so taut that one single movement conveys your every wish to him who will always be

> your slave,
> Felipe

24

October 1824

My dear friend, you who in the space of two months married a poor
wretch and made yourself his mother, you know nothing of the terrible twists and turns of the drama played out in the depths of the
human heart, a drama called love, in which everything can turn tragic
at a moment's notice, in which death lurks behind one single glance,
one thoughtless answer. I still had one final test in store for Felipe—
a cruel test, but a decisive one. I wanted to know if I was loved *all the
same*, to use the Royalists' (and so why not the Catholics'?) great,
sublime phrase.[36] He spent an entire night walking with me under
the lindens at the end of our garden, and I saw not so much as the
shadow of a second thought cross his face. I was even more loved the
next day than the day before, and so far as he knew every bit as chaste,
every bit as fine, every bit as pure; he earned nothing from it. Oh! he
is a true Spaniard, a genuine Abencerrage. He scaled my wall for a
chance to kiss the hand extended into the shadows from my balcony,
at the risk of falling and injuring himself, but how many young men
would do just the same? That's nothing at all: Christians endure the
most horrific martyrdoms in hopes of a place in paradise.

The evening before last, then, I went to the king's future ambassador to the Spanish court, my very honored father, and said to him
with a smile, "Monsieur, a small circle of friends has heard tell that
you plan to marry your dear Armande to an ambassador's nephew;
that ambassador has long wished for and sought that alliance, and
so bequeaths his vast fortune and titles to the happy couple in the
marriage contract, with an advance of one hundred thousand livres

113

per year, writing off the bride's eight hundred thousand franc dowry. Your daughter weeps at the prospect, but she bows down before the irresistible force of your majestic fatherly authority. Certain slanderers maintain that your daughter is concealing a venal and ambitious soul behind her tears. This evening we will be at the Opéra, in the box of the nobles, and Monsieur le Baron de Macumer will come in."

"So he won't . . . ?" my father answered with a sly smile, as if admiring my stratagem.

"Father, you're confusing Clarissa Harlowe with Figaro!" I said, giving him a look of pity and disdain. "When you see me remove my right glove, you will denounce that impertinent rumor and express deep offense."

"I may rest easy on the subject of your future: you no more have the mind of a girl than Joan of Arc had the heart of a woman. You will be happy, you will love no one, and you will allow yourself to be loved!"

I let out a great laugh.

"What is it, my little coquette?" he asked.

"I tremble for the interests of my country . . ." and, seeing that he didn't understand me, I added, ". . . in Madrid!"

"Incredible how little this nun fears her father after only a year," he said to the duchess. "Armande fears nothing," my mother replied, looking at me.

"What do you mean?" I asked her.

"Why, you're not even afraid of the damp night air, when you know it can give you rheumatism," she said, casting me another glance.

"Ah, but the afternoons are so warm," I answered.

The duchess lowered her eyes.

"It's high time we married her off," said my father, "and I hope it will be before I go away."

"It will be, if you will allow it," I answered simply.

Two hours later, my mother and I were sitting with the Duchess of Maufrigneuse and Madame d'Espard, like four roses lined up along the balustrade. I had chosen a place to one side, showing the crowd only one shoulder, able to see without being seen in that large box, which occupies one of the two bays cut out in the back of the theater, between two columns. Macumer came in, stood stock-still, and clapped his opera glass to his eyes so as to look at me unseen. At the first intermission we were visited by a man I call the King of the Roués, a young man of feminine beauty: Count Henri de Marsay walked in with an epigram in his eyes and a smile on his lips, his face aglow with merriment. He first complimented my mother, then Madame d'Espard, the Duchess de Maufrigneuse, Count d'Esgrignon, and Monsieur de Canalis; he then turned to me.

"I don't know," he said, "if I am the first to congratulate you on an event that will earn you a good deal of envy."

"Ah! you must mean a marriage," I said. "Do you need a girl fresh from the convent to inform you that the marriages people talk about never come to pass?"

Monsieur de Marsay bent toward Macumer's ear, and from the movements of his lips I easily made out what he was saying: "Baron, you may be in love with this little coquette, who has used you, but since this is a question of marriage, not a simple affair, I believe it's best to know what's what."

Macumer gave that slanderous meddler one of those glances that to my mind are a poem in themselves, and answered with words to the effect of "I am in love with no little coquette!"

Perfectly enchanted with his manner, I took off my glove and glanced at my father. Felipe had felt not the slightest fear, nor the slightest suspicion. He did just what I expected of him; he has faith in me alone. Society and its lies cannot touch him. The Abencerrage never blinked, his blue blood did not color his olive face.

The two young counts went out. I then said to Macumer with a laugh, "Monsieur de Marsay seems to have whispered some epigram about me in your ear."

"Far more than an epigram," he answered, "an epithalamium."

"You're speaking Greek to me," I told him, smiling and rewarding him with a special gaze that never fails to fluster him.

"I should say so!" my father cried, speaking to Madame de Maufrigneuse. "There are vile rumors going about. The moment a young woman is introduced to society everyone is hell-bent on marrying her off, and they come up with the most outlandish ideas! I will never marry Armande against her will. I must go out for a stroll around the lobby, lest anyone think I am spreading this rumor to put a flea in the ambassador's ear. Caesar's daughter must be above suspicion, even more than his wife, who must be above all suspicion."

Madame d'Espard and the Duchess de Maufrigneuse looked first at my mother and then at the baron with an eager, sly, teasing air, full of unspoken questions. Those vigilant snakes had sensed something. Love is the most public of all private things, and I believe it radiates visibly from a woman. Only a monster could hide it! Our eyes say even more than our tongues. Having tasted the delight of finding Felipe every bit as grand as I'd wished, I naturally wanted more. I then gave him a sign we'd established as an order to come to my window by the perilous route you know well. A few hours later I found him standing straight as a statue, his back pressed to the wall, his hand on the corner of my balcony, his eye fixed on the light from my rooms.

"My dear Felipe," I said to him, "you were fine tonight: you did just as I would have, had I heard you were to be married."

"I thought you would surely have told me before anyone else," he answered.

"And by what right do you have that privilege?"

"The right of a devoted servant."

"And is that what you are?"

"Yes," he said, "and I always will be."

"Well, suppose such a marriage was necessary, suppose I'd resigned myself...."

The gentle moonlight was as if brightly lit up by the two glances he cast, first at me, then at the sort of sheer cliff that the wall formed before us. He seemed to be wondering if the fall could kill us both, but after flashing like a lightning bolt on his face and darting from his eyes, that emotion was repressed by a force even greater than passion.

"An Arab's word is forever," he said in a thick voice. "I am your servant, and I belong to you: I will live my entire life for you."

The hand holding the balcony seemed to loosen its grip; I placed mine atop it, saying, "Felipe, my friend, by my will alone, I am your wife from this moment forward. Go and ask my father for my hand tomorrow afternoon. He means to keep my inheritance; promise to forgo it, and he will surely approve of you. I am no longer Armande de Chaulieu. Hurry down from that wall: Louise de Macumer does not wish to commit the slightest imprudence."

He paled, his legs appeared to go weak, he threw himself to the ground from a height of ten feet without hurting himself in the least; after causing me the most dreadful emotion, he gave me a wave and ran off. "And so I am loved," I said to myself, "as no woman has ever been!" And I fell asleep as happy as a child, my destiny fixed forever.

At around two in the afternoon, my father had me summoned to his study, where I found the duchess and Macumer. The necessary words were very elegantly exchanged. I simply answered that, if Monsieur Hénarez had come to an agreement with my father, I had no cause to object. With that, my mother invited the baron to stay for dinner; afterwards the four of us went out for a drive through the Bois de Boulogne. I shot Monsieur de Marsay a taunting look when he passed by on horseback, for he had spied Macumer and my father in the front seat of the calèche.

My adorable Felipe has had new calling cards printed up:

Hénarez

of the Dukes de Soria, Baron de Macumer

Every morning he personally brings me a splendid bouquet of flowers, amid which I find a letter with a Spanish sonnet in my honor, written by him during the night. So as not to make this envelope too thick, I am sending you as a sample only the first and the latest of those sonnets, which I have translated word for word and line by line.

FIRST SONNET

More than once, clad in a thin silken jacket,
my sword held high, my heart beating not one beat faster,
I have awaited the onrush of the furious bull,
and its horn, sharper than Phoebe's crescent.

Humming an Andalusian seguidilla, I have climbed
the steep slope of a redoubt, iron raining down around me;
I have wagered my life at the gaming table of chance,
thinking no more of it than I would a mere quadruple.

I would gladly have pulled the cannonballs from the weap-
    on's mouth by hand;
but I believe I have grown more timorous than a startled hare,
than a child who sees a ghost in the folds of his curtains,

For, when you look at me with your gentle eye,
an icy sweat floods my brow, my knees buckle beneath me,
I tremble, I retreat, all my courage is gone.

SECOND SONNET

Last night I wanted to sleep, and dream of you,
but jealous sleep fled my eyes;
I came to the balcony and looked at the sky:
when I think of you, my gaze always turns heavenward.

By some strange phenomenon that love alone can explain,
the firmament had lost its sapphire hue;
the stars, lusterless diamonds in their setting of gold,
now scarcely gleamed, dull and faint, their rays gone cold.

The moon, its lily-white and silver makeup washed away,
was hanging sadly over the drear horizon,
for you have stripped the heavens of all their splendors.

The white of the moon gleams on your charming brow,
all the azure of the sky is concentrated in your irises;
and your lashes are the rays of the stars.

Is there a more graceful way for a man to prove to a girl that his thoughts revolve around her alone? What do you think of this love that expresses itself with an offering of the mind's flowers along with the earth's? For some ten days now, I have known what is meant by that once-celebrated Spanish gallantry.

Now, my dear, what is happening at La Crampade, where I so often go walking, observing our agriculture's progress? Have you nothing to tell me of our mulberry trees, of last winter's plantings? Is everything working out as you wish? Have the flowers bloomed in your wifely heart along with those in our garden plots? I dare not say *flower beds*. Has Louis kept up his methodical madrigals? Do you suit each other? Is the gentle murmur of your trickle of conjugal tenderness better than the turbulence of my love's torrents? Have I angered my sweet professor in skirts? I would have great difficulty believing it, but if so I would dispatch Felipe to kneel at your feet and bring me back your head or my pardon. My life here is beautiful, dear love, and I would so like to know how yours is in Provence. We have just added to our family a Spaniard the color of a Havana cigar,[37] and I am still awaiting your congratulations.

In all honesty, my lovely Renée, I am worried, I fear you may be holding back certain sorrows so as not to put a damper on my joys, you cruel thing! Write me a few pages at once, and paint me a picture of your life, down to its tiniest detail; tell me if you are still resisting, if your free will is on its two feet or on its knees, or sitting down, which would be a terrible thing. Do you believe I take no interest at all in the events of your marriage? The things you have written sometimes leave me thoughtful. Often, when I seemed to be watching the dancers pirouette at the Opéra, I was thinking: Here it is half past nine, she might be going to bed at this moment, what's she doing? Is she happy? Is she alone with her free will? Or is her free will lying in that place where free wills go when we no longer care about them?... A thousand tendernesses.

25

October

Impudent girl! Why should I have written you? What would I have
said? As you lead a life illuminated by the celebrations and torments
of love, by its rages and bouquets, with me looking on as if watching
a well-acted play, my days are as orderly and unchanging as those of
the convent. We are always in bed by nine o'clock and up at daybreak.
We take our meals at depressingly regular hours, with never the
slightest disruption. I have grown used to that schedule, and without
too much difficulty. Perhaps it is simply the way of things; what would
life be without this obedience to fixed rules that, according to the
astronomers and Louis, govern the cosmos itself? Order never grows
wearisome. Indeed, I have imposed on myself a beauty regimen that
occupies my every hour between rising and breakfast: I am determined
to offer a charming appearance at table, out of deference to my wifely
duty; I find pleasure in that, and I give heartfelt pleasure to that sweet
old man and Louis. After breakfast we go out for a stroll. When the
newspapers come, I disappear to see to my household tasks, or to
read—for I read a great deal—or to write you. I reappear one hour
before dinner, after which we play cards, receive visitors, or go calling.
I spend my days between a happy old man who wants nothing and a
man for whom I am happiness itself. Louis is so contented that in
the end his joy warmed my own soul. For us, pleasure is not the true
source of happiness. Some evenings, when I am not needed at the
card table and so settle comfortably into a *bergère*, my thought is
powerful enough to place me inside you; I follow your beautiful life,
so rich, so varied, so tumultuous, and I wonder where these turbulent

prologues will lead you—will they not spoil the book? My dear darling, you may enjoy the illusions of love; I myself have only the realities of the household. Yes, your love seems to me a dream! Which is why I find it difficult to understand why you insist on making it so like a novel. You want a man with more soul than sense, more greatness and virtue than love. You want the man every girl dreams of as she nears adulthood; you demand sacrifices so that you may reward them; you test your Felipe to learn if desire, anticipation, and curiosity can last. But, my child, behind all your fantastical adornments stands an altar at which an eternal bond is to be forged. The day after the wedding, the terrible deed that changes a girl to a wife and a lover to a husband can easily topple the elegant scaffolding of your ingenious precautions. You must realize that two lovers, no less than two married people such as Louis and me, are, beyond the festivities of the wedding party, setting off in search of something very like Rabelais's *great perhaps*![38]

However heedless the act, I do not fault you for speaking with Don Felipe at the far end of the garden, for questioning him, for spending a night on your balcony with him on the wall, but you are playing with life, child, and I fear that life may well end up playing with you. I dare not advise you to do what experience tells me would be best for your happiness, but allow me to tell you once again, from the depths of my valley, that the key to marriage is to be found in these two words: resignation and devotion! For in spite of all your tests, all your coquetry and petulance, you will marry exactly as I have, I can see it. By prolonging one's desire, one simply digs the hole a little deeper, nothing more.

Oh! how I would like to meet Baron de Macumer, to have a long talk with him, so badly do I want you to be happy!

26

March 1825

By forswearing my inheritance, with typical Saracen generosity, Felipe
has furthered my parents' designs, and the duchess is even friendlier
with me than before. She calls me *little slyboots, little vixen*, tells me
I have a gift for wrapping men around my finger.

"But, dear Mama," I said to her the day before the papers were
signed, "you are crediting ruse and maneuvers and cleverness with
what is simply the natural outcome of the truest, most naive, most
disinterested, most entire love that ever was! You must understand,
I am not the vixen you do me the honor of taking me for."

"Come now, Armande," she answered, placing her hand on the
back of my neck, drawing me to her, and kissing my brow, "you didn't
want to go back to the convent, you didn't want to remain unmarried,
and, like the great, beautiful Chaulieu you are, you wanted to do your
part for your father's house." (If you only knew, Renée, how those
words sought to flatter the duke, who was close by, listening!) "Through
an entire winter I saw you sniffing the air at every quadrille, astutely
appraising the men, studying the state of French society. You thus
sought out the only Spaniard who could offer you the ideal life, that
of a wife who rules in her home. My dear girl, you treated him exactly
as Tullia treats your brother."

"What a school is that convent of my sister's!" cried my father.

I shot him a glance that silenced him at once, then turned back
to the duchess and answered, "Madame, I love my suitor Felipe de
Soria with all my soul. I never chose that love, and indeed I struggled
mightily against it when it arose in my heart, but I swear that I sur-

rendered to it only when I recognized in Baron de Macumer a soul worthy of my own, a heart whose sensitivity, generosity, devotion, character, and sentiments mirrored mine."

"But my dear," she broke in, "he is as ugly as—"

"As whatever you please," I answered sharply, "but I love that ugliness."

"Well, Armande," said my father, "if you love him, and if you have found the force to contain your love, you must take care not to imperil your happiness. Now, happiness depends a great deal on the first days of a marriage—"

"Why not say the first nights?" my mother cried. "Leave us alone, monsieur," the duchess added, looking at my father.

"In three days you will be married, my dear girl," my mother whispered in my ear. "I must therefore now give you the serious advice all mothers give their daughters, but with no bourgeois sentimentality. You are marrying a man you love, and so I need not feel sorry for you, nor for myself. I have known you for only a year, long enough to love you but not enough to weep at the thought of losing you. Your intelligence has outshone even your beauty; you have flattered my maternal pride; you have been a good and lovable daughter, and you will always find me an excellent mother. Ah, that makes you smile? Often, alas, though the mother and daughter lived together happily, the two wives cannot see eye to eye. I want you to be happy, so listen to me closely. The love you now feel is a girl's love, the love natural to all women who are born to cleave to a man, but alas, my little girl, there is only one man in the world for us, not two, and the man we are meant to adore is not always the man we have taken as a husband, however sure we were that we loved him. These words may seem strange to you; reflect on them all the same. If we do not love the man we have chosen, the fault is ours and not his; sometimes it must be blamed on circumstances that depend neither on him nor on us. Nonetheless, nothing prevents the man who speaks to our heart, the man we love, from being the man given us by our family. The barrier that later distances us from him often comes from a lack of perseverance, on our part and his. It is every bit as difficult an undertaking to make a lover out of your husband as it is to make a husband out of your lover, and you have just performed it magnificently. Now, I repeat: I want you to be happy. You must thus reflect that three months into your marriage you may find yourself unhappy, if you do not submit to your marriage with the obedience, tenderness, and intelligence you have shown in your love. For, my little vixen, you have indulged in all the innocent pleasures of clandestine love. Should you first find in sanctified love only disillusionments, displeasures, perhaps even sorrows, well then, come and see me. Do not hope for too much from the early days of your marriage; it may well give you more pain than joy. Your happiness must be cultivated, no less than your love. But even were you to lose the husband, you would still be gaining the father of your children. That, my dear child, is the very soul of life in society. Sacrifice everything to the man whose name is yours, whose honor and standing cannot be harmed without wounding you cruelly. Sacrificing all to a husband is not only an absolute duty for women of our rank; it is also the shrewdest move. The finest attribute of great moral principles is to be true and profitable from whatever angle one considers them. Enough said of that. Now, I believe you are inclined to jealousy; I am a jealous woman myself! . . . But I would not want you to be foolishly jealous. Listen to me: A jealousy revealed is like a politician who divulges his strategy. If you say you are jealous, if you let it be seen, are you not showing your cards, knowing nothing of your opponent's hand? In all things, it is vital that we know how to suffer in silence. On the eve of your wedding, of course, I will have a serious talk about you with Macumer."

I took my mother's lovely arm and kissed her hand, dampening it with a tear brought to my eye by her tone. In that admirable moral lesson, worthy of her and of me, I glimpsed the deepest wisdom, a tenderness without social pieties, and above all a genuine esteem for my character. In those simple words she summed up all the knowledge she'd acquired, perhaps at a very dear price, from her life and experience. Moved, she looked at me and said, "Dear thing! you will soon cross over from girlhood to womanhood; it is a difficult crossing.

And most ignorant or disabused women are perfectly capable of imitating the Count of Westmoreland."

We laughed. In order to explain this little joke, I must tell you that, at dinner the evening before, a Russian princess had told us that the Count of Westmoreland, having greatly suffered from seasickness as he was crossing the Channel, and wanting to travel to Italy, turned and started for home at once when he heard mention of crossing the Alps. "I've had more than my fill of crossings, thank you very much!" he said. As you must surely understand, Renée, your dour philosophy and my mother's lesson could not help but reawaken the fears that so plagued us in Blois. The nearer my wedding day drew, the more I screwed up my strength, will, and emotions in view of that fearsome crossing. I recalled all our conversations, I reread your letters, and I found in them a certain hidden melancholy. Those apprehensions had the merit of turning me into the conventional fiancée one finds in engravings and in the mind of the public. Everyone found me very charming and proper the day the papers were signed. This morning, at the city hall to which we had gone without ceremony, only our witnesses were present. My gown is being readied for dinner as I finish these lines. We will be married in Sainte-Valère church at midnight tonight, after a glittering reception. I confess that my fears give me the air of a victim, along with a deceptive modesty for which, though I cannot see why, I will be greatly admired. I am tickled to see my poor Felipe as girlish as I. The crowd of guests torments him, he's like a bat in a crystal shop. "Fortunately, there is a day after this one!" he whispered in my ear, meaning nothing wicked. He would rather see no one, so timid and bashful is he. The Sardinian ambassador, there to sign our contract, took me aside and gave me a necklace of pearls clasped by six magnificent diamonds, a gift from my sister-in-law, the Duchess de Soria. That necklace is accompanied by a sapphire bracelet, engraved on the underside with the words *I know you not, but I love you!* Two charming letters were wrapped around those presents, which I did not want to accept until I was sure Felipe would allow it.

"For," I told him, "I would never want to see you wear something that did not come from me."

He kissed my hand, greatly moved, and answered, "Wear them for the words and the sentiments, which are sincere. . . ."

Saturday evening

Here then, my poor Renée, are the last lines the maiden will write. After midnight Mass, we will leave for a property that Felipe has gallantly acquired for us in the Nivernais, on the road to Provence. My name is already Louise de Macumer, but I will leave Paris in a few hours as Louise de Chaulieu. Whatever my name, for you there will always be only

Louise

27

October 1825

My dear, I have not written you a line since that ceremony at the city hall, some eight months ago. And from you, not a word! That is a horrible thing, madame.

Here we are, then. We set off by coach for the Château de Chantepleurs, the property Macumer bought in the Nivernais, sixty leagues from Paris, on the banks of the Loire. Apart from my chambermaid, all our servants were there waiting, and we made excellent time, arriving the next evening. I slept from Paris to past Montargis. The only liberty taken by my lord and master was to put his arm around my waist and place my head on his shoulder, on which he had laid several handkerchiefs. The almost maternal attention with which he fought off his own need to sleep filled me with a strange, deep emotion. Having fallen asleep by the fire of his dark eyes, I awoke to their flames: the same ardor, the same love, but thousands of thoughts had traversed them! He kissed my brow twice.

We breakfasted in our coach, at Briare. At seven thirty that evening, after a long talk of the sort you and I so often had in Blois, admiring the same Loire we admired there, we turned into the long, graceful avenue of lindens, acacias, sycamores, and larches that leads to Chantepleurs. By eight we were dining, by ten we were in a charming Gothic bedroom enhanced by all modern luxury's inventions. My Felipe, whom everyone finds ugly, seemed to me very handsome, thanks to his goodness, his grace, his tenderness, his exquisite sensitivity. Of love's desires I saw not a trace. All through our journey he behaved like a good friend I'd known for fifteen years. He recounted, as only he can (he is still the same man as the one who wrote that first letter), the violent turmoils he had repressed, which I saw come to his face and then fade away.

"So far, there's nothing so frightening about marriage," I said, going to the window and seeing a charming park imbued with heady perfumes, lit by a magnificent moon.

He came to my side, once again took my waist, and said, "And why should you be frightened? Have I ever broken my promises, by word or deed? Will I ever?"

Never did any voice, any gaze hold such magnificent power: the voice stirred the most delicate fibers of my body and reawoke all my emotions; the gaze had the force of the sun. "Oh!" I answered, "how much Moorish treachery there is in your perpetual enslavement!" My dear, he understood me.

And so, my dear doe, if I have gone several months without writing you, you will now understand why. I must remember the girl's strange past to tell you of the woman. Renée, I understand you today. A happy bride cannot speak of her happy marriage, not to an intimate friend, not to her mother, perhaps not even to herself. We must leave that memory in our souls like one more emotion that is ours alone, one that has no name. How odd that anyone should use the word "duty" to refer to the sweet follies of the heart, to the conquering force of desire! Why should that be? What awful power conceived the idea that we must sully the beauty of longing, the thousand secrets of woman, by transforming those delights into duties? How can we ever owe those flowers of the soul, those roses of life, those poems of the exalted sensibility to one we do not love? The very idea of speaking of rights in such sensations! No, they are born and they flourish in the sunshine of love, or else their seeds die in the chill of repugnance and aversion. Only love can keep such magic alive! Oh my sublime Renée, I find you very great at this moment! I bend my knee before you; I marvel at your depth, your clear-sightedness. Yes, a woman who does not engage in a secret marriage of love hidden beneath the legal, public vows must throw herself into motherhood, just as a soul sundered from the earth launches itself into the heavens! From all that you have written me, one cruel principle emerges: Only superior men know how to love. Today I see why. Man obeys two principles: he has in him need and emotion. Weak or inferior men mistake need for emotion, while superior men conceal need beneath the admirable effects of emotion: by its violence, emotion instills in them an excessive reserve and inspires an adoration for the woman. Sensitivity depends on the force of the inner nature, and so only the man of genius can begin to approach woman's natural delicacy: he sees her, he hears her, he understands her, he lifts her up on the wings of his tender, respectful desire. And when we are thus swept away by intelligence, by the heart, and by the senses, all equally intoxicated, we do not fall back to earth but ascend into the celestial spheres, where alas we never stay long enough. There, my dear soul, is the philosophy I have acquired in the first three months of my marriage.

Felipe is an angel. I can think out loud with him. I mean no rhetorical flourish when I say that he is another me. He is finer than words can say: he grows more fondly attached to what he possesses, and in his happiness discovers ever new reasons to love. To him I am the finest part of himself. I can see it: years of marriage, far from altering the object of his passions, will heighten his faith, will develop new sensibilities, and will strengthen our union. What a happy delirium!

My soul is made in such a way that pleasures leave a bright glow inside me, they warm me, they imprint themselves on my inner being; the interval that separates them is like the short night of high summer. The sun that gilded the peaks as it set finds them still warm when it rises. By what happy twist of fate should it be this way for me from the start? My mother awakened in me a thousand fears; her predictions—which seemed to me riddled with jealousy, though no bourgeois small-mindedness—have been disproved by the event. Your fears and hers, and mine, it all faded away! We stayed at Chantepleurs for seven and a half months, like two lovers, one spirited away by the other to flee their parents' wrath. Our love has been crowned by the roses of pleasure, they fill our life together. One morning when I was more deeply happy than usual, I found myself looking back. I thought of my Renée and her marriage of convenience, and I could imagine your life, I entered into it! Oh my angel, why do we speak two different languages? Your marriage is a purely social affair, mine nothing more than the fullest fruition of love: two worlds that can no more understand each other than the finite can understand the infinite. You are on earth, and I in the heavens! You are in the realm of the human, and I of the divine. I reign by love, and you reign by calculation and duty. I am so high up that I would break into a thousand pieces should I ever fall. But here I must say no more, for I would blush to tell you of all the wonder, the richness, the fresh, glowing joys of such a springtime of love.

For ten days we have been in Paris, in a charming house on the rue du Bac, decorated by the same architect Felipe engaged for Chantepleurs. I have just gone to hear the celestial music of Rossini, which I once heard with an unquiet soul, tormented by the curiosities of love and not even knowing it, but which I now hear with a soul fulfilled by the legitimate pleasures of a happy marriage. I was judged more beautiful than before in every way, and I am like a child when I hear myself called *madame*.

Friday morning

Renée, my beautiful saint, my happiness always brings my thoughts back to you. I think myself a better friend than ever before: see how devoted I am! I have thoroughly examined your married life by way of the beginning of mine, and I find you so great, so noble, so magnificently virtuous, that I consider myself your inferior, your sincere admirer, and your friend as well. Having seen what my marriage is, I am very nearly convinced that I would have died had it been otherwise. And yet I find you still alive! Living on what sentiment, tell me? And so I will never ridicule you in any way. Alas! ridicule, my angel, is the daughter of ignorance, we mock what we do not know. "A green recruit is always quick to laugh; the seasoned soldier is somber," I learned from Count de Chaulieu, a poor captain in the cavalry, whose journeys have so far taken him only from Paris to

Fontainebleau and back again. I have an inkling, then, my dear, that you have not told me all. Yes, you are hiding more than one wound from me. You are unhappy, I can feel it. I have written whole novels of ideas about you in my mind, striving, from a distance and from the little you've told me of your life, to discover the reasons for your behavior: she gave marriage a try, I told myself one evening, and what has turned out to be joy for me, was misery for her. Her sacrifices have cost her dearly, and she wants to limit them. She is disguising her sadness beneath the pompous axioms of societal morality. Ah! Renée, here is a curious thing: pleasure needs no religion, no finery, no grand words, it is everything in itself, whereas men have piled up all manner of theories and maxims to justify the atrocious calculations of our enslavement and serfdom. If your renunciations are beautiful and sublime, does that make of my happiness, protected by the church's gold-and-white veil and confirmed by the dourest mayor of all time, a monstrous wrong? For the sake of the law's honor, and for your sake as well, but above all so that my pleasures will be complete, I want you to be happy, my Renée. Oh! Tell me you can feel a little love creeping into your heart for that Louis who adores you so! Tell me the symbolic, solemn torch of the wedding ceremony did not simply reveal all the darkness around you! For love, my angel, is to our inner selves exactly what the sun is to the earth. I cannot stop telling you of the Light that illuminates me, which I fear may consume me. Dear Renée, in your ecstasies of friendship, you used to tell me beneath the bower at the back of the convent garden: "I love you so, Louise, that if God were to appear here before us, I would ask for all the torments of life, and pray that you have all the joys. It's true, I have a passion for suffering!" Well, my dear, today I turn the tables on you, and cry out to God to divide my pleasures between us.

Listen, now: I suspect that you have become an ambitious woman under the name of Louis de l'Estorade; see to it, then, that he is named *député* at the next elections, for he will be nearly forty years old, and since the National Assembly will not convene until six months after, he will be exactly the age required. You will come to Paris, what more need I say? You will be a great success with my father and the friends

I'll soon make, and if your aged father-in-law is willing to promise a *majorat*, then we will have Louis made a count. That will be a start! Not to mention that you and I will be together again.

28

December 1825

My happy Louise, you have taken my breath away. For a few moments I sat holding your letter, the paper glistening with a few teardrops in the setting sun, my arms limp, alone beneath the arid little crag where I have installed a bench. The Mediterranean gleams like a steel blade in the endless distance. That bench is sheltered by a little grove of aromatic trees; I have had an enormous jasmine transplanted there, along with honeysuckle and Spanish broom. One day the wall of rock behind it will be wholly covered by climbing plants. We have already planted Virginia creeper. But winter is coming, and all that greenery is as faded as an old tapestry. No one ever disturbs me when I am there; they know I want to be alone. That bench is known as Louise's bench, which will tell you that I am never alone there, even though I am.

If I tell you these details, so trivial to you, if I depict the green expectations already bedecking that bare, severe rock, atop which the whimsy of the vegetable kingdom has placed a most beautiful umbrella pine, it is because in that place I have discovered images to which I have grown attached.

As I was rejoicing in your happy marriage, as (why should I not tell you all?) I was envying it with all my might, I felt the first movement of my child, which from the depths of my physical being reacted on the depths of my soul. That vague sensation, at once a warning, a pleasure, a pain, a promise, a reality; that happiness, mine alone in all this world, a secret between me and God, that mystery told me the rock would one day be covered with flowers, that it would ring with a family's joyous laughter, that my entrails had been blessed and would give life in abundance. I felt I was born to be a mother! This first certainty that I was bearing another life inside me brought me a healing consolation. Deep joy had at last crowned the long days of devotion that had already brought joy to Louis.

"Devotion!" I said to myself. "Are you not greater than love itself? Are you not the deepest pleasure of all, because you are an abstract pleasure, a productive pleasure? Are you not, O Devotion, the one human faculty that is greater than its visible effects? Are you not the mysterious, tireless divinity hidden among the countless spheres in some unseen center, through which all the worlds pass in turn?" Devotion, alone in its seclusion, full of pleasures savored in silence, on which no one casts a profane eye, whose existence no one suspects; Devotion, that jealous, omnipotent god, that strong, triumphant god, inexhaustible because it partakes of the very nature of things and so never weakens, even as it expends all its strength; Devotion, there is the guiding light of my life.

Love, Louise, is an action that Felipe exerts on you, but as my life radiates onto my family that little world will return it, in a never-ending reaction, to me! Your beautiful golden harvest will be fleeting; will mine, delayed though it be, not prove more enduring? For with each passing moment it will begin anew. Love is the prettiest thing Society has managed to steal from Nature, but is maternity not Nature in all its joy? A smile dried my tears. Love makes my Louis happy, but marriage has made me a mother, and I will be happy too! With that, I wandered back to my green-shuttered white *bastide* to write you these lines.

And so, my dear, the most natural, most astonishing element of a woman's life has been with me for the past five months, but—to you I can say this, very quietly—it has changed nothing in my heart or mind. I see everyone around me happy. The grandfather-to-be, encroaching on the rights of his grandchild, has become like a child himself; the father puts on grave, preoccupied airs; both are at my beck and call, everyone talks of the joys of motherhood. Alas, I alone feel nothing, and I dare not speak of my insensibility. I lie a little, so as not to dull their joy. Since with you I may be frank, I must confess that there is no motherhood in my present state but an imagined one. Louis was as surprised as I to learn that I was with child. Is that not to say that this child came along of its own will, summoned only by its father's impatiently expressed wishes? The god of motherhood, my love, is Chance. Our doctor claims that these chances are attuned to the wishes of Nature, but he does not deny that what are so prettily called "children of love" can only be clever and handsome, that often their existence is in a way protected by the happiness that shone, O brilliant star!, at their conception. Perhaps then, my Louise, you will find in your own motherhood joys I will never know in mine. Perhaps we feel more love for the child of a man we adore as you adore your Felipe than for the child of a husband married in a spirit of reason, to whom we give ourselves out of duty, and so as to be a woman at last! Those thoughts, buried deep in my heart, compound the gravity that is already mine as an expectant mother. But, since without a child there is no family, my desire wishes it could hasten the moment when the pleasures of the family begin for me, as those pleasures will be my only existence.

For now, my life is a life of waiting and wondering, in which nauseous misery no doubt prepares the woman to endure other torments. I observe myself. Despite Louis's best efforts, despite the constant attention, care, and tenderness his love offers me, I am full of nameless anxieties, compounded by the repugnances, the discomforts, and the singular cravings of pregnancy. If I must tell you things as they are, at the risk of inspiring in you a certain distaste for the business of motherhood, I will admit that I am mystified by the taste I have acquired for certain oranges, an aberrant appetite that seems to me perfectly natural. My husband goes off to Marseille to buy me the world's finest oranges; he has ordered oranges from Malta, from Portugal, from Corsica, but those oranges I never touch. I hurry to Marseille, sometimes on foot, to devour horrible, cheap little half-rotten oranges in a back street that runs down to the port, just by the town hall. To my eye their blue or green mold shines like diamonds: I look at it and see flowers, I pay no mind to their cadaverous odor and find in them a teasing tang, a warmth like wine, a delectable flavor. Those, my angel, are the first feelings of love I have ever known. Those horrid oranges are my loves. You cannot possibly desire Felipe as much as I yearn for one of those moldering fruits. Sometimes I even slip out of the house and scurry off in secret to Marseille; I quiver with longing as I draw near the street, fearing the fruit lady has no more rotten oranges to sell. I throw myself on them, I eat them, I devour them there in the street. I feel as though they must come from paradise and contain the most exquisite nourishment. I have seen Louis turn away to flee their foul smell. I remembered that awful sentence from *Obermann*, a somber elegy I wish I had never read: *The roots draw their sustenance from fetid water!*[39] Ever since I began eating that fruit, my nausea has disappeared and my health has returned. There is a meaning behind that madness, since it is an effect of nature, and half of all women feel such cravings, which can sometimes be monstrous. Once my pregnancy cannot go unnoticed I will stop leaving La Crampade; I would not like to be seen in such a state.

I am exceedingly curious to know just when motherhood begins. It cannot be in the midst of the horrible pains I am dreading.

Farewell, my happy friend! Farewell, you in whom I am reborn and through whom I imagine those beautiful ardors, those jealousies born of a single glance, those words whispered in the ear, those pleasures that envelop us like another atmosphere, another blood, another light, another life! Ah! my darling, I too understand love. Never weary of telling me all. Let us remain true to our pact. For my part, I will spare you nothing. And so I will say, to end this letter on a serious note, that a deep, insurmountable terror seized hold of me as I reread your words. I could only see that splendid love of yours as a challenge to God. Will this world's sovereign master, Sorrow, not be angry to have been offered no share of your feast? Is there one superb fortune he has not overturned? Oh, Louise, amid all your happiness, do not forget to pray to God. Do good, be charitable and kind; ward off all adversity by your modesty. I myself, since my wedding, have become still more pious than I was at the convent. You have made no mention of religion in Paris. In your adoration of Felipe, I sense that you are turning more to the saint than to God, contravening the proverb. But my terror is simply an effect of excessive friendship. You do go to church together, and you do perform good works in secret, do you not? You will perhaps find me very provincial in these last lines of my letter, but remember that my fears conceal only a deep friendship, friendship as La Fontaine understood it, the sort of friendship that worries and frets over things merely imagined, over nebulous suspicions. You deserve to be happy, since you think of me in your happiness, just as I think of you in my monotonous life, slightly gray but full, sober but productive—and bless you for that!

29

December 1825

Madame,

My wife did not want you to learn by an ordinary printed announcement of an event that has filled us with joy. She has given birth to a strong, healthy son, and we will delay his baptism until you return to Chantepleurs. It is our hope that you will continue on to La Crampade and become our firstborn's godmother. In that anticipation, I have just had his birth recorded under the name Armand-Louis de l'Estorade. Our dear Renée suffered a good deal, but with angelic patience. You know her: she was supported in that first trial of motherhood by her certainty of the happiness she was giving us all. Without falling into the faintly ridiculous exaggerations of fathers who are fathers for the first time, I can assure you that little Armand is a very handsome boy, but you will have no difficulty believing it when I tell you he has Renée's features and eyes. That is a sign of good sense in itself. Now that the doctor and the obstetrician have assured us that Renée is out of danger—for she is nursing, the child took readily to the breast, the milk is abundant, nature is so powerful in her!—my father and I can abandon ourselves to our joy. Madame, that joy is so great, so strong, so complete, it so animates the entire household, it has so changed my dear wife's existence, that for the sake of your happiness I hope you will very soon experience it for yourself. Renée has had rooms prepared for you; I do wish they were more worthy of our guests, but you will be received here with fraternal cordiality, if not great luxury.

Renée has told me, madame, of the aid you intend to give us, and

I am all the more eager to seize this occasion to thank you in that the timing is opportune. The birth of my son has convinced my father to make the sort of sacrifices to which old men resolve themselves with difficulty: he has just bought two new tracts of land. La Crampade is now an estate with an annual revenue of thirty thousand francs. My father will seek the king's permission to establish it as a *majorat*, but if you obtain for him the title you alluded to in your last letter you will already have done much for your godson.

As for me, I will take your advice solely so that you might be reunited with Renée while the assembly is in session. I am studying seriously, trying to develop some useful area of expertise. But nothing will encourage me more than the knowledge that you are the protector of my little Armand. Promise us, then, to come and play the role of a good fairy—you who are so beautiful and so gracious, so fine and so wise—for my eldest son. In so doing, madame, you will add undying gratitude to the respectful affection with which I have the honor to be

> your very humble and very obedient servant,
> Louis de

30

January 1826

Macumer woke me just now with your husband's letter, my angel.
Let me begin by saying *yes*. We will leave for Chantepleurs toward
the end of April. It will be one pleasure on another for me to travel,
to see you, and to be the godmother of your first child, but I want
Macumer as his godfather. I would find Catholic alliance with any
other man odious. Ah! if you'd seen the look on his face when I told
him that, you would know how deeply that angel loves me.

"I am all the more eager to leave with you for La Crampade, Felipe,"
I told him, "in that we will perhaps have a child there. I too want to
be a mother... although between a child and you I would have a great
deal on my hands. To begin with, if I saw you prefer any other creature
to me, even my own son, I can't say what would happen. Medea may
well have been right. Those ancients knew a thing or two!"

He laughed. And so, dear doe, you've had the fruit without the
flowers, and I have the flowers without the fruit. The contrast of our
two destinies goes on. We are philosophical enough to seek the meaning and moral of that one day. Bah! I have been married only ten
months, and we must agree, there is no such thing as time wasted.

We lead the frivolous but full life of happy people. The days always
seem too short. Seeing me back in its midst disguised as a wife, Parisian society found Baroness de Macumer far more beautiful than
Louise de Chaulieu: happy love is a cosmetic in itself. When, in the
beautiful sunlight and beautiful frost of a January day, the trees on
the Champs-Élysées abloom with sparkling white sprays, Felipe and
I drive past in our coupé before all of Paris, together where we were

apart only last year, then thousands of thoughts fill my mind, and I fear I am being a little too insolent, as you suggested in your last letter.

If I know nothing of the joys of motherhood, you will tell me of them, and I will be a mother through you, but if you want my opinion, nothing compares to the pleasures of love. You will think me very odd, but ten times in ten months I have found myself hoping to die at thirty, when life is at its most splendid, the roses of love in full bloom, amid pleasure and desire, to go away sated, never disappointed, having lived my whole life in the sunshine, the ether, and perhaps even killed by love itself, my crown still intact, not a single leaf missing, my illusions unbetrayed. Imagine what it must be to have a young heart in an old body, to see only cold, mute faces where once everyone smiled at you, even those of no consequence, to be a respectable lady... it is a very foretaste of hell.

Felipe and I had our first quarrel on that subject. I wanted him to be strong enough to kill me when I am thirty, as I sleep, unsuspecting, so that I might pass from one dream into another. The monster refused. I threatened to leave him alone in the world, and he went pale, poor child! That great minister has become a true babe in arms, my dear. It is incredible how much youthfulness and simplicity he was hiding. Now that I think aloud with him just as I did with you, now that we tell each other all, we are forever surprised by each other.

My dear, the two lovers, Felipe and Louise, want to send a present to the new mother. We'd like to have something made that would please you. Tell me frankly what you desire, then, for we have no taste for those surprises so dear to the bourgeoisie. We want to continually remind you of us with some adorable memento, something you will find useful every day and which will not lose its luster over time. Our happiest and most intimate meal is breakfast, for then we are alone; I thus thought of sending you a special service, known as a breakfast service, whose ornaments would be little children. If you approve, let me know me promptly. If I am to bring it to you, I must order it, and the artisans of Paris are like lazy kings. That will be my offering to Lucina.[40]

Farewell, dear nurse, I wish you all the pleasures of motherhood, and I am eager to read your first letter, in which you will tell me all, will you not? That obstetrician sends a shiver down my spine. The word fairly leapt out from your husband's letter, not at my eyes but at my heart. Poor Renée, a child costs us dearly, doesn't it? I will be sure to tell that godson of mine how much he must love you. A thousand tendernesses, my angel.

31

It will soon be five months since my delivery, and, dear soul, I have
not found one moment to write you. When you are a mother, you
will find more forgiveness for me than you have, for you have punished
me a little with the scarcity of your letters. Write me, my dear darling!
Tell me your pleasures, paint your happiness in the most vivid colors,
do not spare the ultramarine, and have no fear of offending me, for
I am happy, and happier than you will ever imagine.

I went with great ceremony to the parish church for an end-of-
confinement Mass, as is the custom in old Provençal families. The
two grandfathers, Louis's father and my own, offered me their arms.
Oh! never have I knelt down before God with such consuming gratitude. I have so many things to tell you, so many sentiments to depict,
that I cannot think where to begin, but one radiant memory arises
from that morass of confusion: the prayer I offered in that church!

When—there in the very spot where I knelt as a girl, doubting in
life, in my future—I found myself metamorphosed into a joyous
mother, I thought I saw the Virgin on the altar nodding and showing
me the holy infant, who seemed to be smiling at me! With what a
sacred effusion of celestial love I held out our little Armand for the
curé's blessing, who sprinkled him with holy water in anticipation
of the baptism proper. But you will already have pictured the two of
us, my Armand and me.

My child—here I am calling you my child! But that is indeed the
sweetest word there is in the heart, in the mind, on the lips of a mother.
So, my dear child, for the two months before my delivery I drifted
listlessly through our gardens, drained, wearied by the weight of that

burden I never realized was so precious and sweet, for all those two months' torments. I was so full of apprehensions and dark forebodings that curiosity could not drown them out: I tried to talk sense to myself, I assured myself that there is nothing to fear in what nature wants, I tried to cheer myself with the reflection that I would be a mother. Alas! I felt nothing in my heart, even as my thoughts were full of that child, who was giving me some rather vigorous kicks; no doubt, my dear, one can relish those kicks when one has had a child before, but when one first feels them, those thrashings of an unknown life bring more shock than pleasure. I speak only for myself, I who am neither insincere nor melodramatic, I whose fruit came more from God—for it is God who gives children—than from a cherished man. But let us forget those past sorrows, which I am convinced will never come again.

When the crisis came, I summoned up such endurance, I had girded myself for such horrible pains, that I am told I withstood the cruel ordeal wonderfully well. There came a moment, my darling, something like an hour, when I surrendered to a prostration whose effects were those of a dream. I felt as if I were two things at once: a strained, torn, tortured vessel and a soul at peace. In that strange state, pain blossomed like a crown above my head. I felt as if an enormous rose had sprouted from the top of my skull, growing ever larger, enveloping me. The air was suffused with the color of that blood-drenched flower. I could see nothing but red. Having reached the point where a separation seems to want to take place between body and soul, I felt a sudden explosion of pain, of a sort that convinced me my final hour had come. I let out a horrible scream, and then I found a new strength against these new pains. That awful clamor was suddenly silenced inside me by the sweet song of the little creature's silvery cries. No, nothing can paint that moment for you; I felt as if the entire world was crying out with me, that there was nothing in the world but shrieking and pain, and then that child's small cry stilled it all.

I was returned to my big bed, which felt like paradise, though I was exceedingly weak. I saw three or four joyous faces around me, tears in their eyes; they showed me the child. My dear, I cried out in horror. "What a little monkey!" I said. "Are you sure that's a child?" I rolled onto my side, distressed to feel no more a mother than that.

"Don't worry, my dear," said my mother, who had volunteered to watch over me, "you've given birth to the most beautiful child in the world. Don't torment your imagination; you must devote all your thoughts to becoming an animal, you must make of yourself nothing other than a cow, grazing to make milk."

Hearing these words, I drifted off to sleep with the firm intention of letting nature take me in hand. Oh! my angel, how divine it was to wake from all those pains, those tangled feelings, those first days when all is dark, raw, and unclear. That darkness was soon brightened by a sensation whose pleasure surpassed that of my child's first cry. My heart, my soul, my being, an unknown *me* came to life in its once gray, aching shell, just as a flower erupts from its seed on hearing the shining call of the sun. The little monster took my breast and suckled, and with that, *fiat lux!*, suddenly I was a mother. Here is happiness, joy, ineffable joy, though it is not without its pains. Oh! my jealous beauty, how you will savor a joy that is known only to us, to the child, and to God. That little thing knows nothing in this world but the breast. That glowing point is all there is, he loves it with all his strength, he thinks of nothing but that font of life, he comes to it, then turns away to sleep, then wakes to come to it once more. There is inexpressible love in his lips, and when they cling to it, they cause a pain and a pleasure at once, a pleasure so strong as to be pain, or a pain that becomes a pleasure; I do not know how to make you understand a sensation that spreads from the breast into me and then on to the very sources of life, for from that central point a thousand beams seem to radiate, exalting heart and soul alike. Giving birth is nothing; to nurse is to give birth at every moment. Oh! Louise, no lover's caress can rival those little pink hands so gently roaming over us, clinging to life. Oh! the child's gaze, turning from our breast to our eyes and back again! The dreams that come into our minds as we watch him clutching his treasure with his lips! It is as much mental as physical: it draws on our blood and our intelligence, it satisfies us far beyond our desires. I relived the glorious feeling of hearing his first cry, which was for me what the first ray of sunlight was for the earth, as I felt my milk filling his mouth; I relived it again when he first looked into my eyes; I have just relived it once more as I saw his first smile and so treasured his first thought. For he laughed, my dear. That laugh, that gaze, that bite, that cry, those four ecstasies have no end; they go to the very depths of the heart, and they stir strings they alone can stir! The spheres must cleave to God as a child cleaves to every fiber of his mother: God is an enormous mother's heart. Nothing can be seen or sensed in conception, nor even in pregnancy, but nursing, my Louise, is a happiness that never ends. One sees what becomes of the milk, it becomes flesh, it blooms at the tips of those sweet little fingers, so like flowers, and every bit as delicate; it grows in the fine, transparent fingernails, it unravels into hair, it tosses and wriggles in the feet. Oh! there is a whole language in a child's feet. It is with them that the child first expresses himself. Oh, Louise, nursing is a transformation you can see hour by hour, dazzling to the eye. It is not with your ears but with your heart that you hear the child's cries; you understand the smile in his eyes or on his lips or in his wriggling feet as if God had written letters of fire in the air for you! Nothing in the world can interest you now. The father? You would kill him if he dared wake the child. You are this child's entire world unto yourself, just as the child is yours! You are so certain that your life is shared, you are so generously rewarded for the trouble you go to and the pains you endure, for pains there are, may God spare you a fissure of the breast! That wound, reopening with every touch of those pink lips, so slow to heal, so painful that you might lose your mind were it not for the joy of seeing the child's mouth dripping with milk, is one of the most appalling punishments that can be inflicted on beauty. My Louise, reflect on that, it affects only the tenderest and most delicate skin.

Over the past five months, my little monkey has become the prettiest creature a mother ever bathed with tears of joy, or washed, brushed, combed, primped; for God knows with what indefatigable ardor one primps, dresses, brushes, washes, changes, kisses those little flowers! My monkey is no longer a monkey, but a *baby*, as my

English nursemaid says, a pink-and-white *baby*, and since he feels that he is loved he never cries too much, but in truth I am nearly always beside him, and I strive to fill him with my soul.

My dear, what I now feel for Louis in my heart is not love but a sentiment that must be love's fullest consummation in a loving woman. I am in fact not sure that this tenderness, this selfless gratitude, does not go beyond love. From what you have told me, my darling, love is a horribly earthly thing, whereas there is something religious and divine in the affection a happy mother feels for the man who is the source of those long, those endless joys. A mother's joy is a light that spills out onto the future, showing her the way, but reflecting onto the past as well, to offer her the charm of its memory.

The elder l'Estorade and his son are more thoughtful than ever, I am like a new person to them: their words and gazes go straight to my soul, for they celebrate me anew each time they see me and speak to me. The old grandfather is becoming a child, I believe: he looks at me with wonderment. The first time I came down to breakfast, he wept to see me eating and nursing his grandson. That tear in those two dry eyes, so often lit by no thought other than money, did me more good than I can tell; I felt that the old man understood my joys. As for Louis, he could easily have told the trees and the pebbles on the road that he had a son. He can gaze on your sleeping godson for hours on end. He tells me he wonders if he will ever grow used to it. These excessive demonstrations of joy showed me the depth of their earlier fears and uncertainties. Louis finally admitted that he had doubted in himself, and thought he had been condemned never to have children. My poor Louis has suddenly changed for the better, he is studying even more seriously than before. The child has doubled the father's ambition. As for me, my dear soul, I am happier with each passing moment. Every hour brings a new bond between a mother and her child. What I feel inside me proves that this sentiment is imperishable, natural, and constant, whereas love, I suspect, wanes and waxes. One does not love in the same way at every moment; love does not embroider the fabric of life with inevitably glowing flowers. Love can and must end, but motherhood need fear no decline, it grows in concert with the child's needs, it develops along with him. Is it not all at once a passion, a need, an emotion, a duty, a necessity, happiness itself? Yes, darling, there is the life that is women's alone. In it our thirst for devotion is sated; in it we find none of the turmoils of jealousy. For us, then, it is perhaps the only point at which Nature and Society coincide. And indeed, here Society has enriched Nature: to maternal sentiment it has added the family spirit, through the continuity of the family name, bloodline, and fortune. What love must a woman not lavish on the dear creature who first made her know such joys, who made her deploy the forces of her soul and taught her the great art of motherhood? I believe that primogeniture—an ancient right even in Antiquity, and a founding principle of all human societies—must never be questioned. Ah! a child teaches his mother so much. So many promises are made between virtue and us in our unceasing protection of a frail creature that woman is in her true sphere only when she is a mother; only then does she make use of all her forces; she sees to the duties of her life, she has all of life's happi- nesses and all its pleasures. A woman who is not a mother is an in- complete, failed person. Hurry, my angel, and become a mother! You will be multiplying your current happiness by the joys I now feel.

Eleven o'clock at night

I left you on hearing a cry from your godson; I can hear that cry from the farthest point in the garden. I do not want this letter to go off without a word of farewell to you. I have just reread it, and I am mortified by the sentimental commonplaces I found. Alas, I believe every mother has felt just what I feel, and no doubt they express it in just the same way; I fear you may mock me, in the way people mock the naiveté of fathers who inevitably praise the intelligence and beauty of their children as if they were utterly unique. In any case, dear darling, here is the great message of this letter, which I will tell you again: I am as happy now as I was unhappy before. This *bastide*, soon to become an estate and a *majorat*, is for me the Promised Land. My time in the desert has come to an end. A thousand tendernesses, dear darling. Write me. Today I can read of your love and your happiness without weeping. Farewell.

32

March 1826

My dear, can it be? Three months have gone by, and I've neither writ-ten nor had a letter from you.... My fault is the greater, for I never answered you, but I do not believe you are easily hurt. Macumer and I took your silence as an approval of the breakfast service decorated with children, and will have those pretty things sent off to Marseille this morning; it took the artisans six months to make them. I thus woke with a start when Felipe suggested we go and inspect that service before the goldsmith boxed it up. It suddenly occurred to me that we'd said not a word to each other since your last letter, which made me feel a mother alongside you.

My excuse, angel, is the tyranny of Paris; I await yours. Oh! what an abyss is the social world. Have I not already told you that in Paris one has no choice but to be a Parisienne? In Paris society crushes all sentiment, takes up all your time, it will devour your heart if you don't take care. What an astonishing stroke of genius is the role of Célimène in Molière's *The Misanthrope*! She is the worldly woman of Louis XVI's age and our own, indeed the worldly woman of all ages. Where would I be without my shield, my love for Felipe? As I told him this morning, reflecting on all this, he is my savior. My evenings are taken up with parties and balls, concerts, the theater, and then when we come home I rediscover the joys and the follies of love, which bring a bloom to my heart and erase the bite marks left by society. I've dined at home only when we were receiving what people call friends, and I've stayed in only for my at-home days. I have my day, Wednesday, when I am at home for visitors. I have entered into competition with Mesdames d'Espard and de Maufrigneuse, and the aged Duchess de Lenoncourt. My house is considered an amusing place. I allowed myself to fall in with fashion on seeing my Felipe happy at my successes. I give him the first half of the day, for from four in the afternoon to two in the morning I belong to Paris. Macumer is an admirable host; he is so witty, so grave, so exceptional, so perfectly gracious that he could inspire love in the heart of a woman who married him purely for convenience. My father and mother have left for Madrid. With the death of Louis XVIII, the duchess had no difficulty obtaining a position for her charming poet from our good Charles X; he will be accompanying her as an attaché of the embassy. My brother the Duke de Rhétoré deigns to consider me an eminent person. As for the Count de Chaulieu, that make-believe soldier owes me his eternal gratitude: before my father set off, he used my inheritance to acquire enough land for a *majorat* with an annual income of forty thousand livres, and his marriage to Mademoiselle de Mortsauf, an heiress from the Touraine, is now definitively settled. So as to prevent the disappearance of the de Lenoncourt and de Givry houses, the king will issue a proclamation conferring their names, titles, and coats of arms on my brother. How, indeed, could those two fine crests be allowed to perish, and that sublime device, *Faciem semper monstramus!*[41] Mademoiselle de Mortsauf, the granddaughter and sole heiress of the Duke de Lenoncourt-Givry, is said to have an inheritance in excess of one hundred thousand livres a year. My father asked only that the Chaulieu family crest be placed *en abîme* in the center of the Lenoncourt crest. My brother will thus be the Duke de Lenoncourt. The young de Mortsauf son, for whom all this fortune was intended, is in the final stages of consumption; he is expected to die any day. The wedding is planned for next winter, after the period of mourning. They say I will have a charming sister-in-law in Madeleine de Mortsauf. As you see, then, my father was right in every way.

This outcome has earned me the admiration of a great many people, and my marriage is no longer seen as a mystery. Out of affection for my grandmother, Prince de Talleyrand is promoting Macumer;

our success is complete. Once derided by Parisian society, I am now admired on all sides. At long last I reign over this place, I who was of so little consequence here just two years ago. Macumer finds his happiness the envy of all, for I am *the most sparkling woman in Paris*. You know that there are twenty *most sparkling women in Paris* in Paris. All the men purr words of love at me, or simply express it with longing glances. Truly, this concert of desires and admirations offers so constant a satisfaction of one's vanity that I now understand the excessive expenses women incur to gain these small, ephemeral advantages. That triumph is an intoxicant for human pride, vanity, and self-love, for all the sentiments bound to our *ego*. So violently heady is this perpetual deification that I am no longer surprised to see women turn selfish, thoughtless, and superficial amid the festivities. Society goes to one's head. You lavish the flowers of your mind and your soul, your most precious time, your most generous efforts on people who repay you with jealousy and smiles, who give you the counterfeit coin of their well-turned sentences, their compliments and adulations in exchange for the gold ingots of your courage, your sacrifices, all the ingenuity you devote to being beautiful, well-dressed, witty, affable, and agreeable. You know how dearly that commerce is costing you, you know you're being robbed, but you abandon yourself to it all the same. Ah! my beautiful doe, how one thirsts for the heart of a true friend, and how precious is Felipe's love and devotion! How I adore him! How happily one makes preparations for a trip to Chantepleurs and a respite from the playacting of the rue du Bac and the salons of Paris! In short, I who have just reread your last letter, I will have said all you need know of the infernal paradise that is Paris by telling you that no society woman could possibly be a mother.

Goodbye for the moment, my dear: we will be staying at Chantepleurs for a week at most, to be by your side around the tenth of May. We will thus be seeing each other again after more than two years! And so many changes! We are both of us women now: I the happiest of all mistresses, you the happiest of all mothers. To be sure, my dear, I have not written you, but I have not forgotten you. And my godson, that monkey, is he still pretty? Does he do me proud? He will be more than nine months old now. I would so like to see his first steps in the world, but Macumer tells me that even the most precocious children are scarcely walking at ten months. We will have a good chinwag, in the old manner of Blois. I will see if, as they say, a child plays havoc with the figure.

P.S. If you answer me, sublime mother, address your letter to Chantepleurs, as I am to leave at any moment.

33

Well, my child, if ever you become a mother, you will see if the first
nine months of nursing offer a single opportunity to write. There is
never a moment's peace for my English maid *Mary* and me. I have
not told you, it is true, that I insist on doing everything myself. Before
the event, I sewed all the baby clothes with my own fingers, I embroidered and trimmed the bonnets with my own hand. I am a slave, my
darling, a slave day and night. For one thing, Armand-Louis nurses
whenever he wants to, and he always wants to; for another, he so
often has to be changed, cleaned, dressed, and his mother so loves to
look at him as he sleeps, and to sing him songs, and to take him out
walking when the weather is fine, holding him in her arms, that she
has not a moment to herself. In other words, you have been busy with
society, and I with my child, our child! What a full, rich life! Oh, my
dear, soon you will be here, and then you shall see! But I fear that he
may begin teething soon, and that you will find he wails and weeps
a great deal. Until now he has cried little, because I am always there.
Children cry only when they need something that no one has realized, and I forever seek to anticipate his every wish. Oh! my angel,
how my heart has grown, while you were shrinking yours by making
of it a servant of Paris! I await you as impatiently as one who lives
alone. I want to know what you think of l'Estorade, as you no doubt
want to know what I think of Macumer. Write me from your last
stop on the way. My men want to go out and meet our illustrious
guests on the road. Come, queen of Paris, come to our poor little
bastide, where you will be loved!

34

April 1826

My dear, as you will see from this letter's address, my solicitations have borne fruit. Your father-in-law is now Count de l'Estorade. I didn't want to leave Paris before I'd fulfilled your wish; I write you this letter in the presence of the Keeper of the Seals, who has come to tell me that the proclamation has been signed.

I shall see you soon.

35

Marseille, July

You will have been greatly surprised by my sudden departure, and I am ashamed, but because I am sincere above all else, and because I love you as much as I ever did, I will candidly tell you all in four words: I am desperately jealous. Felipe was looking at you too much. The two of you were often at the foot of your bluff, having little talks that tormented me terribly, that so filled me with spite that I scarcely knew myself. Your genuinely Spanish beauty must have reminded him of his homeland, not to mention Maria Hérédia, of whom I am jealous, for I am jealous even of the past. Your magnificent black hair, your beautiful brown eyes; that brow on which the joys of motherhood accent your poetic past sorrows, which are like shadows in a radiant light; that fresh southern complexion, fairer than my blond fairness; those vigorous forms, that breast glowing amid the lace like some delicious fruit, and my godson clinging to it: all of that hurt my eyes and my heart. I put cornflowers in my hair, I tried to enliven my drab blond locks with cherry-red ribbons, all in vain. No matter what I did, it paled before a Renée I never expected to find in the oasis that is La Crampade.

Furthermore, Felipe was too envious of that child, whom I found myself despising. Yes, that insolent life that fills your house, animates it, makes it ring with shouts and laughter, I wanted all that for myself. I could see regret in Macumer's eyes; for two nights I wept in secret. It was torture to be in your house. You are too beautiful a woman and too happy a mother; I cannot stay with you. And here you were complaining, imposter! First of all, your l'Estorade is fine, his conversation is pleasant, his salt-and-pepper hair is pretty, he has beautiful eyes, and there is in his southern ways the je ne sais quoi that never fails to please. From what I have seen of him, he will surely be named *député* for the Bouches-du-Rhône district sooner or later, and will make his way in the National Assembly, for I am forever at your service where your ambitions are concerned. The miseries of exile have given him the calm, steady air that I believe is half of all success in politics. If you want my opinion, my dear, there is nothing more to politics than a grave demeanor, which is why I told Macumer he must be a very great statesman indeed.

Satisfied that you are happy, I am now contentedly racing back to my beloved Chantepleurs, where Felipe will find some way to become a father. I want to welcome you there only when I have a child like yours at my breast. I deserve all the names you might call me: I am silly, ignoble, absurd. Alas! one is indeed all of that when one is jealous. Through no fault of yours, I was suffering, and you will forgive me for fleeing that pain. Two days more and I would have done something terrible—yes, something gauche. Despite the rage gnawing at my heart, I am glad I came, glad to have found you such a beautiful, fertile mother, still my friend amid all your maternal joys, just as I remain yours amid all the raptures of my love. Here I am just a stone's throw away from you, in Marseille, and already I'm proud of you, proud of the magnificent mother you'll be. How perceptive of you to see your true vocation! For to my mind you were born to be a mother more than a lover, just as I was born more for love than for motherhood. Some women, too ugly or dull, can be neither one. A good mother and a mistress-wife both require a quick mind, sound judgment, and an ability to draw as needed on all womankind's most exquisite qualities. Oh! I studied you closely: is that not to say, my kitten, that I admired you? Yes, your children will be happy and well-bred, they will be bathed in the effusions of your tenderness, caressed by the gleaming light of your soul.

Tell Louis truthfully why I left in such haste, but find a few decent pretexts with which to varnish that truth for your father-in-law, who seems to be your steward, and above all for your family, the very image

of the Harlowe family, albeit with a touch of the Provençal spirit.
Felipe does not yet know why I left, and he never will. If he asks, I
will invent some excuse. Very likely I will tell him you were jealous
of me. Please allow me that little white lie. Farewell, I must hurry to
finish this letter: I want it to reach you at breakfast, and the coachman, who has promised to deliver it to you, is here drinking and
waiting. Kiss my dear little godson for me. Come to Chantepleurs
in October: I will be there alone while Macumer is away in Sardinia,
for he has ambitious improvements in mind for his lands. Such at
least is his project of the moment; he makes it a point of pride always
to have a project, as it makes him feel independent—hence his anxiety when he speaks of it to me. Farewell!

36

My dear, there are no words to express our surprise when we learned
at breakfast that you had gone on your way, and particularly when
the coachman who drove you to Marseille handed me your extraordinary letter. But, you wicked thing, your happiness was the one
single subject of all those conversations at the foot of the bluff—on
Louise's bench—and you were very wrong to take umbrage. *Ingrata!*
I sentence you to return here the moment I summon you. You did
not say, in that odious letter scrawled on some inn's common paper,
just where you would be stopping, and so I am sending this answer
to Chantepleurs.

Listen to me, dear chosen sister, and know, above all, that I want
you to be happy. Dear Louise, there is in your husband a greatness of
soul and of mind as striking as his natural gravity and noble face;
there is, too, a truly majestic force in his expressive homeliness, his
velvet gaze. It took me some time to draw him into the familiarity
without which two people cannot observe each other in depth. That
man was once a first minister, and he adores you as he adores God.
He must be a master of dissimulation, and if I wanted to go fishing
for secrets in that diplomat's depths, among the stones of his heart,
I needed as much skill as ruse; in the end, however, without our man
having guessed, I discovered many things my darling would never
suspect. Of we two, I am in a way Reason where you are Imagination;
I am grave Duty where you are unbridled Love. Once that contrast
of mind existed only for us, but Fate has chosen to extend it into our
respective destinies. I am a humble country viscountess of considerable ambition, who must lead her family down the road to prosperity,

whereas society knows that Macumer was once the Duke de Soria, and so, as a duchess by right, you reign over that Paris where not even kings have an easy time reigning. You have a fine fortune, which Macumer will double if he sees out those plans for his vast holdings in Sardinia, whose resources are well-known in Marseille. You must admit, if one of us should be jealous, it is I! But let us give thanks to God that our two hearts are elevated enough to maintain our friendship above vulgar pettiness. I know you: you are ashamed to have left. But flee me or not, I will not spare you even one of the words I was planning to say to you today beneath the bluff. I beg you, then, read this letter closely, for its subject is even more you than Macumer, though he has a great deal to do with its message.

First of all, my darling, you do not love him. You will have wearied of this adoration before two years are out. You will never see Felipe as a husband but only as a lover, and you will scorn him without a second thought, as all women do with their lovers. No, he does not inspire in you, and you do not feel, the deep respect and fearful tenderness a true lover has for the man in whom she sees a God. Oh! I have made a close study of love, my angel, and more than once I have sounded the very depths of my heart. Now that I have carefully examined you, I can tell you: You do not love him. Yes, dear queen of Paris, like all queens, you will yearn to be treated like a shopgirl, you will yearn to be dominated, led along by a strong man who, rather than adoring you, bruises your arm as he grasps it in a jealous rage. Macumer loves you too much to rebuke or resist you. His will dissolves with one single glance from you, one beguiling word. Sooner or later you will despise him for loving you too much. Alas! he is spoiling you, as I spoiled you at the convent, for you are one of the most charming women and one of the most captivating minds that can be imagined. Above all, you are sincere, and for our own happiness the world often demands untruths to which you will never stoop. For instance, the world demands that a woman never show the power she holds over her husband. Socially speaking, a husband must no more seem his wife's lover, even if he loves her like one, than a wife must play the role of a mistress. And as it happens neither one of you obeys that law. For one thing, my child, what society least forgives—from what you have told me of it—is happiness, and so it must be concealed, but this is nothing. Two lovers are equal in a way that, I believe, must never be seen in a wife and her husband, lest they lose their social standing and suffer irreparable sorrows. An undistinguished man is a sad thing, but an extinguished man is far worse. In time you will make of Macumer a mere shadow of a man, stripped of his will, no longer himself but a thing fashioned for your use; you will have assimilated him so fully to yourself that there will be not two but one person in your household, and that person will of necessity be an incomplete one; you will regret that, and when you do finally open your eyes the damage will be beyond repair. Try as we might, our sex will never have the qualities peculiar to men, and those qualities are not simply necessary but indispensable to the Family. In spite of his blindness, Macumer is now glimpsing that future, and he feels his love has diminished him. His voyage to Sardinia seems to me a sign that he wants a brief separation, so that he might find himself again. You do not hesitate to make use of the power love has handed you. Your authority shows in a gesture, a glance, a tone of voice. Oh! my dear, you are, as your mother said, a bold vixen. To be sure, I believe you understand that I am greatly superior to Louis, but have you ever once seen me contradict him? In public, am I not a wife who respects him as the master of the family? Hypocrisy! you will say. First, any advice I think fit to give him, my opinions, my ideas, I submit to him only in the shadow and silence of the bedroom, but I can swear to you, my angel, that even then I treat him with no superiority. If I did not remain his wife, both in secret and in the eyes of the world, he would have no faith in himself. My dear, true charity requires a self-effacement so complete that the recipient never thinks himself inferior to the giver, and there is joy without end to be found in that secret devotion. My greatest pride, then, is that I deceived even you and heard you tell me of Louis's many qualities. Indeed, over the past two years, prosperity, happiness, and hope have allowed him to recover everything he had lost through sorrow, poverty, solitude, and doubt.

In light of my observations, then, I now find that you love Felipe for yourself, not for him. There is a certain truth in what your father told you: your egoism, the egoism of a true grande dame, is merely disguised by the springtime flowers of your love. Ah! my child, no one who did not love you could tell you such cruel truths. Let me inform you, on the condition that not one word of what I say will ever be whispered to the baron, of the end of my last talk with him. We had sung your praises in every key, for he could clearly see that I loved you like a sister who is loved, and after drawing him unawares into a discussion of more secret thoughts, I said to him, "Louise has not yet had to struggle with life; fate treats her like a favored child, and she may well be unhappy if you cannot be a father for her, just as you are a lover." "But can I?" he answered! He said no more, like a man who sees the abyss into which he is about to tumble. That exclamation told me all I needed to know. Had you not left, he would have told me more a few days later.

My angel, when that man's strength is gone, when he grows sated with his pleasures, when he feels, I shall not say degraded but robbed of his dignity in your eyes, then the rebuke he will hear from his conscience will fill him with a remorse that will hurt you precisely because you will blame yourself. In the end, you will feel only disdain for one you have not come to respect. Reflect on that. Disdain is the first form assumed by a woman's hatred. Your heart is noble, you will always remember the sacrifices Felipe made for you, but having, so to speak, served himself up in that first feast, he will have nothing more to sacrifice, and woe to the man or woman who leaves nothing to be desired! For then everything has been said. To our shame or our glory—a difficult question, that, which I cannot answer—we demand much only of the man who adores us!

Oh, Louise, change: there is still time. If you do with Macumer as I do with l'Estorade, you can bring the lion hidden in that truly fine man leaping out. As it is, you might almost be seeking vengeance for his superiority. Will you not be proud to exercise your power for reasons other than your own gain, to transform a great man into a genius, as I make a superior man from an ordinary one?

I would have written you this same letter had you not left us; in conversation, I would have feared your petulance and sharp wit, whereas I know that on reading my thoughts you will reflect on your future. Dear soul, you have everything you need to be happy. Do not spoil your happiness—and do go back to Paris as soon as November comes. The cares and intrusions of society, which I have so often disparaged, are diversions necessary for your perhaps overly private life. A married woman must have a coquettishness all her own. The mother who does not leave her family wanting more of her by making herself slightly scarce risks allowing boredom into her home. If I have several children—and for the sake of my happiness I hope I shall— then I swear that once they are old enough I will set aside several hours each day to be alone, for it is important to be sought after by everyone, even one's own children! Farewell, dear jealous one! Do you know that an ordinary woman would be flattered to have caused you this fit of jealousy? Alas! I myself can only regret it, for I am a mother and a sincere friend, and nothing else. A thousand tendernesses. Explain your sudden departure however you please: you may not be sure of Felipe, but I am sure of Louis.

37

Genoa

My dear beauty, the fancy took me to see a bit of Italy, and to my great joy Macumer allowed himself to be talked into it, his Sardinian projects put off for another day.

This country enchants and delights me. There is something ardent and seductive in the churches here, and especially the chapels, something that must fill the heart of any Protestant girl with a longing to convert. Macumer was given a warm welcome; everyone was elated to have gained such a subject. If I wished, Felipe could be the Sardinian ambassador in Paris, for the court has been charming with me. If you write, send your letters to Florence. I do not quite have time to tell you anything in detail; I will give you a full account when you first come to Paris. We will be here only a week, then we leave for Florence by way of Livorno; after one month in Tuscany and another in Naples, we will set off for Rome in November. On our way home we will stop in Venice, where we will spend the first half of December, and then we will continue on to Milan and Turin, arriving in Paris at the beginning of January. We travel like a couple of lovers. The newness of these places puts us in mind of our wonderful honeymoon. Macumer knew nothing of Italy; our first sight of it was that magnificent Grande Corniche road, which might have been built by fairies. Farewell, my dear. Do not be angry if I fail to write. I cannot find a moment for myself when I travel; I have only the time to see, to feel, and to savor my impressions. Once they have taken on the colors of memory, I shall tell you of them.

38

September

My dear, awaiting you at Chantepleurs is a rather long answer to the letter you wrote me from Marseille. Your second honeymoon has done so little to assuage the fears I expressed in that reply that I would ask you to write your people in the Nivernais and have them forward it to you at once.

Word has it that the ministry has decided to dissolve the National Assembly. This is a setback for the king, as the current assembly is sympathetic to his cause, and he was counting on them to enact laws that would strengthen his power, but it is a setback for us as well: Louis will not turn forty until the end of 1827. Fortunately, my father has agreed to have himself named *député*, and will then submit his resignation when the time comes.

Your godson took his first steps without his godmother. He is a wonder and is beginning to make charming little gestures that tell me he is no longer a mere organ sucking down a primordial life but a soul: there are thoughts to be seen in his smiles. I am finding such success as a nurse that our Armand will be weaned by December. One year of milk is enough. A child who nurses too long will end up simpleminded. I have every faith in popular sayings. You must be a sensation in Italy, my beautiful blond. A thousand tendernesses.

39

Rome, December

I have your horrid letter, which my steward sent down from Chantepleurs at my request. Oh! Renée.... But I will spare you all the
thoughts my indignation inspired in me. I will tell you only of your
letter's effect. On our return from the charming party thrown for us
by the ambassador, where I shone so brightly that Macumer came
home more intoxicated with me than I can tell you, I read him your
horrible answer, and as I read I wept, at the risk of spoiling my beauty.
My dear Abencerrage fell at my feet, calling you a nag; he led me to
the balcony of the palace where we are staying, overlooking a part of
Rome, and there he spoke words in every way worthy of the view we
saw before us, for it was a superb moonlit night. We have already
learned Italian, and so it was in that languid tongue, so conducive to
passion, that he expressed his love; it was a sublime thing to my ears.
Even were you a prophet, he told me, he would trade an entire lifetime
for one sweet night with me, or one delicious afternoon. By that
measure, he had already lived a thousand years. He wanted me to
remain his mistress and wanted no other title than my lover. Each
and every day, he is so proud and so happy to find himself my favorite that, if God appeared to him and gave him the choice between
living another thirty years by your system, with five children, and
living only another five years but years filled with our flower-decked
love, he would make his choice at once: better to be loved as I love
him and die. As he was whispering these protestations in my ear,
encircling my waist with one arm, my head on his shoulder, we suddenly heard the shriek of a bat under attack by a wood owl. So cruel

an impression did that death cry make on me that Felipe carried me half conscious to my bed. But fear not! That horoscope had resounded through my very soul, but this morning I feel fine. On rising, I knelt before Felipe, and clasping his hands in mine and looking up into his eyes, I said to him, "My angel, I am a child, and Renée may well be right: perhaps what I love in you is simply love, but know, at least, that there is no other emotion in my heart, and so I do love you, in my own way. But if ever, in my behavior, in the tiniest aspects of my life and my soul, there is anything contrary to what you wanted or hoped from me, you have only to say so! Tell me! I will take pleasure in hearing your words, and in guiding my acts only by the light of your eyes. Renée loves me so, she's frightened me!"

Macumer had no voice to answer with: he was dissolving into tears. Now I must thank you, Renée; I hadn't realized how deeply I was loved by my handsome, regal Macumer. Rome is the city for love. When you have a passion, this is the place to indulge it: you have God and the arts as your accomplices. In Venice we will meet up with the Duke and Duchess de Soria. Should you write, write me in Paris, as we will be leaving Rome in three days. The ambassador's soirée was a farewell.

P.S. Dear imbecile, your letter clearly shows that you know love only as an idea. Understand, then, that love is a principle whose effects are so disparate that no theory could ever hope to encompass or direct them. I say this for the benefit of my little professor in a corset.

40

January 1827

My father has his appointment, my father-in-law is dead, and I am
again about to give birth; such are the great events of the end of this
year. I tell them to you straight off so as to dispel at once the ideas
given you by this black-bordered paper.

My darling, your letter from Rome made me tremble. You are two
children. Felipe is either a diplomat who concealed his true feelings
or a man who loves you as he would love a courtesan to whom he is
prepared to abandon his fortune, knowing full well she is betraying
him. But enough of that. You think me a nag, so I will hold my tongue.
But allow me to tell you that from my study of our two lives I have
derived a cruel law: If you wish to be loved, then do not love.

Louis, my dear, was awarded the cross of the Legion of Honor on
being named to the Regional Council. Since he will soon have served
for three years, and since my father, whom you will no doubt see in
Paris during the session, would like to see his son-in-law promoted
to an officer of that Legion, please be so kind as to approach whatever
bigwig it is who oversees these things and take care of that little matter. Do not under any circumstances intercede for my very honored
father, Count de Maucombe, who aspires to the title of marquis; save
your favors for me alone. Next winter, when Louis becomes a *député*,
we will come up to Paris and move heaven and earth to find him a
place in some directorate-general, so that we may save up our revenues
and live on the appointments of his position. My father has a seat
between the Center and the Right, he wants only a title. Our family
was already well-known under King René,[42] so King Charles X will

not refuse a Maucombe, but I fear that my father might take it into his head to seek some favor for my younger brother, and if the brass ring of the marquessate is kept just slightly out of his reach, he will be able to think only of himself.

January 15

Ah! Louise, I am just back from hell! If I have the courage to tell you of my torment, it is only because I think of you as a second self. And even then, I am not sure I will ever allow my thoughts to turn back to those five awful days! The mere word *convulsion* sends a shiver through my soul. I have just endured not five days but five centuries of pain. Until a mother has suffered that martyrdom, she will not know the meaning of the word *suffering*. There were moments when I counted you lucky for not having children—you see how far I was from my right mind!

The eve of that terrible day, the weather, which was still and humid, almost hot, seemed to be discommoding my little Armand. Ordinarily so sweet and affectionate, he had turned grumpy; he cried for virtually no reason, he wanted to play and then smashed his toys. Perhaps among children all illnesses are foretold by such changes of mood. Alerted by his strange misbehavior, I saw Armand's face now red, now pale, which I attributed to the four large teeth all coming in at the same time. I kept him beside me as I slept, waking often to see to him. He had a slight fever during the night, which little worried me; I was still blaming it on his teeth. Toward morning he said "Mama!" and made a gesture to ask for some water, but in his voice there was a sharpness and in his gesture a twitch that chilled my blood. I leapt out of bed to make him some sugar water. Imagine my terror when he made no move as I held out the cup; he simply said "Mama" once again, in that voice that was no longer his voice, no longer even a voice at all. I took his hand, but it would not obey, it was going stiff. I put the cup to his lips. The poor child drank in a strange and alarming way, taking three or four spasmodic little sips, and the water made an odd noise in his throat. All at once he clutched at me desperately; I saw his eyes go white, pulled back by some inner force, and I felt no flexibility in his limbs. I let out an awful cry. Louis came running. "Send for a doctor! Send for a doctor! He's dying!" I shouted. Louis disappeared, and once again my poor little Armand said "Mama! Mama!" as he clung to me. That was the last moment in which he knew he had a mother. The pretty veins of his temples swelled up, and the convulsion began. With an hour to wait before the doctors arrived, that child—once so lively, so pink and so white, that flower who filled me with pride and joy—lay in my arms as stiff as a log, and those eyes! I tremble as I remember them. Deep red, clenched, shrunken, mute, my dear Armand was a mummy. A doctor, then two more doctors brought from Marseille by Louis stood over him like birds of ill omen. They sent a shiver down my spine. One spoke of a brain fever, the other saw nothing more than the sort of convulsions to which children are sometimes prone. Our local doctor seemed to me the wisest, for he had no recommendations. "It's his teeth," said the second doctor. "It's a fever," said the first. In the end, they agreed to put leeches on his neck and ice on his head. I thought I might die, seeing before me a discolored cadaver, not a cry, not a movement, instead of the bright, noisy creature he was! Half out of my mind, I fell into hysterical laughter when I saw leeches biting that pretty neck I had so often kissed, and a cap of ice placed on that charming head. My dear, they had to cut off the pretty hair we so admired, the hair you caressed, so they could put on that ice. Like my labor pains, his convulsions returned every ten minutes, and the poor child writhed, now livid, now purple. When they struck each other, his limbs made a sound like two pieces of wood. That lifeless creature had once smiled at me, spoken to me, called me Mama! Gales of pain ripped through my soul with those thoughts, lashing it as a hurricane lashes the sea, and I felt a shudder run through the bonds by which a child holds fast to our hearts. My mother might have been able to help me, advise me, or console me, but she is in Paris. I believe mothers know more about convulsions than doctors. After four days and four nights of uncertainties and fears that nearly killed me, the doctors all agreed that a horrible pomade should be applied to his skin, to raise blisters! Oh! blisters on my poor Armand, who just five days before was playing, laughing, trying his best to say *Godmother*! I refused, preferring to trust in nature. Louis took me to task: he had faith in the doctors. A man is always a man. But at certain moments, these terrible illnesses take on the look of death, and in one such moment, that loathsome remedy seemed Armand's only chance. My Louise, his skin was so dry, so rough, so arid that the unguent would not stick. I then wept over the bed for so long that the mattress grew wet. And all this time the doctors were at dinner! Finding myself alone, I wiped my child clean of all their medical ointments and took him in my arms, half mad, pressing him to my breast, putting my forehead to his, praying God to give him my life, striving to impart that life to him. I held him that way for a few moments, wanting to die along with him, so that we would not be separated in life or in death. My dear, I felt his limbs move; the convulsions eased, my child stirred, those horrible, sinister colors disappeared! I cried out just as I had when he fell ill; the doctors came up, and I showed them Armand.

"He is saved!" cried the oldest of the doctors.

Oh! What a word! What music! The heavens opened. And indeed, two hours later, Armand was coming back to life, but I was destroyed, I required the balm of joy so as not to fall into some illness. Dear God! With what horrible pains you attach the child to his mother! What nails you drive into our hearts to hold him in place! Was I then not yet mother enough, I who wept with joy on seeing that child's first steps, on hearing him stammer out his first words? I who study him for hours at a time so as to properly perform my duties and learn the sweet trade of motherhood? What need was there to inflict these terrors, these horrible visions, on one who makes an idol of her child? As I write you this letter, our Armand is playing, shouting, laughing. And I am trying to discover the cause of that horrible childhood illness, remembering that I am pregnant. Is it teething? Is it some strange process at work in the brain? Do children who suffer convulsions have some manner of imperfection in their nervous systems? These ideas worry me as much for the present as for the future. Our country doctor thinks it a nervous excitement, set off by teething. I would give every one of my own teeth to see our little Armand's come in safely. When I see one of those white pearls poking through his inflamed gum, I now break into a cold sweat. From the heroism that dear angel shows in his suffering, I know that he will have my character exactly; he gives me glances that break my heart. Medicine knows very little about the causes of that sort of paralysis, which ends as abruptly as it begins and can be neither cured nor prevented. Let me repeat, one thing alone is certain: the sight of a child in convulsions is a mother's hell. How desperately I embrace him! Oh! how long I keep him on my arm when we go out walking! To make my torture all the more horrible, I was forced to endure that ordeal knowing I would deliver again in six weeks: I trembled for the child to come! Farewell, my dear, beloved Louise. Do not wish for children, that is my final word.

41

Paris

Poor angel, Macumer and I have forgiven you all your meanness on learning of your ordeal. I shivered, I suffered as I read the details of that double torment, and now I am a little less sorry not to be a mother. Let me inform you at once of Louis's promotion: he may now wear the rosette of the officer. You wanted a little girl; very likely you will have one, happy Renée! My brother's wedding to Mademoiselle de Mortsauf was celebrated on our return. Our charming king, who is indeed a wonderfully good man, granted my brother succession to the charge of first gentleman of the chamber, which came to him from his father-in-law. "The charge must be passed on with the titles," he told the Duke de Lenoncourt-Givry. He asked, however, that the Mortsauf family crest be placed back to back with the de Lenoncourts' on the coat of arms.

My father was a hundred times right. Without the aid of my inheritance, none of this would have happened. My father and mother came from Madrid for the wedding and will return after the party I shall be hosting tomorrow for the newlyweds. It will be a glittering gala. The Duke and Duchess de Soria are in Paris; their presence worries me a little. Maria Hérédia is certainly one of the most beautiful women in Europe, and I don't like the way Felipe looks at her. I have thus doubled my love and tenderness for him. I take great care not to say "*She* would never have loved you like this!," but those words are written in my every glance, my every move. God knows I am elegant and enticing enough. Madame de Maufrigneuse said to me yesterday, "Dear child, we can only lay down our arms to you." I keep

Felipe so amused that he will find his sister-in-law as stupid as a Spanish cow. I regret all the less not having produced a little Abencerrage in that the duchess will no doubt bear her child in Paris and will be unlovely to behold; if it is a boy, he will be named Felipe in honor of the exile. And so, by a curious twist of fate, I will be a godmother for a second time. Farewell, my dear. I will go to Chantepleurs early this year, for we spent an exorbitant sum on our travels; I leave toward the end of March to go and live economically in the Nivernais. In any event, Paris bores me. Felipe sighs no less than I for the beautiful solitude of our gardens, our fresh meadows, and our sand-spangled Loire, a river like no other. Chantepleurs will seem delicious after the pomp and vanity of Italy, for, after all, magnificence grows tedious and a lover's gaze is more beautiful than any *capo d'opera*, any *bel quadro*![43] We will be expecting you, and I promise I will never be jealous of you again. You may fish about in my Macumer's heart all you like, reel in his exclamations, haul his scruples to the surface: I place him in your hands with serene confidence. Felipe loves me all the more since that scene in Rome; he told me yesterday (he is looking over my shoulder) that his sister-in-law, the Maria of his youth, his onetime fiancée, Princess Hérédia, his first dream, was dull-witted. Oh! dear, I am worse than an opera girl, that insult tickled me pink. I observed to Felipe that she doesn't speak French properly; she says *essemple* for *exemple*, *san* for *cinq*, *sheu* for *je*; she is beautiful, but she has no grace, she has not the slightest quickness of mind. When you pay her a compliment, she looks at you as if she's not used to receiving them. His character being what it is, he would have left Maria after two months of marriage. The Duke de Soria, Don Fernand, is a very fine match for her; he is generous, but he is a spoiled child, one can see it. I could be cruel and make you laugh, but I say only what is true. A thousand tendernesses, my angel.

42
FROM RENÉE TO LOUISE

My little girl is two months old; my mother is the godmother and one of Louis's old great-uncles the godfather of that little child, whose name is Jeanne-Athénaïs.

As soon as I am able, I will leave to come and visit you at Chantepleurs, since you are not afraid of a nursing woman. Your godson sometimes speaks your name: he pronounces it *Matoumer*! for that is as close as he can come to the letter *c*. You will adore him; he has all his teeth and eats meat like a big boy, runs and scurries like a rat, but my anxious gaze is forever fixed on him. I despair that I will not have him at my side during my confinement, which will keep me closed up in my room for more than forty days, owing to certain precautions the doctors have prescribed. Alas! my child, one never gets used to labor! The same pains return, and the same fears. Nevertheless (do not show this letter to Felipe), there is a bit of me in that little girl, who will perhaps show up your Armand.

My father thought Felipe was looking a bit thinner, and my dear darling as well. But the Duke and Duchess de Soria have gone on their way; there is nothing more to be jealous of! Are you hiding some secret sorrow from me? Your letter was neither as long nor as affectionately turned as the others. Is this one more little caprice of my dear capricious friend?

I have written too much, my caretaker is scolding me for having written you, and Mademoiselle Athénaïs de l'Estorade would like her dinner. Farewell, then; write me nice long letters.

43

For the first time in my life, dear Renée, I wept alone beneath a wil-
low tree, on a wooden bench by my long pond at Chantepleurs, a
delicious view that you will make lovelier still when you come, for
merry children are the only thing missing. Your fruitfulness has
forced me to consider myself, I who have no children after what will
soon be three years of marriage. Oh! I thought, even if I had to suffer
a hundred times more than Renée suffered as she gave birth to my
godson, even if I had to see my child in convulsions, please, God, give
me an angelic creature like that little Athénaïs, whom I am now
picturing in my mind, beautiful as a sunlit day, for you have told me
nothing of her! In that I recognized my Renée. You seem almost to
have sensed my sorrows. Each time that my hopes are dashed, I fall
prey to a black grief for several days. Sitting on that bench, I lost
myself in the composition of melancholy elegies. When will I embroider little bonnets? When will I pick out the fabric for my baby's
clothes? When will I sew together pretty pieces of lace to wrap a
little head? Am I then never to hear one of those charming creatures
call me Mama, pull my dress, rule over me? Will I never see the marks
left in the sand by the wheels of a little carriage? Will I never pick up
broken toys from my courtyard? Will I never visit the fancy-goods
stores, as I have seen so many mothers do, to buy swords, dolls, tiny
furniture? Will I never observe the growth of that life, that angel,
who will be another Felipe, even more dearly loved than the first? I
would like a son, so that I might learn how a man can be loved even
more in a second incarnation than in the first. My gardens, my château
feel empty and cold. A woman without children is a monstrosity; we

are made only to be mothers. Oh! professor in corsets that you are, you have truly understood life. Sterility is indeed horrible in all things. My life is a little too like those pastoral love poems by Gessner or Florian, of which Rivarol said that one wishes there were a few lurking wolves.[44] I too want to devote myself! I sense within myself forces unknown to Felipe; if I am not soon a mother, I will have to do something rash. So I have just said to my relic of the Moors, whose eyes filled with tears; his only punishment was to hear himself called a sublime beast, not to be teased where his love is concerned.

I sometimes find myself wanting to say novenas, to seek fruitfulness from some Madonna or curative water. Next winter I will consult the doctors. I am too furious with myself to say more to you. Farewell.

44

FROM THE SAME TO THE SAME

Paris, 1829

What, my dear, a year with no letter? ... I am a little put out. Do you believe that your Louis, who has come to see me nearly every other day, is any replacement for you? It is not enough for me to know you're not ill and your affairs are going well: I want your sentiments and your ideas just as I offer you mine, even if it means being scolded or criticized or misunderstood, for I love you. I am deeply concerned by your silence and your retreat to the countryside, when you could be here reveling in the parliamentary triumphs of Count de l'Estorade, whose diligence and gift for *speechifying* have earned him some influence, and who will no doubt be placed in a very high position after the session. Do you perhaps spend all your time writing up instructions for him? Numa was not so distant from his Egeria.[45] Why have you not seized the opportunity to visit Paris? I could have been enjoying your company for the past four months. Louis told me yesterday that you would be coming to join him, and that you would deliver your third child here, you rabbit! After many questions, sighs, and laments, Louis, wily diplomat though he be, came out and told me that his great-uncle, Athénaïs's godfather, is very ill. And I have every confidence that you, ever the good mother, will know just how to vaunt the *député*'s successes and obtain an advantageous legacy from your husband's last maternal relative. Fear not, my Renée, the de Lenoncourts, the de Chaulieus, Madame de Macumer's entire salon are working to further Louis's ambitions. Martinac will very likely appoint him to the Court of Audit. But if you do not tell me why you are staying in the provinces, I will be angry. Do you not want to be recognized as the real political genius in the house of l'Estorade? Do you want to cultivate the uncle as you oversee his will? Do you fear you will be less a mother in Paris? Oh! how I would like to know if you simply prefer not to make your first appearance in society as a pregnant woman, you coquette! Farewell.

45

You complain of my silence; have you forgotten the two little ones in my care, and I in their thrall? But you have indeed discovered a few of my reasons for keeping to my house. Apart from our precious uncle's condition, I did not want to drag a four-year-old boy and a little girl not far from three off to Paris while I am pregnant. I did not want to encumber your life and your household with such a family, I did not want to appear to my disadvantage in the glittering world you reign over, and I have a horror of furnished rooms and hotels. On learning that his great-nephew had been named officer, Louis's great-uncle made me a present of half of his savings, two hundred thousand francs, so that we might buy a house in Paris; Louis has been given the task of finding one in your neighborhood. My mother has given me some thirty thousand francs to furnish it. I will be in my own home when I come to Paris for the session. And I will try to prove in every way worthy of my dear *soeur d'élection*, no pun intended.[46]

I thank you for having so well helped Louis on his way, but despite the esteem shown him by Messieurs de Bourmont and de Polignac, who want him in their new ultra-Royalist ministry, I would prefer to have him less in the public eye: he would be too vulnerable there. I prefer a place in the Court of Audit, for its permanence. Our affairs here will be in very good hands, and once our steward has been fully filled in I will come and assist Louis in Paris, fear not.

As for writing you long letters, how can I at present? This one, in which I hope to depict the events of an ordinary day in my life, will sit on my writing table for a week. Armand may well use it to make paper hens, of which he has whole regiments lined up on the rug, or little boats for the fleets that ply his bathwater. But I need recount for you only one day in my life, for each is like the next, and there are only two states of affairs: the children are well, or the children are not. For me, here in this lonely *bastide*, minutes are quite literally hours or hours minutes, depending on the children's state. Delicious hours to myself can be found only when they are napping, when I am not busy rocking the one and telling stories to the other to put them to sleep. Once they are sleeping close by me, I tell myself: Now there is nothing to fear. For, my angel, all day long mothers invent dangers. The moment they no longer have their children before them, then suddenly there are razors Armand has stolen to play with, or a flame catching hold of his frock, a slowworm that might bite him, a tumble as he is running that might cause an abscess on his head, basins in which he might drown. As you see, motherhood is a series of poems, some sweet, others frightful. No hour goes by without its joys and its terrors. But then comes the evening, and the moment when I sit in my room and spin out their destinies in my daydreaming mind. Their life is then lit by the smiles of the angels I see at their bedside. Sometimes Armand calls for me in his sleep, and unbeknownst to him I come and kiss his brow, and then his sister's feet, gazing at them both in all their beauty. Those are my parties! Yesterday I believe it was our guardian angel who made me race frantically to Athénaïs's cradle in the middle of the night, for her head was not propped up high enough, and our little Armand had thrown off all his covers, his feet purple with cold. "Oh! little Mother!" he said as he woke, and he gave me a kiss. There, my dear, is what I call a nocturnal love scene.

How useful it is for a mother to have her children beside her! What nursemaid could take them in her arms, reassure them, and then put them back to sleep when they have been woken by some horrible nightmare? For they do have their dreams, and it is all the more difficult to explain away one of those terrible imaginings in that the child is listening to its mother with eyes at once sleepy, frightened, intelligent, and innocent. Such moments are interludes between two bouts of sleep. My own sleep has grown so light that I can see and hear my two little ones through the veil of my eyelids. One single sigh, one start, and I am awake. In my mind, the monster of convulsions is forever crouched at the foot of their beds.

Morning comes, and with the first birdsongs my children's peeping begins. Through the mists of the last moments of sleep, their babble is like the dawn chorus, the quarreling swallows, merry or plaintive little cries that I hear less with my ears than with my heart. Naïs tries to come to me, fording the gap between her cradle and my bed on hands and knees or uncertain feet; meanwhile, Armand climbs right up, nimble as a monkey, and gives me a kiss. Those two dears then colonize my bed for their games, with their mother close by for their every whim. The little girl pulls my hair, is forever trying to nurse, and Armand guards my breast as if it were his alone. They strike poses I cannot resist, their laughter explodes like a rocket, and sleep is soon driven away. Then we play ogress: mother ogress devours that tender, white young flesh with caresses, she hungrily kisses those sweet, sparkling eyes, those pink shoulders, giving rise to the most charming little fits of jealousy. Some days I try to put on my stockings at eight o'clock and by nine have yet to pull on even one.

Finally, my dear, we get up. The ablutions begin. I put on my peignoir, roll up my sleeves, don the oilcloth apron; I bathe and clean my two little flowers, with Mary standing by. I alone judge whether the water is too hot or too tepid, for half of a child's cries and tears come from the temperature of the water. And then out come the paper fleets and the little glass ducks. Children must be kept amused if they are to be properly washed. If you knew all the pleasures that must be invented for those absolute monarchs simply so that you can run a soft washcloth over their tiniest folds, you would be shocked at the cleverness and skill accomplished motherhood requires. You beg, you scold, you promise, you acquire a gift for trumpery all the more admirable in that it must be kept perfectly hidden. Who knows what would become of us had God not counterbalanced the child's cunning with the mother's! A child is as wily as any politician, and one masters him just as one masters any politician: by his passions. Happily, it takes nothing to make those angels laugh: a dropped scrub brush, a cake of soap sliding into the water, and suddenly there are bursts of joy! As you see, a mother's triumphs may be hard-won, but triumphs there are. Nevertheless, God alone—for the father knows nothing of all this—you, God, or the angels alone will understand the glances I exchange with Mary when the two little ones are all dressed and we see them clean and tidy in the midst of the soaps, the washcloths, the combs, the basins, the blotting paper, the flannels, all the thousand little accessories to be found in a *nursery* worthy of the name. In that way, and that way alone, I have become English: I will concede that the women of that land have a genius for childcare. Although they consider the child only in terms of his material and physical well-being, their innovations are excellent. My children will thus always be shod in flannel, and their legs will be bare. They will never be crowded or constrained, but neither will they ever be alone. The French child's imprisonment in his swaddling bands is the nurse's freedom—a loaded word if ever there was! A true mother is never free: that is why I do not write you, having the estate to oversee and two children to raise. There are many silent merits to be found in a mother's wisdom, unknown to all, never vaunted, a virtue in every tiny detail, a devotion that knows no timetable. The soups cooking before the fire need my close attention. Do you think me the sort of woman to shirk her duties? There is tenderness to be gleaned from even the tiniest task. Oh! how pretty is the smile of a child enjoying his little meal. Armand has a way of nodding his head that is as good as a whole lifetime of love. How could I leave to some other woman the right, the task, the pleasure of blowing on a spoonful of soup that will be too hot for Naïs, whom I weaned seven months ago, and who still remembers the breast? When a nursemaid burns the child's tongue and lips with something hot, she tells the alarmed mother who comes running that the child is simply crying from hunger. How on earth can a mother sleep in peace knowing that an impure breath might touch the spoonfuls her child will swallow, she to whom nature allowed no intermediary between her breast and her newborn's lips! It takes a certain patience to cut up a cutlet for Naïs, whose last teeth are just coming in, and then to mix that well-done meat with potatoes;

often only a mother can make a fussy child finish his meal. No English nursemaid, no houseful of servants can absolve her of the obligation to take her place on the field of battle, where gentleness must combat childhood's many little sorrows and pains. Indeed, Louise, one must tend to these dear innocents with one's very soul; one must believe only one's own eyes, only the touch of one's own hand for their washing, their feeding, their tucking into bed. In principle, a child's cry is an unappealable rebuke of the mother or nursemaid, if that cry is not caused by some distress imposed by nature. Now that I have two and soon three to look after, I have nothing in my soul but my children; you yourself, you whom I so love, exist only in the form of a memory. I am not always dressed by two in the afternoon. I will thus never trust a mother whose rooms are tidy, who has all her collars, gowns, and affairs in order.

Yesterday, with April beginning, the weather was fine, and I wanted to take them out for a walk before my delivery, whose hour will soon sound; for a mother, an outing is a veritable poem, one you already look forward to the day before, making plans for the morrow. Armand was to wear his first black velvet jacket, with a new ruff I embroidered myself, and a tam in the colors of the Stuarts, ornamented with rooster feathers; Naïs was to be dressed in white and pink, with her delicious *baby* bonnet, for she is still a *baby*—she will lose that pretty name with the arrival of the little one, who is forever kicking at me, and whom I call *my beggar*, for he will be the last-born. I have already seen that child in my dreams, and I know I will have a son. Bonnets, ruffs, jacket, the little stockings, the adorable shoes, the pink swaddling bands, the silk-embroidered chiffon dress, everything was carefully laid out on my bed. When those two lighthearted, cheerful little birds had their brown hair curled in one case and gently combed onto the forehead and along the edge of the pink-and-white bonnet in the other, when the shoes were buckled, when those little bare calves, those neatly shod feet trotted through the *nursery*, when those two *cleanes* faces[47] (as Mary says)—when, in limpid French, those bright eyes said "Let's go!," I quivered with anticipation. Oh! the sight of two children made ready by your own hands, the sight of that fresh skin, those glowing blue veins, when you have bathed them, steamed them, dried them yourself, highlighted by the lively colors of the velvet or silk, why it is better than a poem! With what passion, two seconds after your eagerness has been satisfied, you call them back to plant one more kiss on those necks, made far prettier than the neck of the most beautiful woman by a simple ruff! Such tableaux, which can make any mother stare transfixed with joy at the most idiotic sentimental lithograph, are a part of my life every day!

Once outside, as I was congratulating myself on my handiwork, admiring my little Armand, who looked just like the son of a prince as he led the *baby* down that little path you know well, a carriage came along, and I tried to pull them to one side. My two children tumbled into a mud puddle, and my masterpiece was ruined! There was nothing to do but to take them home and change them into fresh clothes. I picked up Naïs, not seeing that I was ruining my dress; Mary took Armand, and a moment later we were inside again. When a *baby* cries and a child is wet, there is nothing more to say; a mother no longer thinks of herself, all her thoughts are occupied elsewhere.

The dinner hour comes, and most often I have done nothing to prepare for it; how can I alone serve them both, lay out the napkins, roll up their sleeves, ensure that they eat? I answer that question two times a day. What with all these unending tasks, these joys or disasters, everyone in the house is seen to but me. Often, when the children have been misbehaving, I never take out my curlers. My toilette depends on their mood. If I have a moment to write you these six pages, it is only because they are busy cutting out pictures from my romances, or making castles from books or chessmen or mother-of-pearl tokens, or Naïs has to be winding up my silk or wool thread in her own way, which, I assure you, is so complicated that she throws all her little intelligence into it, and never makes a sound.

But I have nothing to complain of: my two children are healthy, free, and it takes less to keep them amused than people suppose. Everything makes them happy: more than toys, what they need is a well-supervised freedom. A few pink, yellow, purple, or black pebbles, some little shells, they are enthralled by the wonders of sand. Their wealth is to own lots of little things. I study Armand; he talks to the flowers, the flies, the chickens, he imitates them, he is friends with the insects, which captivate him without end. He is fascinated by anything small. Armand is beginning to ask me the *why* of all things, he has just stopped by to see what I was saying to his godmother; indeed, he takes you for a good fairy, and as you see, children are always right!

Alas! my angel, I never meant to make you sad by telling you of my happiness. Here is a little portrait of your godson. The other day, a poor man was following us, for the poor know that a mother with a child in tow will never refuse them alms. Armand has yet to learn that it is possible to lack for bread, he has no idea what money is! But as I had just bought him a little trumpet he wanted, he regally held it out to the old man and said, "Here, take this!"

"May I keep it?" the poor man said to me.

What is there on this earth that can outweigh the joy of such a moment?

"Because, madame, I've had children of my own," the old man said, taking what I then gave him, which I had entirely forgotten.

When I think that a child like Armand will have to be sent to school, that I have only three and a half years more to keep him by my side, I shudder. Public education will mow down the flowers of that perpetually blessed childhood, will *denaturalize* those graceful ways, that adorable innocence! They will cut off that curly hair I so cared for, washed, and kissed. And Armand's soul, what will they do with that?

And what news of you? You have told me nothing of your life. Do you still love Felipe? For where the Saracen is concerned I have no worries. Farewell—Naïs has just fallen, and if I were to go on this letter would take up a whole volume.

46

1829

My good and tender Renée, you will have learned from the newspapers of the horrible sorrow that has befallen me; I could not write you a single word. For twenty days and nights I sat at his bedside, I heard his last sigh, I closed his eyes, I piously kept watch over him with the priests, and said the prayers for the dead. I have brought the punishment of this cruel grief down on myself, and yet, seeing the serene smile he gave me before he died, I could not believe that my love had killed him! But in any case, *He is no more*, and *I am*! To you who knew us so well, what more need I add? Those two sentences say it all. Oh! if someone would only tell me he might be brought back to life, I would give up my share of heaven just to hear that promise, for it would be as good as seeing him again! ... And if I could hold him, if only for two seconds, then I could take a breath with no dagger in my heart! Won't you come soon and tell me that? Don't you love me enough to lie to me? ... But no! you told me in advance of the harm I was doing him. ... Is that true? No, I never deserved his love, you're right, I stole it. I smothered happiness in my frantic embraces! Oh, I am no longer mad as I write you these lines, but I feel so alone! Lord, what more can there be in your hell than that single word?

Once he was taken away from me, I lay down in the same bed, hoping to die, for there was only one door between us, and I thought myself still strong enough to push it open! But alas! I was too young, and after a convalescence of forty days, during which the inventions of a sad science sustained me with detestable efficacy, I now find

myself in the country, sitting at my window amid the beautiful flowers he had our servants cultivate for me, enjoying the magnificent
view over which his eyes so often wandered, which he applauded
himself for finding, since it pleased me. Ah! my dear, one can scarcely
stir when one's heart is dead: the pain is unspeakable. The damp soil
of my garden makes me shiver, the earth is like a vast grave, and I feel
I am walking on *him*! The first time I went out, I took fright and
stood frozen in place. How sad to see *his* flowers without *him*!

My mother and father are in Spain, you know my brothers, and
you cannot leave your house in the country, but you needn't worry:
two angels had flown to my side. The Duke and Duchess de Soria,
those two charming people, sped here to be with their brother. The
last nights found our three conjoined sorrows silent and calm around
the deathbed of a truly noble and genuinely great man, a rare man,
in every way superior to his fellows. My Felipe bore his illness with
divine patience. The sight of his brother and Maria eased his soul for
a moment and soothed his pain.

"My dear," he said to me, with the simplicity he showed in all
things, "I nearly forgot to give Fernand the barony of Macumer before
I die. I must rewrite my will. My brother will forgive me, he knows
what it is to be in love!"

I owe my life to the care of my brother-in-law and his wife; they
want to take me to Spain!

Ah! Renée, only to you can I speak of the enormity of this disas-
ter. An awareness of my own errors weighs heavy on me, and it is a
bitter consolation to confide them to you, my poor unheard Cassandra. I killed him with my demands, my absurd fits of jealousy, my
continual teasing. My love was all the more heartless in that we had
the same exquisite sensibilities, we spoke the same language, he understood everything wonderfully, and often my japes hurt him in the
depths of his heart, and I had no idea. Never will you imagine how
far that slave pushed his obedience: I sometimes told him to go away
and leave me alone, and off he went, never questioning a caprice that
may well have been torture for him. He blessed me until his very last
sigh, saying once again that a single day alone with me was better

than a long life with any other, even Maria Hérédia. I weep as I write you these words.

Now I rise at noon, I retire at seven, I take an absurdly long time with my meals, I walk slowly, I spend an hour before a plant, I look at the leaves, I quietly, gravely fill my thoughts with nothing at all, I love shadows, silence, and night; I do battle with the passing hours and with grim pleasure consign them to the past, one by one. I want no other company than the tranquillity of my garden, for there, everywhere I look, I find the sublime images of my happiness, now gone dark and invisible to all others but bright and eloquent for me.

My sister-in-law threw herself into my arms when I told them one morning: "I can't bear having you here! The Spanish soul is so much stronger than ours!"

Ah! Renée, if I am not dead, it is because God measures out unhappiness in proportion to the strength of the afflicted. Only we women can know the depth of our loss when we lose a love with no trace of dishonesty, a love of the highest order, an enduring passion whose pleasures satisfied nature and the soul at once. When will we meet a man of such quality that we can love him without lowering ourselves? Meeting such a man is the greatest happiness that can come to us, and we do not meet him twice. O truly great, truly strong men, your virtue concealed by your poetry, your souls stamped with a superior charm, O men who were made to be loved, you must never fall in love, for you will only bring sorrow to the woman and yourself! Such is my cry as I stroll the pathways of my woods! And no child from him! That inexhaustible love, always smiling on me, covering me with nothing but flowers and joys, that love was sterile. I am a cursed creature! Is pure, violent love—as it is when it is entire—thus as infertile as aversion, just as the extreme heat of the desert sands and the extreme cold of the pole are equally hostile to existence? Must one marry a Louis de l'Estorade to have a family? Could God be jealous of love? I'm talking nonsense.

You alone, I believe, I can bear to have with me. Come to me, then: a grieving Louise must have no other company than you. How horrible was the day I donned the widow's bonnet! Seeing myself in black,

I fell onto a chair and wept until night, and I weep anew as I tell you of that terrible moment. Farewell. It exhausts me to write you; I'm tired of my ideas, I don't want to put them into words any longer. Bring your children, you can nurse the new one here, I won't be jealous, since *he* is here no more, and it will be a pleasure to see my godson, for Felipe wanted a child just like that little Armand. Come, then, and shoulder your share of my sorrows! ...

47
FROM RENÉE TO LOUISE

My dear, by the time this letter is in your hands I will not be far, for I will leave a few moments after I have sent it off. We will be alone. Louis must remain in Provence for the upcoming elections; he wants to be reelected, and already the Liberals are scheming against him.

I come not to console you but simply to bring you my heart, so that it might keep yours company and help you to live. I come to compel you to weep. That is the price to be paid for the happiness of rejoining him one day, for he is only traveling toward God; henceforth, every single step you take will bring you nearer to him. Every duty you accomplish will break a link of the chain that separates you. Come, my Louise, you will recover from this in my arms, and you will go to him pure, noble, forgiven your unmeaning wrongs, and accompanied by the good works you will do here below in his name.

I write these lines in great haste, as I prepare for my departure, with Armand crying out "Godmother! Godmother! Let's go see Godmother!" until I find myself jealous: he is almost your son!

PART TWO

48

October 15, 1833

Well, my Renée, it's true, you've heard right. I have sold my house in Paris, I have sold Chantepleurs and the farms in the Seine-et-Marne, but there is no truth to the rumor that I am ruined and mad. Shall we count it all up? Having burned all my bridges behind me, I found myself with some one million two hundred thousand francs from my poor Macumer's fortune. I will give you a faithful account of my investments, like a sensible sister. I put one million francs into three-percent bonds when the going rate was fifty francs, and have thus assured myself an annual income of sixty thousand francs, rather than the thirty thousand I had from my land. Spending six months each year in the provinces, drawing up leases, listening to the farmers' complaints—they who pay when it pleases them—feeling as bored as a hunter on a rainy day, having produce to sell and selling it at a loss; living in a Parisian house that represented an income of ten thousand livres, overseeing investments, waiting for dividends, having to sue for payments, studying the proposed mortgage laws, in short having financial affairs to keep up with in Paris, in the Seine-et-Marne, and in the Nivernais, what a burden, what a bore, how many possible missteps and enormous losses for a twenty-seven-year-old widow! Now my fortune is invested in the national budget. Rather than pay taxes to the state, it is the state that pays me, every six months, at the Public Treasury: a handsome little clerk smiles when he sees me coming, and then hands me thirty thousand-franc notes, free and clear. Suppose France goes bankrupt, you will ask? Well, for one thing, *Such distant misfortunes I cannot foresee.*[1] But also, France would then deprive me of half of my revenue at most; I would still be as rich as I was before my investment, and besides, between now and that catastrophe, I will have earned twice the revenue I made before. Catastrophes come only once in a century; if I live frugally, there is more than enough time to amass a capital sufficient to see me through. And then, is Count de l'Estorade not a peer of the July Monarchy's semi-republican France? Is he not one of the rivets in the crown offered by "the people" to the king of the French? Need I worry when I have as a friend a presiding officer at the Court of Audit, a great financier? Dare tell me that I am mad! I can calculate nearly as well as your Citizen King. And what is it that endows a woman with this algebraic erudition? It is love!

Alas, the time has come to explain the mysteries of my conduct, whose reasons defied your discernment, your affectionate curiosity, and your perceptive mind. I will soon marry in secret, in a village not far from Paris. I am in love, and I am loved. I love as only a woman who knows what love is can love. I am loved as a woman must be loved by the man she adores. Forgive me, Renée, for hiding myself away from you, and from everyone. If your Louise eludes every eye, frustrates every curiosity, you must see that this deceit was required by my passion for my poor Macumer. You and l'Estorade would have pelted me with misgivings, smothered me with reproaches. And the circumstances would only have strengthened your case! You alone know how jealous I am, and you would have tormented me to no purpose. What you will call my folly, dear Renée, is a thing I wanted to do all on my own, obeying my head and my heart, like a young girl evading her parents' vigilance. My lover's fortune amounts to thirty thousand francs in debts, which I have paid off. What perfect grounds for concern! You would have set out to prove that Gaston is an adventurer, and your husband would have spied on the poor boy. I preferred to study him myself. He has been courting me for the past twenty-two months; I am twenty-seven years old and he twenty-three—an enormous difference, when the woman is older. Another cause for alarm! And finally, he is a poet, who was living off his work, which is to say on next to nothing. That dear lazy lizard of a poet spent more time sunning himself and building castles in Spain than toiling over his poems in the gloom of his garret. Now, among practically minded people, writers and artists and all those who live by their ideas are often thought of as inconstant. They imagine and embrace so many fanciful thoughts that it is only natural to suppose that their hearts are as unbound as their minds. In spite of the paid-off debts, in spite of the age difference, in spite of the poetry, after nobly defending myself for nine months, never allowing him even to kiss my hand, after the most chaste and most delicious of love affairs, I will in a few days not surrender myself, inexperienced, ignorant, and curious, as I did eight years ago, but give myself to him, by my own choice, and I am awaited with such deference that I could well delay my wedding by a year—but there is no servility in that: servitude, yes, but no submission. I have never known a man with a nobler heart than my intended, with more eloquence in his tenderness or more soul in his love. Alas, my angel! It runs in his family! I will tell you his story in a few words.

My beloved has no name beyond Marie Gaston.[2] He is the son, not illegitimate but adulterous, of the beautiful Lady Brandon, whom you must have heard of; Lady Dudley's vengeance ended up killing her of chagrin, a horrible business of which this dear child knows nothing.[3] Marie Gaston's brother Louis enrolled him in the Collège de Tours, which he left in 1827. A few days after entrusting him to that school, the brother sailed off in search of his fortune, as Marie learned from an old woman who was his own Providence. That brother became a sailor, and now and then wrote him truly fatherly letters, the emanations of a beautiful soul, but his labors kept him far from France. In his last letter, he announced that he had been named ship's captain in some American republic, and enjoined his brother not to lose hope. Alas! three years have now gone by with no further word from him, and my lizard so loves his brother that he wanted to sail away and go looking for him. Our great writer Daniel d'Arthez prevented that act of madness and nobly took Marie Gaston under his wing, often providing him *grub and a roof*, as the poet told me in his vigorous language. And indeed, imagine the child's difficult straits:

he thought genius was the quickest way to fortune, is that not enough to make you laugh for twenty-four hours straight? And so, from 1828 to 1833, he tried to make a name for himself in literature, and naturally he led the most appalling life of doubt, hope, work, and privation that can possibly be imagined. Driven by excessive ambition and despite all d'Arthez's wise advice, he only added to his pile of debts. His name was nonetheless beginning to become known when I met him at the Marquise d'Espard's. There, though he saw nothing, I found myself sympathetically drawn to him on first sight. How is it that he has never been loved? How could he have been left to me? Oh! he has genius and wit, he has heart and pride; women are always skittish of such complete greatness. Did it not take a hundred victories for Josephine to glimpse Napoleon in her little Bonaparte? The innocent believes he knows the depth of my love for him! Poor Gaston! He has no idea, but you I will tell. It is important that you know, for there is something of the last will and testament in this letter, Renée. Heed these words closely.

At this moment I am certain of being loved as much as any woman can be loved on this earth, and I have every faith in the magical marriage that will be mine, to which I bring a love I did not know before.... Yes, at long last I know the pleasure of a passion fully felt. Marriage is giving me what women today seek from love. I feel for Gaston the very adoration I inspired in my poor Felipe! I am not my own mistress, I tremble before that boy as the Abencerrage trembled before me. To put it plainly, I love more than I am loved; I am afraid of everything, I have the most ridiculous terrors, I fear he will leave me, I tremble to think of turning ugly and old when Gaston is still young and handsome, I tremble to think I may not please him enough! Nonetheless, I think myself sufficiently talented, devoted, and clever not only to maintain but to increase that love, far from Parisian society, in isolation. Should I fail, should the magnificent poem of that secret love come to an end—what am I saying, an end?—should Gaston one day love me less than the day before, and should I see it, Renée, know that it is not him but myself I will blame. The fault will be mine, not his. I know myself: I am more a lover than a mother. I must tell you, then, in advance: if his love waned I would die, even if I had children. Before I make this bargain with myself, dear Renée, I therefore beseech you, should that calamity come, to serve as a mother to my offspring, for I will have bequeathed them to you. Your devotion to duty, your exceptional goodness, your love of children, your affection for me, everything I know of you will make my death less bitter, I dare not say sweet. That pact I have made with myself adds something fearsome to the solemnity of this marriage; for that reason, I want no witnesses who know me, and my wedding will be celebrated in secret. In that way I may tremble at my ease, not seeing the concern in your sweet eyes, and I alone will know that as I sign this second certificate of marriage I may well be signing my death warrant.

I will never reconsider this agreement made between myself and the *me* I will become; I tell you of it so that you might know the full extent of your duties. I marry with my property in my own name; while I know I am rich enough that we may live at our ease, Gaston has no idea of my fortune. In twenty-four hours I will divide it as I see fit. As I do not want him humiliated, I have established an annuity of twelve thousand francs in his name; he will find that sum in his desk the day before our wedding. Should he refuse it, I will call everything off. Only by threatening not to marry him did I acquire the right to pay off his debts. Writing these confessions has wearied me; in two days I will tell you more, for tomorrow I must go to the country.

October 20

Here are a few of the measures I have taken to hide our happiness away, for I wish to deny jealousy any chance to raise its head. I remind myself of that beautiful Italian princess who ran off like a lioness to devour her love in some Swiss city, after pouncing like a lioness on her prey.[4] I tell you of these preparations so as to ask of you another favor, which is to never come and see us unless I have summoned you myself and to respect the solitude in which I wish to live.

Two years ago I arranged to purchase some twenty arpents of pastureland, along with a stretch of woods and a fine orchard, on the road to Versailles, overlooking the ponds of Ville-d'Avray. At the far end of the fields, the earth has been moved in such a way as to create a three-arpent pond, with a gracefully shaped island in the middle. Delightful little brooks flow from the two wooded hills that enclose this little valley; my architect has cunningly guided them through my garden and into the ponds on the king's grounds, which can be seen through the trees. This little park, wonderfully laid out by my architect, is surrounded by hedges, walls, or ditches, depending on the terrain, never spoiling the view. Halfway up the hill, flanked by the wood of La Ronce, deliciously exposed to the sun and facing a meadow that slopes down to the pond, I now have a chalet, identical from the outside to the one travelers admire on the road from Sion to Brig, which so charmed me on my way home from Italy. Inside, its elegance rivals the most illustrious of such houses. A hundred paces from that rustic abode, a charming house with the look of a garden pavilion communicates with the chalet by a tunnel, concealing the kitchen, stables, storage sheds, and other outbuildings. Of all those brick constructions, the eye sees only a single, harmonious façade, surrounded by flower beds. The gardeners' house is another pavilion, masking the entrance to the orchards and vegetable gardens.

The door to my grounds, concealed in the outer wall on the wooded side, is nearly impossible to find. The plantings are already tall; within two or three years they will completely conceal the houses. Passersby will discover our nest only on seeing the smoking chimneys from the hilltops, or in the winter when the leaves have fallen.

My chalet is set in the middle of a landscape copied from what is known as the King's Garden in Versailles,[5] but with a view of my pond and my island. On all sides the hills proudly display of verdure, their fine trees so carefully maintained by your new Civil List.[6] My gardeners have orders to cultivate only scented flowers around me, flowers by the thousands, making a perfumed emerald of this patch of land. The chalet, ornamented by a Virginia creeper that runs over the roof, is literally wrapped in climbing plants, hops, clematis, jasmine, azalea, and cup and saucer vine. Anyone who makes out our windows may boast of fine eyesight indeed!

That chalet, my dear, is a fine, beautiful house, with a heater and all the comforts modern architecture has devised, which can make a palace of a hundred square feet. There are rooms for Gaston and rooms for me. On the ground floor is an antechamber, a parlor, and a dining room. Above us are three bedrooms destined for the nursery. I have five beautiful horses, a little light coupé, and a two-horse cabriolet, for Paris is forty minutes away, and whenever we wish to go and hear an opera or see a new play, we can leave after dinner and be back that very evening. The road is lovely, shaded by our hedge. My servants—my cook, my coachman, the stableman, the gardeners, my chambermaid—are entirely trustworthy people, whom I have spent the past six months seeking out; they will be overseen by my old Philippe. Although I have no doubt of their devotion and discretion, I have bound them by their self-interest: their wages are small, but increase each year by what we give them on New Year's Day. They know that any misstep, any doubt about their discretion, will cost them dearly. Lovers never push their servants too far; they are indulgent by nature, and so I can rely without fear on our staff.

Everything that was valuable, pretty, and elegant in my house on the rue du Bac has been moved to the chalet. The Rembrandt, neither more nor less than a daub, is displayed on the stairway; the Hobbema is in *his* rooms, facing the Rubens; the Titian, sent to me from Madrid by my sister-in-law, Maria, adorns the boudoir; the beautiful furniture found by Felipe is prettily arranged in the parlor, which my architect has decorated in the most charming way. Everything in the chalet is wonderfully simple, with the kind of simplicity that costs a hundred thousand francs. Built over cellars of millstones laid on concrete, our ground floor, scarcely visible beneath the flowers and bushes, is deliciously cool but never damp. And finally, a fleet of white swans glides over the pond.

Oh, Renée! There is in that valley a silence that could charm the dead. You are awakened by birdsong or the rustle of poplars in the breeze. As he was digging the foundations for the wall on the wooded side, my architect discovered a little spring, which now feeds a stream that runs down from the hill and then over silvery sand to the pond, between two cress-covered banks: I don't know that such a thing could be bought for any sum of money. Might Gaston come to hate that too-perfect bliss? Everything is so beautiful that I tremble; worms burrow into the finest fruits, the most magnificent flowers are devoured by insects. Is it not always the pride of the forest that is eaten by the horrible brown larva, voracious as death itself? I know all too well that a jealous, invisible force attacks the most perfect felicities. Indeed, you wrote me just that long ago, and your words proved prophetic.

The day before yesterday I went to see if my latest whims had been understood. I felt tears in my eyes, and to my architect's great surprise I wrote on his invoice "Pay in full."

"Your accountant will never allow it, madame," he said. "The bill is for three hundred thousand francs." Beneath my words I added "Without argument!" in the manner of a true Chaulieu of the seventeenth century.

"However, monsieur," I said to him, "I place one condition on my gratitude: you must never tell anyone of these buildings and this park. No one is to know the owner's name. Promise me upon your honor to observe that codicil to my payment."

Do you now understand my sudden disappearances, my secret comings and goings? And all those beautiful things everyone thought had been sold, do you now see where they are? Have you grasped the imperious reason behind the change in my fortune? My dear, love is serious business, and if you want to love properly you must have no other. I need never trouble myself over money again; I have made life an easy and peaceable thing, and just this once I have played the role of mistress of the house so that I will never have to play it again, save for ten minutes each morning with my old butler, Philippe. I have fully observed life and its dangerous turns; death one day taught me its terrible lesson, and I mean to put it to good use. My sole occupation will be to please and to love *him*, to create variety in what ordinary people find so monotonous.

Gaston knows nothing for the moment. Like me, he has taken up lodging in Ville-d'Avray, at my request; tomorrow we leave for the chalet. Our life there will cost little, but if I told you the sum I have devoted to my wardrobe, you would say, quite rightly: She is mad! I want to adorn myself for him every day, just as women adorn themselves for society. My country attire for one year will cost twenty-four thousand francs, and my daywear is not the costliest part. He can go about in a smock if he likes! Do not conclude from all this that I mean to make a duel of my new life and exhaust myself in calculations to keep his love alive; I simply want nothing to reproach myself for. I have thirteen years left to be a fine-looking woman, and I want to be loved on the last day of the thirteenth year even more than the day after my mysterious wedding. This time I will be ever humble, ever grateful, never a stinging word; I am making of myself a servant, since mastery destroyed me the first time. Oh Renée, if Gaston has like me understood the boundlessness of love, I know that my life will be happy forever. The nature around the chalet is very beautiful, the woods are beguiling. With every step the fresh countryside and woodland prospects please the soul and awaken charming ideas. Those woods are full of love. Let us hope I haven't simply built myself a magnificent pyre! The day after tomorrow, I will be Madame Gaston. Dear God, I wonder if it is quite Christian to love a man so. "It's legal, at any rate," I was told by our accountant, who will be one of my witnesses, and who, finally understanding my reasons for liquidating my fortune, cried, "This is costing me a client!" For your part, my fine doe—I dare no longer say "my dear doe"—you may say, "This is costing me a sister."

My angel, henceforth send your letters to Madame Gaston, care of general delivery, Versailles. We will go and collect our mail every day. I do not want us to be known in the area. We will send the servants to Paris for provisions. I hope in this way to live our lives shrouded in mystery. Over the past year, as my retreat was being constructed, no one has ever been seen there, and the purchase was made in the midst of the upheavals that followed the July revolution. The only person who has shown himself in the area is my architect: people here know only him, and soon he will come back no more. Farewell. As I write that word, I feel as much sorrow as pleasure in my heart; does it not mean I will soon miss you as powerfully as I love Gaston?

49

FROM MARIE GASTON TO DANIEL D'ARTHEZ

October 1833

My dear Daniel, I require two witnesses for my wedding; be so kind as to come to my rooms tomorrow evening, and bring our great and glorious friend Joseph Bridau with you. It is my future wife's intention to live far from the world of men, utterly forgotten. She has anticipated my fondest wish. I have told you nothing of my love, you who lightened the hardships of my poverty; now you will understand why this absolute secrecy was essential, and why we have seen so little of each other in the past year. The day after our wedding, you and I will be parted for some considerable time. Daniel, your soul will not fail to understand me: The friendship will go on, even without the friend. I may sometimes need you, but I will never see you, at least not in my house. Here too *she* has made our fondest wishes come true. For my sake she has sacrificed her friendship with a schoolmate, a veritable sister to her; I was obliged to give up my friend as well. What I have just told you will give you an idea not of a passion but of a profound love, unmingled, complete, and divine, founded on the intimate mutual understanding of the two people thus binding themselves. My happiness is pure and limitless, but, as some secret law forbids us unalloyed felicity, I conceal, deep in my soul, buried in the furthest recess, a thought that gnaws at me alone, of which she knows nothing. You too often came to my aid in my perpetual penury not to know my desperate financial condition. Where did I find the courage to go on, when my hopes were so often dashed? In your past, my friend, by your side, where I found so many consolations and such thoughtful support. My dear friend, she has chosen to pay off all my debts. She is rich, and I have nothing. How many times have I said, in my fits of laziness, "Ah! if only some rich woman would take me on!" Well, now that it has come to pass, the young man's facetious joke, the amoral pauper's compromise, all of that faded away. I am humiliated, for all her ingenious cajoleries. I am humiliated, however wholly convinced I am of the nobility of her soul. I am humiliated, even as I know that my humiliation is proof of my love. She saw that I did not recoil from that ignominy. In that one way, I am not the protector but the protected. I tell you of this regret in strictest confidence.

Apart from that, my dear Daniel, my dreams have been realized down to the tiniest detail. I have found beauty without tarnish, goodness without flaw. The bride is, as they say, too good to be true; there is a mind behind her tenderness, she has the sort of charm and grace that brings constant variety to love; she is educated, understands everything; she is pretty, blond, slender, slightly fleshy: as if Raphael and Rubens had come together to create a woman! I do not believe I could ever love a brunette so much as a blond: I have always thought brunettes somewhat mannish. She is a widow, she has never had children, she is twenty-seven years old. Although she is lively, bright, and tireless, she can nonetheless take pleasure in melancholic reflections. These wondrous gifts imply no lack of dignity or nobility: she is a most regal woman. She belongs to one of France's most nobility-riddled old families, but she loves me enough to overlook the unfortunate circumstances of my birth. We have long loved in secret, testing each other; we are both equally jealous, our thoughts are indeed the two flashes of a single thunderbolt. We are both in love for the first time, and we found in the springtime just past a delicious setting for all the longed-for moments the imagination decorates with its happiest, sweetest, deepest inspirations. Loving emotion heaped its flowers on us. Every day that went by was a full day, and when we parted, we wrote poems to each other. I never thought of allowing desire to tarnish that sunlit season, although it bedeviled my soul without end. She was a widow, she was free, she fully understood the reverence implied by that restraint; often it moved her to tears. In all I have told you of her, my dear Daniel, you will have seen a truly superior creature. We have yet even to exchange a first kiss: each of us feared the other.

"We both have something to regret in our past," she told me.

"I don't see yours."

"My marriage," she answered.

You who are a great man, you who love one of the most extraordinary women of the same aristocracy in which I found my Armande, that sentence alone will give you a sense of her soul, and of the future happiness of

your friend,
Marie Gaston

50

Can it be, Louise, that after all the private sorrows you brought down
on yourself by making of marriage a mutual passion you now want
to live with a husband in solitude? You killed one in the midst of
society, and now you want to hide yourself away to devour another?
What torments you are preparing for yourself! But, by the way you
have gone about it, I can see there is nothing now to be done. Any
man who can make you overcome your aversion for second marriages
must have an angelic soul, a divine heart; you must be allowed to
cling to your illusions, but have you forgotten what you once said of
young men, who have traveled all manner of vile backwaters, their
innocence lost at the most sordid crossroads? Who changed, you or
they? You are very lucky to believe in happiness; I have no force to
fault you for it, although the instincts of my affection compel me to
talk you out of that marriage. Yes, a hundred times yes, nature and
society work together to destroy any perfect felicity, because perfect
felicities go against nature and society, perhaps because heaven allows
no interlopers in its realm. In any case, my friendship foresees some
sorrow awaiting you, of what sort I cannot say; I know not where it
will come from, nor who will cause it, but, my dear, without question,
an immense, boundless happiness will destroy you in the end. Excessive joy is an even heavier burden than the most massive grief. I say
nothing against him: you love him, and of course I have never seen
him, but you will, I hope, some day when you find yourself unoccupied,
write me a portrait of that strange, beautiful animal.

If you see me blithely accepting all this, it is because I have no
doubt that once the honeymoon is over you will both do just as

everyone else does, and by a common accord. One day, two years from now, as we are out for a ride and drive past that road, you will say to me, "Oh look, there's that chalet I was never going to leave!" And you will laugh your heartfelt laugh, showing your pretty teeth. I have said nothing of all this to Louis; we would be giving him too many good reasons to snicker. I will very neutrally inform him of your marriage and your desire to keep it a secret. Unfortunately, you require neither a mother nor a sister to prepare the bridal chamber. Here it is October: you are starting with winter, brave woman that you are. Were there not a marriage involved here, I would say you are taking the bull by the horns.[7] In any case, you will have in me the most discreet and intelligent friend. The mysterious heart of Africa has devoured many travelers, and I believe that, sentimentally speaking, you are setting off on a voyage very like those that have cost many explorers their lives, at the hands of the savages or in the desert sands. Your own desert is but two leagues from Paris, and so I can say to you, light of heart: Bon voyage! You will be back.

51

FROM COUNTESS DE L'ESTORADE TO MADAME MARIE GASTON

1835

What news of you, my dear? After a silence of two years, Renée is permitted to feel some concern for Louise. Ah, there's love for you! It sweeps away, it erases a friendship like ours. You must admit, even if I adore my children still more than you love your Gaston, maternal sentiment is expansive enough to diminish no other affection, and to permit a married woman to remain a sincere and devoted friend. I miss your letters, your sweet, charming face. O Louise, I am reduced to trying to guess how you live!

As for us, I will explain everything as succinctly as I can.

Rereading your next-to-last letter, I found a subtle little jab at us, occasioned by our current political situation. You mocked us for not having renounced the post of presiding officer at the Court of Audit, which we had acquired, along with the title of count, by the good graces of Charles X, but could I have suitably established Athénaïs and that poor little beggar René on forty thousand livres a year, thirty of them set aside in a *majorat*? Were we not duty bound to live off the wages of our position, meanwhile patiently saving up the revenues from our lands? In twenty years we will have amassed some six hundred thousand francs, which will serve as an endowment for both my daughter and for René, whom I have destined for the navy. My little beggar will have an annual interest income of ten thousand livres; perhaps we will find a way to leave him enough capital to make his share even with his sister's. When he is a ship's captain, my beggar will marry a wealthy woman and will enjoy a social rank every bit as elevated as his brother's.

These calculations showed us that it was wisest to accept France's new political order. Naturally, the new dynasty has named Louis a peer of France and a grand officer of the Legion of Honor. From the moment l'Estorade first took his oath, he could do nothing halfway; he did yeoman service in the National Assembly, and now he has attained a position that he will go on holding untroubled till the end of his days. He has a certain talent for finance; he is more an agreeable speaker than an orator, but that is enough for what we seek from the political world. His finesse, his skills in both government and administration are appreciated, he is considered irreplaceable by all sides. I can tell you that he was recently offered an ambassadorship, but I had him decline. Armand is now thirteen years old and Athénaïs eleven; I must stay in Paris for their education, and I mean to remain here through René's, which is now only beginning.

Only if we did not have three children to raise and establish could we have remained faithful to the Bourbons and retired to our lands. My angel, a mother must not imitate Decius, especially in an age when Deciuses are few and far between.[8] In fifteen years, l'Estorade will be able to return to La Crampade with a fine pension, installing Armand as an auditor in the Court of Audit. As for René, the navy will no doubt make of him a diplomat. At seven years of age that little boy is already as shrewd as an aged cardinal.

Ah! Louise, I am such a happy mother! My children continue to give me joys never darkened by shadow. (*Senza brama sicura ricchezza.*) Armand is at the Collège Henri IV. I wanted to put him into public education but could not bring myself to be separated from him, and so I have done what the Duke d'Orléans did before he was—perhaps so that he could become—Louis-Philippe. Lucas, that old servant whom you know, takes Armand to school each morning at the hour of the first study hall, then brings him back to me at four thirty. A wise old tutor, who lives with us, oversees his work in the evenings and wakes him at the hour when schoolboys rise. Lucas brings him his lunch at noon recess. I thus see him at dinner and then before he goes to bed in the evening, and I see him off every morning. Armand is still the charming child you love, full of heart and devotion; his tutor is pleased with him. I have my Naïs and the little one with me, both forever underfoot, but I am as much a child as they. I cannot do without the sweetness of my dear children's caresses. The possibility of running to Armand's bed whenever I please, to watch him as he sleeps, or to steal or seek or receive a kiss from that angel is to me a vital necessity of existence.

Nonetheless, there are drawbacks to the system of keeping one's children at home, and I have noted them well. Like Nature, Society is jealous; it allows no one to trample on its laws or tamper with their order. Children not sent off to school are exposed at too young an age to the fires of the social world: they see its passions, they study its ruses. Unable to make out the fine distinctions that govern the conduct of adults, they submit the world to their passions and sentiments, rather than submit their desires and demands to the world; they adopt a false showiness, which shines more brightly than solid virtues, for the world prizes nothing so much as appearances dressed in deceptive guise. When a child of fifteen has the self-assurance of a man of the world, he is a monstrosity; at twenty-five he is an old man, and by that precocious sophistication he makes himself inapt for the sort of sincere studies on which real and serious talents are founded. Society is a great actor, and like any actor, it absorbs and sends back, preserving nothing. A mother who keeps her children at home must therefore firmly resolve to shield them from society, must have the courage to oppose their desires and her own, to avoid showing them off. Cornelia had to keep her jewels well hidden.[9] I will do the same, for my children are my entire life.

I am thirty years old; the heat of the day has passed, the hardest stretch of road is behind me. In a few years I will be an old woman, and I draw great strength from the sense that I have done my duty. Those three little dears seem to know my thoughts and conform to them. There are mysterious connections between us, for they have never left me. And of course they smother me with delights, as if fully realizing how much they owe me for all I have done.

For the first three years of his schooling Armand was slow and dreamy; he worried me, but now he has taken wing. No doubt he has realized those preparatory labors' true purpose, something children do not always see, which is to habituate them to hard work, to sharpen their intelligence, and to mold them to obedience, the guiding principle of all successful societies. My dear, a few days ago I had the intoxicating sensation of seeing Armand triumph at the *concours général*, in the Sorbonne itself! Your godson took first place in translation from Latin. At the Collège Henri IV's annual prize ceremony he took first place in both verse and Latin composition. I went pale as I heard his name read out, and I wanted to shout: *I am the mother!* Naïs was squeezing my hand so hard that it hurt, or would have, if pain were possible at such moments. Ah! Louise, that joy is worth any number of lost loves.

Those triumphs have stimulated my little René, who wants to go to school just like his older brother. Sometimes the three children scream and tear through the house, and they make such a din I feel my head might split. I do not know how I put up with it, because I am always with them; I have never entrusted anyone with the care of my children, not even Mary. But there are so many joys to be had from that beautiful business of motherhood! To see a child breaking off his play to come give me a kiss, as if driven by some urgent need ... what a joy! I can also study them far more closely this way. One of a mother's duties is to determine her children's aptitudes, nature, and vocation from their earliest age—something no teacher could ever do. Children raised by their mothers invariably display self-assurance and sociability; those two acquired traits are a vital supplement to native intelligence, whereas native intelligence can never replace what men learn from their mothers. Even now I can spot those differences among the men I meet in drawing rooms, and I can immediately make out a woman's touch in a young man's manners. How could I possibly rob my children of that advantage? As you see, there are many pleasures, many fulfillments to be found in simply doing my duty.

I have no doubt that Armand will be the most excellent magistrate, the most upright administrator, the most conscientious *député* ever to be found, and my René the bravest, boldest, and at the same time the craftiest sailor in the world. That little scamp has an iron will; he gets everything he wants, he makes a thousand detours to arrive at his goal, and if those thousand do not take him there, he finds a thousand and first. Where my dear Armand calmly resigns himself and seeks to understand why things are as they are, my René rages, contrives, calculates, sweet-talking all the while, and in the end discovers a crack; if it is wide enough for a knife blade, he is soon driving his little coach straight through it.

As for Naïs, she is so like me that I cannot distinguish her flesh from my own. Ah! that little dear, that beloved girl I am happily turning into a coquette, braiding and curling her hair, throwing all my love into the task, I want her to be happy; she will be given only to one who loves her and whom she loves. But, my God! when I allow her to primp herself, when I thread berry-red ribbons through her hair, when I put shoes on those dainty little feet, my mind and my heart are assailed by a thought that nearly brings me to my knees. Is a mother truly the mistress of her daughter's fate? Perhaps she will love a man who is unworthy of her, perhaps she will not be loved by the man she loves. Often I find my eyes filling with tears when I look at her. Imagine losing a charming creature, a flower, a rose who lived in your breast like a bud on the rosebush, imagine giving her to a man who steals it all away! It is you—who in two years have never written me the words "I am happy!"—it is you who reminded me of the great wrench that is marriage, a formidable blow for any mother as much a mother as I. Farewell. I do not see why I should be writing you, you do not deserve my friendship. Oh! answer me, my Louise.

52

The Chalet

Two years of silence have roused your curiosity, you ask why I've not written, but my dear Renée, there is no word, no sentence, no language to express my happiness. Our souls are strong enough to withstand it, there is no more to be said. Our happiness requires no effort; we agree about everything. In three years there has been not the slightest dissonance in that harmony, the tiniest disparity in the expression of our sentiments, the faintest discord in even our most trivial wishes. In short, my dear, not one of those thousand days has failed to bear its own special fruit, not one moment has been made anything but delicious by our fancies. Not only will our life never be monotonous—of that we are certain—but it will also perhaps never be long enough to contain all the poetry of our love, which is as fertile as nature and similarly varied. No, not one misunderstanding! We are even more drawn to each other than the very first day, and with every passing moment we find new reasons to love each other. Every evening, out for a stroll after dinner, we vow that we will soon go to Paris, out of curiosity, as one might say, "I'm going to see the sights in Switzerland."

"Really!" Gaston cries. "Such-and-such boulevard is being rebuilt, La Madeleine has been finished. We must go have a look."

And then, ah well, the next day we spend the morning in bed, take our breakfast in our room; noon comes, the weather is warm, we allow ourselves a little nap, and then he asks me to let him look at me, and he looks at me precisely as if I were a painting, lost in that contemplation—which is reciprocated, as you must have guessed. And with that tears come to our eyes, we think of our happiness and we tremble. I am still his mistress, which is to say that I seem to love less than I am loved. A delicious little deception! How endearing to a woman's eye is the sight of sentiment quelling desire, how charming to see the master, still intimidated, stop where we will it! You asked me to describe him for you, but my Renée, one cannot possibly draw the portrait of a man one loves, one could never hold fast to the truth. And then, just between us, let us acknowledge without shame a sad, strange effect of our society's mores: there is nothing so different as a man in public and a man in the private world of love. So great is the difference that you might never recognize the one in the other. The man who strikes the most graceful dancer's most graceful poses to speak love to us one evening by the fireside may well turn out to have none of the secret graces a woman most desires. On the other hand, a man who seems ugly and gauche, ridiculously dressed in an ill-fitting black suit, often hides a lover with the true spirit of love, who will never be ridiculous in any posture, even those fatal to us women, for all our exterior beauties. To find in a man a mysterious harmony between what he seems and what he is, to find a man who in the secret life of marriage displays the kind of innate grace that cannot be given, that cannot be learned, that the ancient sculptors deployed in the chaste and voluptuous marriages of their statues, the innocent abandon that the ancient poets put into their verse, and which seems to find in nakedness still another adornment for the soul, the ideal that springs from us and derives from the world of harmonies, which is no doubt the genius of all things, that immense problem pondered by every woman's imagination—well, Gaston is its living solution. Ah! my dear, I had no idea how powerful love, youth, wit, and beauty all rolled up together could be. My Gaston is never affected; elegance is instinctive, it grows without effort. When we go out for a quiet stroll in the woods, his arm around my waist, my hand on his shoulder, his body pressed to mine, our heads touching, we walk with precisely the same gait, at a regular pace so smooth and united that anyone who saw us pass by would take us for one single creature gliding over the sand of the alleyways, like Homer's immortals. That same harmony marks our desires, our thoughts, our words. Sometimes, beneath the verdure still damp from a passing shower, the wet grass gleaming in the evening light, we have taken whole walks in perfect silence, simply listening to the falling droplets, marveling at the red glow draped over the treetops or daubed on the trunks by the setting sun. Our only thoughts were surely a secret, uncertain prayer, rising up to heaven like an apology for our happiness. Sometimes we cry out together at the same moment, seeing the path make a sudden turn up ahead and revealing a delicious prospect in the distance. If you knew all the sweetness and profundity there is in an almost timid kiss bestowed amid that sacred nature ... it's as if God made us only so that we might pray to Him in that way. And then we go back home, even more in love than before. In Paris, such a love between two spouses would seem an affront to society; one must partake of it as lovers do, in the secret depths of the woods.

Gaston, my dear, has the medium build found in all men of great energy, neither fat nor thin, beautifully proportioned, vigorous and solid; his movements are nimble, he jumps a ditch with the ease of a wild animal. No matter his position, he has a sort of innate sense that allows him to keep his balance, a rare thing among men given to deep thought. Although his hair and eyes are dark, his skin is quite white. His jet-black hair contrasts strikingly with the pallor of his neck and brow. He has the melancholy visage of a Louis XIII. He has grown out his mustachios and his royale,[10] but I had him shave off his sideburns and beard: that has become common. His saintlike poverty kept him pure for me, unmarked by the scars that spoil so many young men. He has magnificent teeth, he is as healthy as a horse. His blue eyes, so piercing but for me so magnetically gentle, flash like a lightning bolt when his soul is inflamed. Like all strong, powerfully intelligent people, he has an even temperament that would surprise you as it surprised me. Many wives have confided to me the unhappiness in their homes, but those changeable moods, those anxieties and regrets of men who are not happy with themselves, who do not want or do not know how to age, who still harbor who knows what eternal sad reminders of their wild youth, their veins full of poison, whose gaze always conceals a sadness in its depths, who lash out to hide their insecurity, who sell you an hour of tranquillity at the cost of a whole day of unpleasantness, who take their vengeance on women for their own unlovability, who conceive a secret hatred for our beauty—youth knows nothing of those sorrows, they are peculiar to ill-matched marriages. Oh! my dear, only marry Athénaïs to a young man. If you knew the sustenance I find in that constant smile, forever varied by a keen and sensitive mind, a smile that speaks, with loving thoughts and unspoken gratitude nestling in its corners, forever uniting joys past and present! Nothing is ever forgotten between him and me. We have made the slightest things of nature accomplices in our felicity: everything is alive, everything speaks to us of ourselves in those magnificent woods. A mossy old oak, near the gatehouse on the road, reminds us that we once sat down to rest in its shade, where Gaston told me of the moss at our feet, its history, and from those mosses we ascended, one science to the next, to the very ends of the earth. There is such a kinship between our two minds that I believe they are two editions of a single work. As you see, I've grown literary. It is a habit or a gift for us both to see each thing in its entirety, to grasp all it contains; again and again we reveal the purity of that inner sensibility to each other, and it is a pleasure that never palls. We have come to see this oneness of mind as an expression of love, and should it ever fail us, that would be for us what infidelity is for any other marriage.

My life is full of pleasures, but no doubt you would find it excessively given over to labor. First of all, my dear, know that Louise-Armande-Marie de Chaulieu makes up her own room. Never would I allow some mercenary hand, some unknown woman or girl to violate the sanctity of my bedchamber (literary indeed!). My religion reveres even the smallest objects required for its worship. This is not jealousy; it is simple respect for oneself. I keep up my room with the same care a young woman in love might devote to her finery. I am as meticulous as an old spinster. My powder room is not a disorderly jumble but a delicious boudoir. My attentions have anticipated every eventuality. At any moment the master, the sovereign may enter; his eye will not be offended, nor surprised nor disenchanted: flowers, perfumes, elegance, everything pleases the eye. While he lies sleeping in the morning, I rise at first light—he has yet to catch me in the act—and slip into that powder room, where, well-taught by my mother's inventions, I wash away the lingering traces of sleep with splashes of cold water. When we sleep, our skin is less stimulated and so performs its functions less perfectly; it grows warm, it exudes a sort of fog visible to a mite's eye, a sort of atmosphere. A woman emerges from beneath the dripping washcloth as a young girl. There, perhaps, is the explanation for the myth of Venus emerging from the waters. Water thus gives me the piquant charms of dawn; I comb and perfume my hair, and after that fastidious toilette I slip like a garden snake back into bed, so that on waking the master will find me as fresh as a spring morning. He is charmed by that freshness, like a newly opened flower, and has no idea how it came to be. Later comes my daytime toilette, seen to by my chambermaid in a dressing room. And, as you must already suspect, there is also the bedtime toilette. Three times a day, then, I make myself up for my husband—sometimes four, but that, my dear, has to do with certain other myths of antiquity.

We have our work, as well. We take a great interest in our flowers, in the magnificent productions of our greenhouses, in our trees. We are serious botanists, we love flowers with a passion, they fill our chalet. Our lawns are always green, our flower beds as carefully tended as the richest banker's gardens. Nothing could be as beautiful as our grounds. We are exceedingly fond of fruit, we carefully watch over our walled gardens, our hotbeds, our fans and espaliers. Nonetheless, lest these bucolic occupations fail to satisfy my beloved's mind, I have advised him to use this silence and solitude to finish a few of the plays he began as a starving young writer, for they are truly beautiful. In all of literature, drama alone can be put aside and taken up again, for it profits from long reflection and does not require the masterful fashioning high style demands. One cannot write dialogue at every moment; it requires eloquence, understatements, and quips that the mind bears in the same way that a plant bears its flowers, and one finds them more by awaiting them than by seeking them. I quite like that hunt for ideas. I am my Gaston's collaborator, and so I never leave his side, even when he is wandering the vast fields of the imagination. Can you guess now how I fill the long winter nights?

We are such undemanding masters that we have had no cause to speak one word of reproach or complaint to our domestics since our wedding. When they were asked about us, they had the presence of mind to dissemble, passing us off as a lady's maid and a personal secretary, our masters away on a long voyage. Certain that they will not be refused, they never go out without asking permission, and in any case they are happy here and understand that their situation will never change except by their own fault. We allow the gardeners to sell our excess fruits and vegetables. Our milkmaid does the same with the milk, cream, and fresh butter. We reserve only the finest of everything for ourselves. They are entirely happy with their profits, and we enjoy an abundance that no amount of money could buy in that grasping old Paris, where a single fine peach costs the equivalent of a hundred francs' interest income. There is a method to all this, my dear: I want to be Gaston's entire world; Paris is an amusing place, and so it is essential that my husband not be bored in this solitude. I thought I was jealous when I was loved and allowed myself to be loved, but today I feel the jealousy of a woman who loves—genuine jealousy, in other words. I tremble at every glance from him that strikes me as indifferent. Now and then I say to myself "Suppose he stopped loving me? . . ." and I shiver. Oh! before him I am exactly like the Christian soul before God.

Alas! my Renée, I still have no children. No doubt a time will come when the sentiments of a father and mother are required to enliven this retreat, when we both feel a need to see little gowns, little cloaks, little brown or blond heads jumping and running through our flower beds and alleyways. Oh! what a monstrous thing are flowers without fruit. The memory of your beautiful family makes me ache. My life has retracted, where yours has grown and expanded. Love is a deeply selfish thing, whereas motherhood multiplies our emotions. I fully felt that difference as I read your good, tender letter. I envied your happiness, seeing you living in three different hearts! Yes, you are happy: you have patiently followed the laws of society, whereas I am outside of everything. Loving and beloved children are a woman's sole consolation for the loss of her beauty. Soon I will be thirty, the age at which a woman begins to whisper terrible laments to herself. If I am still beautiful, I nonetheless foresee the day when femininity will wane, and then what will become of me? When I am forty *he* will not be; *he* will still be young, and I will be old. When that thought pierces my heart, I sit at his feet for an hour, making him swear that he will tell me the moment he finds his love for me dwindling. But he is a child, he swears at once, as if his love would never fade, and he is so handsome that . . . I believe you understand! Farewell, dear angel, will we go so many years again without writing each other? Happiness is tedious to tell of; perhaps that explains why lovers find Dante greater in his *Paradiso* than in his *Inferno*. I am no Dante, I am only your friend, and I have no wish to bore you. But you can write me, for in your children you have a varied happiness that grows without end, whereas mine. . . . Let us speak no more of this, I send you a thousand tendernesses.

53

FROM MADAME DE L'ESTORADE TO MADAME GASTON

My dear Louise, I have read and reread your letter, and the more I fill my thoughts with it, the more I consider you less a woman than a child; you have not changed, you are forgetting what I have told you a thousand times: Love is a theft inflicted by the social on the natural. It is by its nature so evanescent that society changes its essence, and so noble souls try to make a man of that child, but then Love becomes, as you yourself say, a monstrosity. Society, my dear, wanted to be fruitful. By substituting long-lived sentiments for the ephemeral folly of nature, it created the greatest human invention: the Family, the eternal foundation of all Societies. It sacrificed both man and woman to that task, for—let us make no mistake—the father of a family gives his energy, his strength, all his fortune to his wife. Is it not the wife who profits from every sacrifice? Luxury, wealth, is it not all for her? And the glory, the elegance, the sweetness, all the finery of the house? Oh! my angel, once again you have gravely misunderstood life. Being adored is a young girl's ambition, meant to last a few springtimes, but it cannot be the ambition of a wife and a mother. Perhaps, as a sop to her vanity, a wife need only know that she could cause herself to be adored, should she choose. If you would be a wife and a mother, then come back to Paris. Let me tell you again that you will lose yourself to happiness as others lose themselves to sorrow. Those things that never weary us—silence, bread, air—are faultless because they are without taste; by exciting our desires, things full of flavor wear them down in the end. Listen to me, my child! Today, even if I could be loved by a man who inspired in me the same love you feel for Gaston, I would find the strength to remain faithful to my cherished duties and my sweet family. For the heart of a woman, my angel, motherhood is one of those simple, natural, fertile, inexhaustible things, like the very basics of life. I remember having one day, soon to be fourteen years ago, embraced Devotion as a shipwrecked sailor desperately clings to the mast; today, looking back on the whole of my existence, I would once again choose that sentiment as my guiding principle, for it is the surest and most fruitful of all. The example of your life, founded on a relentless egoism, however hidden behind the poetry of the heart, has only strengthened my conviction. I will never again say these things to you, but I had to say them one last time on learning that your happiness has not yet succumbed to the most punishing of all tests.

Your life in the country, the object of my meditations, has suggested another observation I must share with you. For the body as for the heart, our life is composed of certain regular movements. Any excess introduced into that system causes pleasure or pain, but pleasure and pain are essentially fleeting fevers of the soul, which cannot long be endured. If we make of excess our very life, are we not living in a state of permanent illness? You are doing just that, by maintaining as a passion what should become, through marriage, a pure and unwavering force. Yes, my angel, today I see it: a household's glory lies nowhere other than in that deep, serene mutual familiarity, that sharing of goods and ills for which it is so often mocked by vulgar pleasantries. Oh! how great are those words of the Duchess de Sully, the wife of the great Sully, to whom it was said that her husband, however grave he seemed, was not above having a mistress. "It is very simple," she answered, "I am the honor of the house, and I will not be a courtesan." More pleasure-mad than tender, you want to be both the wife and the mistress. With the soul of Héloïse and the sensibilities of Saint Teresa, you bask in voluptuous excesses that the law unwittingly allows; in a word, you are depraving the institution of marriage. Yes, you who judged me so severely, who thought me immoral when I accepted the means to be happy on the eve of my marriage, today you deserve the rebukes you addressed to me then, for you bend everything to your purpose. What! you want to submit both nature and society to your whim? You remain just as you are, you do not make of yourself what a woman must be. You still have the wants and demands of a girl, and you introduce the most exacting, the most mercantile calculations into your passion; do you not sell your finery for a very dear price? How little trust you must feel, to take such precautions! Oh! dear Louise, if you could only know the joys of the pains mothers endure to be good and tender to their family! My natural independence and pride resolved into a sweet melancholy, which the pleasures of motherhood dissipated as they repaid it. Yes, the day was difficult, but the evening will be pure and serene. I fear that it will be quite the opposite for you.

On finishing your letter I implored God to bring you into our midst for one day, so that you might be converted to the family, to its inexpressible, faithful, eternal joys, because they are real, simple, and natural. But alas! what can my reason do to combat an unreason in which you find happiness? I have tears in my eyes as I write these last words. I honestly believed that a few months of conjugal love would bring you to your senses, for you would be sated, but I see that you are insatiable, and that, having already killed a lover, you will soon have killed love. Farewell, dear lost one, I despair, since the letter in which I hoped to return you to society by depicting my happiness served only to glorify your egoism. Yes, there is only you in your love, and you love Gaston much more for yourself than for him.

54

May 20

Renée, sorrow has come to me; no, it has crashed down on your poor
Louise quick as a lightning bolt, and you understand me: for me,
sorrow is doubt. Certainty would be death. The day before yesterday,
after my first toilette, I came looking for Gaston so we could take a
stroll before breakfast. I couldn't find him anywhere. I went to the
stables, and there I saw his mare bathed in sweat, the groom whisking
away dollops of froth with a knife before drying the animal off.

"Who on earth could have put Fedelta into such a state?" I asked.

"Monsieur," the boy answered.

On the mare's hocks I recognized the mud of Paris, which is nothing like the mud of the countryside. "So he's been to Paris," I told
myself. That thought made a thousand more spring up in my heart
and drained the blood from my face. He went to Paris without telling
me, using the hour in which I leave him to himself, and then came
back in such haste that Fedelta is half dead with exhaustion! . . .
Suspicion laced its terrible corset around me until I could no longer
draw breath. I sat down on a nearby bench, struggling to get hold of
myself. Gaston found me in that state, which must have alarmed him,
for he said "What is it?" so urgently and with such concern in his
voice that I stood and took his arm. But there was no strength in my
limbs, and I had to sit down again; he helped me up and led me into
the parlor a few steps away, with all our domestics following in alarm.
Gaston waved them away. Once we were alone, I staggered to our
bedroom, refusing to speak, and locked the door behind me so I might
weep in peace.

For some two hours Gaston stood by listening to my sobs, questioning his creature with angelic patience, and hearing no reply. "I will see you again when my eyes are no longer red and my voice has stopped shaking," I finally told him, calling him *vous*, which made him race out of the house. I bathed my eyes with ice water, I washed my face, the door to our room opened, and I found him there, back again without my having heard his footsteps.

"What is it?" he asked.

"Nothing," I said. "I recognized the mud of Paris on Fedelta's weary hocks. I couldn't understand why you should go there without telling me, but you are free."

"As a punishment for your criminal doubts, you will not learn my reasons until tomorrow," he answered.

"Look at me," I said. I plunged my gaze into his: the infinite penetrated the infinite. No, I saw no sign of the cloud that infidelity draws over the soul, which cannot help but sully the purity of the pupils. I feigned reassurance, though I was as worried as ever. Men are every bit as skilled in lies and deceit as we! After that, we stayed at each other's side. Oh! my dear, how unalterably attached to him I sometimes felt as I looked at him. How I trembled inside when he reappeared after leaving me alone for a moment! My life is in him, not in me. I cruelly dismissed your cruel letter. Did I ever feel such dependence on that divine Spaniard, for whom I was what this atrocious child is for me? How I hate that mare! How stupid of me to have horses. But I would also have had to cut off Gaston's feet or lock him into the chalet. Idiotic thoughts such as those filled my mind— you see the state I was in! If love has not built a cage around him, no force will ever hold back a bored man.

"Do I bore you?" I asked him, point-blank.

"You're tormenting yourself for no reason," he answered, his eyes full of a gentle pity. "I've never been so in love with you."

"If that's true, my adored angel," I answered, "then allow me to sell Fedelta."

"Go ahead and sell her!" he said.

I was half crushed by that answer, for Gaston seemed to be saying:

You alone are rich here, I am nothing, my will does not exist. Even if he thought no such thing, I believed he was thinking it, and once again I left him to go to bed, for night had come.

Oh! Renée, when one is alone, a single devastating thought can drive one to suicide. Those delicious gardens, that starry night, the cool breeze bringing in the incense of all our flowers, our valley, our hills, everything seemed somber, dark, and empty. I felt as if at the bottom of an abyss, surrounded by snakes and poisonous plants; I saw no God in the sky. A night such as that ages a woman.

"Take Fedelta, run off to Paris," I told him the next morning. "We won't sell her; I love her, for she carries you!" But my tone did not deceive him; the secret rage I was trying to hide pierced through.

"Trust me!" he answered, extending one hand with so noble a gesture, and giving me so noble a look, that I felt utterly flattened.

"We women are so small," I cried.

"No, you love me, that's all," he said, pressing me to him.

"Go to Paris without me," I said, showing him that I was disarming myself of all my suspicions, and off he went. I thought perhaps he would stay.

I will not attempt to describe my misery. There was another woman inside me, one I never realized could exist. For one thing, my dear, to a woman in love, scenes such as these have a tragic solemnity beyond all expression: your entire life lies before you, and the eye sees no horizon; nothing is everything, a glance is a book, great chunks of ice float atop a single word, and you read a death sentence in one twitch of the lips. I was hoping for a little gratitude: was there not a certain nobility and generosity in what I had done? I climbed to the top of the chalet and watched him ride off. Ah! my dear Renée, I saw him disappear not a moment later. "What a hurry he's in!" I couldn't help thinking. Then, once I was alone, I fell back into the hell of conjectures, the tumult of suspicions. From time to time the certainty that I had been betrayed seemed a relief, compared to the horrors of doubt! Doubt is our duel with ourselves, and we inflict the most grievous wounds. I wandered aimlessly through our gardens, returned to the chalet, came running out again like a madwoman. Gaston had left at seven o'clock, and was not back until eleven; clearly, since it takes only half an hour to reach Paris by way of the Parc de Saint-Cloud and the Bois de Boulogne, he had spent three hours in the city. He entered triumphantly, bringing me a rubber riding crop with a gold handle. I'd made do with no riding crop for two weeks; worn and old, mine had broken.

"It was for this that you were torturing me?" I said, admiring the skill that went into that beautiful object, whose tip holds a vinaigrette. I then realized that this present concealed a new deceit; nonetheless, I promptly threw myself into his arms, not without gently rebuking him for inflicting such torments for the sake of a mere bagatelle. He thought himself very clever. I then saw in his manner, his gaze, that sort of private joy one feels on pulling off an act of deceit; it escapes like a glimmer from our soul, like a ray from our mind, and it is reflected in our faces, it emanates from us with every move we make. I went on admiring that pretty crop, and then, at a moment when we were looking straight at each other, I asked, "Who made this lovely thing?"

"An artist friend of mine."

"Ah! here we are: Verdier," I added, reading the merchant's name printed on the crop. Gaston stood looking at me like a little child, blushing. I gave him a tender caress to repay him for his shame at betraying me. I played innocent, and he thought it was all over.

May 25

The next day, toward six o'clock, I put on my riding clothes; by seven I was at Verdier's, where I saw several crops of the very same design. A clerk recognized mine when I showed it to him. "We sold it yesterday, to a young man," he told me. And once I gave him a description of my disloyal Gaston, all doubt was dispelled. I will spare you the palpitations that racked my breast on my way to Paris and all through this little scene, my fate hanging in the balance. I came home at seven thirty, and Gaston found me freshly scrubbed and lovely, with my morning face, strolling in the gardens with deceptive insouciance, certain that nothing would give away my absence, whose secret I had entrusted solely to my old Philippe.

"Gaston," I said to him as we walked around our pond, "I am perfectly capable of seeing the difference between a unique work of art, made with love for one single person, and something that came out of a mold." He turned pale and looked at me as I held out the damning evidence. "My friend," I told him, "this isn't a riding crop, it's a screen, behind which you are concealing a secret." On that, my dear, I allowed myself the pleasure of seeing him lose his way in the bowers of lies and the labyrinths of deceit, never finding an exit, deploying a prodigious ingenuity in search of a wall to scale but forced to remain on the battleground facing an adversary who in the end consented to let herself be deceived. That indulgence came too late, as it always does in such scenes. Besides, I had made the mistake that my mother had always tried to warn me against. By exposing itself, my jealousy had declared a state of war between Gaston and me, with all the attendant ruses and stratagems. My dear, jealousy is essentially a stupid and brutish thing. I then vowed to suffer in silence, to spy on his every move, to arrive at a certainty, and then either be done with Gaston or consent to my unhappiness: no other conduct is suitable for a woman of good breeding. What is he hiding from me? For he is indeed hiding a secret. That secret must involve a woman. Is it some youthful adventure he finds embarrassing? Or what? That *what*, my dear, is engraved in four letters of fire on everything around me. I read that terrible word as I look at the mirror of my pond, I see it in my flower beds, in the clouds of the sky, the ceilings, at table, in the flowers of my rugs. When I am sound asleep, a voice cries out to me: "What?" Starting from that morning, a cruel self-interest came into our life, and I knew the bitterest of all the many thoughts that can corrode the human heart: that of belonging to a man we think unfaithful. Oh! my dear, there is in such a life something of hell and of heaven at the same time. I had never set foot in those flames, I who had heretofore been so sacredly adored.

"Ah! so one day you fancied a look around the dark, burning

palace of torment?" I said to myself. "Well, the demons have heard your fateful wish: walk onward, wretch!"

May 30

From that day on, rather than write in the careless, idle manner of the rich artist toying with his pet project, Gaston has been pushing himself like a writer who must live by his pen. He spends four hours a day working to finish two plays.

"He needs money!" whispered a voice inside me. He spends virtually nothing; we know everything of each other's affairs, there is not one corner of his study that my eyes and fingers cannot probe. His annual expenses never amount to two thousand francs, and I know he has thirty thousand not so much set aside as shoved into a drawer. You can guess what I was thinking. In the middle of the night, as he slept, I went to see if the money was still there. How icy was the shiver that ran through me when I found the drawer empty! In the course of that same week, I discovered that he picks up letters in Sèvres; he must then tear them into tiny pieces, for despite all my Figaroesque machinations I have found not a trace of them. Alas! my angel, after all my promises, all my fine vows concerning the riding crop, I was spurred into action by a sudden reflex of the soul that must be called madness, and I followed him on one of his quick dashes to the post office. Gaston was terrified to find himself caught in the act, still on his horse, paying the postage for a letter he had in his hand. He stared at me for some time, then kicked Fedelta into a gallop so wild that I felt utterly broken when I arrived at the wooden door, and this at a moment when I believed I was beyond bodily fatigue, so terrible was the pain in my soul!

There Gaston said nothing; he rang the bell and waited without a word. I was more dead than alive. Perhaps I was right, perhaps I was wrong; in either case, this espionage was unworthy of Armande-Louise-Marie de Chaulieu. I was tumbling into the social gutter, lower than the shopgirl, the slattern, side by side with courtesans, actresses, creatures with no breeding. How horrible! Finally the door opened, he handed his horse over to the groom, and I dismounted as well, but in his arms, for he stretched them out to me; I held the hem of my riding skirt over my left arm, I gave him my right arm, and we walked on . . . still in silence. The hundred paces we walked in this way count in my mind for a hundred years of purgatory. With each step my soul was assailed by thousands of thoughts, almost visible, swarming around me like tongues of fire, each with its own special stinger, its own venom!

Once we were away from the groom and the horses, I stopped Gaston, looked at him, and, with a gesture you can surely imagine, pointed to the awful letter still clutched in his right hand: "May I read that?" He gave it to me, I opened it, and I found a letter from Nathan, the playwright, telling him that one of our works, accepted for performance, memorized, and put into rehearsals, would be staged the following Saturday. A ticket was enclosed. Although with that I went directly from martyrdom to paradise, the demon was still seeking to trouble my joy with shrieks of "Where are the thirty thousand francs?" And I couldn't bring myself to ask him, held back by dignity, by honor, by all I once was. I could feel the question on my lips; if that thought became words, I knew I would have to throw myself into my pond. At the price of a great struggle, I choked back the urge to speak. My dear, was my suffering not more than a woman can bear?

"You're bored, my poor Gaston," I said, handing back the letter. "If you like, we can move back to Paris."

"Paris?" he replied. "Why should we do that? I simply wanted to know if I had talent and taste the punch of success!"

Someday, when he is at work at his desk, I may well feign astonishment as I open the drawer and see no sign of his thirty thousand francs, but would I not be asking for the answer "I loaned them to some friend or other," which a man as quick-minded as Gaston would not fail to give me?

My dear, the moral of this is that the glittering success of the play all of Paris is now flocking to is owed to us, though the glory goes to Nathan. I am one of the two clusters of stars in the words

AND MESSIEURS *** AND ***. I saw the first performance, hidden deep inside a ground-floor stage box.

July 1

Gaston is still working, still going to Paris; he is writing new plays as a pretext for his outings and a source of income. Three of our plays have been accepted and two more requested. Oh! my dear, I am lost, I am wandering about in the dark. I would set fire to my house for a little light. What does such behavior signify? Is he ashamed to have received a fortune from me? His soul is too great to trouble itself with such trifles. Besides, when a man begins to feel scruples of that sort, they are always inspired by some interest of the heart. A man can accept everything from his wife, but he wants nothing from the woman he is thinking of leaving or whom he no longer loves. If Gaston wants so much money, he must need it to spend on a woman. Were it for himself, would he not simply dig into my purse and think no more of it? We have a hundred thousand francs in savings! My beautiful doe, I have circumnavigated the globe of hypotheses, and in the end I am certain I have a rival. He is leaving me, but for whom? I want to see *her*. . . .

July 10

Now I see clearly: I am lost. Yes, Renée, at thirty years of age, in all the glory of a woman's beauty, rich with all the resources of my mind, adorned with all the charms of my toilette, always fresh, always elegant, I am betrayed, and for whom? For an Englishwoman with big feet, big bones, a big chest—for some British cow! I can doubt it no longer. Here is what has happened to me over these past several days.

Tired of wondering, thinking that if Gaston had simply come to the aid of a friend he'd have no reason not to tell me, seeing him indicted by his silence, and finding him forever at work, forever called to his desk by a continual hunger for money, jealous of that work, alarmed by his perpetual trips to Paris, I took steps, and those steps were so far beneath me that I will tell you nothing of them. Three days ago, I learned that in Paris Gaston makes straight for a house on the rue de la Ville-l'Évêque, where his trysts are protected by a discretion unparalleled in all the city. The close-mouthed porter told me little, but enough to bring me to despair. I then made the sacrifice of my life: I simply had to know all. I went to Paris, I rented an apartment across the street, and with my own eyes I saw him riding his horse into the courtyard. Oh! I didn't have to wait long.

This Englishwoman, who to my eye must be thirty-six years old, goes by the name of Madame Gaston. That discovery was the death blow. Soon I saw her going to the Tuileries with two children . . . oh! my dear, two children who are the living miniatures of Gaston. There is no overlooking that scandalous resemblance. . . . And such pretty children! They are luxuriously dressed, as only an Englishwoman knows how. She has given him children! Now all is explained. That Englishwoman is a sort of Greek statue descended from some monument; she has the whiteness and coldness of marble, she walks solemnly, like a happy mother. She is beautiful, it must be said, but she is as graceless as a warship. There is nothing elegant or refined about her: certainly she is not a *lady*, she is the daughter of some farmer from some wretched village in some distant county, or the eleventh daughter of some poor government minister. I came back from Paris half dead. All the way home, a thousand thoughts prodded at me like demons. Could she be married? Did he know her before he married me? Was she the mistress of some rich man who left her, and did she then suddenly fall back into Gaston's hands? I piled one conjecture on top of another, as if there were any need to guess, given those children. The next day I went to Paris again, and I gave the porter enough money to make him answer the question "Is Madame Gaston legally married?" with the words "Yes, *mademoiselle.*"

July 15

My dear, after that morning, I redoubled my love for Gaston, and I have found him more tender than ever; he is so young! Twenty times, on waking, I am on the verge of asking him, "So you love me more than the woman on the rue de la Ville-l'Évêque?" But I say nothing, and I do not wish to examine the mystery of my silence.

"You love children, don't you?" I asked him.

"Oh! I do, and we'll have some!"

"How?"

"I've consulted all the best doctors, and to a man they advised me to go away on a two-month-long voyage."

"Gaston," I told him, "if I were capable of loving a man who isn't there, I would have stayed in the convent."

He began to laugh, whereas for my part, my dear, that word *voyage* had killed me. Oh! better to jump from my window than tumble down the staircase, struggling to catch myself on every step. Farewell, my angel; I have made my death gentle, elegant, but inevitable. My will has been written since yesterday. You may now come and see me, the sequestration is lifted. Run to me quickly to receive my farewells. Like my life, my death will be stamped with distinction and grace; I will die whole.

Adieu, dear sister spirit, you whose affection has felt no disgust, no highs or lows, always caressing my heart like the steady light of the moon; we have not known the vivacities of love together, but neither have we both tasted its venomous bitterness. You have lived wisely. Adieu!

55

July 16

My dear Louise, I am dispatching this letter by express courier before
I hurry straight to the chalet. Calm yourself. I found your last letter
so distraught that I thought I might, given the circumstances, tell
Louis all: it was a matter of saving you from yourself. If, like yours,
the methods we used were ignoble, the result is so happy that I know
you will approve. I stooped so low as to bring in the police, but this
is all a secret between us, you, and the prefect. Gaston is an angel!
Here are the facts: His brother Louis Gaston died in Calcutta, in the
service of a merchant company, just when he was about to come home
to France rich, happy, and married. His marriage to the widow of an
English trader had given him the most dazzling fortune. For ten years
he worked to send his brother enough to live on, his brother whom
he loved and whom he never told of his disappointments, so as not
to distress him, but then the great house of Halmer abruptly declared
bankruptcy, and the widow was ruined. It was a violent blow, and
Louis Gaston was devastated. His declining spirits left illness the
master of his body, and he succumbed in Bengal, where he had gone
to liquidate what was left of his poor wife's fortune. That loving
captain had entrusted a first installment of three hundred thousand
francs to a banker, with instructions to send it to his brother, but the
banker soon followed Halmer into bankruptcy, and with that the
last trace of his fortune was lost.

Louis Gaston's widow, that beautiful woman you take for a rival,
arrived in Paris with two children—your nephews—and not a sou
to her name. The sale of the mother's jewels scarcely paid for the

family's boat fare. The widow learned of your husband's former address, since it was given to the banker by Louis Gaston. Since your Gaston had vanished without notice, Madame Louis Gaston was sent to see d'Arthez, the only person who might know of his whereabouts. D'Arthez offered the young woman money enough for her needs, all the more generously in that four years earlier, just after your wedding, Louis Gaston had written d'Arthez to ask after his brother, knowing the two of them to be friends: he wanted d'Arthez to tell him how he might have that first installment safely delivered to Marie Gaston. D'Arthez had answered that Marie Gaston was now a rich man, thanks to his marriage to Baroness de Macumer. A handsome face, that wonderful gift handed them by their mother, had rescued the two brothers from poverty, in India as in Paris. Is that not a touching story? Naturally, d'Arthez soon wrote your husband to tell him what had happened to his sister-in-law and his nephews, informing him of the generous intentions the Gaston in India had shown for the Gaston in Paris, intentions aborted only by chance. As you must have imagined by now, your dear Gaston came running to Paris at once. There is the story of his first disappearance. In the past five years he has set aside fifty thousand francs from the revenue you forced him to accept; he used them to buy two bonds in his two nephews' names, for an annual revenue of twelve hundred francs each. He then furnished the apartment where your sister-in-law lives, promising her three thousand francs every three months. Here, then, is the explanation for his theatrical endeavors, and his joy at his play's success.

As you see, Madame Gaston is not your rival; she bears her name quite legitimately. A man as noble and sensitive as Gaston had to keep this adventure hidden from you, fearing your generosity. Your husband does not consider what you gave him to be truly his. D'Arthez read me the letter in which Marie asked him to serve as a witness at your wedding: in that letter, he says that his happiness would be complete if only he had no debts for you to pay, if only he were rich. A virgin soul cannot repress such sentiments; they are or they are not, and when they are, their sting and their insistence are easily imagined. It is entirely understandable that Gaston wanted to secretly offer his brother's widow a decent existence; she had after all given his brother a hundred thousand ecus from her own fortune. She is beautiful, her heart is good, her manners distinguished, but she has no wit. That woman is a mother: little surprise that I felt attached to her the moment I saw her, with one child in her arms and the other dressed like a lord's *baby*. The words *Everything for the children!* are inscribed in the tiniest things she does. Far from being furious at your beloved Gaston, then, you have only new reasons to love him! I caught a glimpse of him; he is the most charming young man in Paris. Oh! yes, dear child, on seeing him I well understood how a woman might be mad about him, for his outward appearance is the very image of his beautiful soul. In your place, I would bring the widow and the two children out to the chalet, and build them a delicious little cottage; I would make them my children! Calm yourself, then, and prepare that surprise—a surprise of your own—for Gaston.

56

Ah! my beloved friend, hear the terrible, fatal, insolent words spoken by the imbecile Lafayette to his master, his king: *Too late!*[11] Oh, my life, my beautiful life! What doctor will give it back to me? I have dealt myself a fatal blow. Alas! was I not a mere will-o'-the-wisp of a woman, destined to flicker out after a brief burst of light? My eyes are two torrents of tears, and ... I can only weep in his absence ... I flee him, and he seeks me. I keep my despair entirely to myself. Dante forgot my torment in his *Inferno*. Come and see me die, will you?

57

The Chalet, August 7

My friend, take the children and leave for Provence without me; I
will stay with Louise, who has only days to live. I owe myself to her
and her husband, who might well lose his senses, I fear.

Since that note I told you of, which sent me racing with doctors
to Ville-d'Avray, I have not left that charming woman's side and have
had no chance to write you, for this is my fifteenth night here.

I arrived to find her with Gaston, radiant and elegant, a smile on
her face, happy. What a sublime lie! Those two beautiful children
had had a long talk. For a moment I was fooled by her brave face, like
Gaston, but Louise pressed my hand and whispered in my ear, "I'm
dying; we mustn't let him know." An icy cold gripped me as I found
her hand burning hot, her cheeks colored only by rouge. I applauded
myself for my prudence: so as to cause no alarm, I had thought to tell
the doctors to go walking in the woods until I sent for them.

"Leave us," she said to Gaston. "Two women who have spent five
years apart have many secrets to confide, and no doubt Renée has
something she'd like to tell me in private."

Once we were alone, she threw herself into my arms, unable to
hold back her tears. "What is it?" I asked her. "In any case, I have
brought you the finest surgeon and the finest doctor of the Hôtel-
Dieu, along with Bianchon; in fact, there are four of them."

"Oh! if they can save me, if there is still time, let them come!" she
cried. "The same emotion that compelled me to die now compels me
to live."

"But what have you done?"

"I've spent the past several days giving myself a serious case of consumption."

"How did you do that?"

"I made myself sweat at night, then ran down to the pond as the dew was falling. Gaston is convinced I have a cold, and I'm dying."

"Send him to Paris; I'll go for the doctors myself," I said, running like a madwoman to the place where I had left them.

Alas! my friend, on finishing their examination, not one of those wise men could give me the slightest reason for hope; they believe that Louise will be dead when the leaves fall. That sweet creature's constitution served her plans singularly well: she had a predisposition to illness, and her actions exacerbated it. She could have lived a long life, but in just a few days she put herself beyond help. I will not tell you my feelings on hearing that unappealable verdict. As you know, I have lived my life as much in Louise as in myself. I sat motionless, stunned and lost, making no move to show those cruel doctors out. My face bathed in tears, I spent I know not how long in tortured meditations. A heavenly voice roused me from my torpor with the words "So I'm doomed," spoken by Louise as she put her hand on my shoulder.

She pulled me to my feet and led me into her little salon. "Stay with me," she said with an imploring gaze. "I want no despair around me; above all, I want to deceive *him*, and I am strong enough to do it. I am full of energy and youth; I will die on my feet. As for me, do not pity me, I am dying just as I often wished: at thirty, young, beautiful, whole. And I would have made him unhappy, I can see it. I am caught in the snares of my love, like a doe strangling itself as it struggles against its captivity; of the two of us, I am the doe . . . and all too wild. My senseless jealousy has already stung his heart and made him unhappy. When the day came that my suspicions met only with indifference, the reward forever lying in wait for jealousy, when that day came . . . I would die. I've got what I wanted out of life. There are some who have spent sixty years at the controls of this world and have lived only two, whereas I seem no older than thirty, but in fact I have sixty years of love behind me. Thus, for me, for him, this is a happy ending. It's different for you and me: you're losing a sister who loves you, and that loss cannot be repaired. You alone, here, must weep for my death.

"My death," she went on, after a long pause during which I saw her only through the veil of my tears, "brings with it a cruel lesson. My dear professor in corsets is right: marriage must not be founded in passion, nor even in love. Yours is a beautiful and a noble existence, you've followed your path, loving your Louis ever more; whereas if one begins married life with fierce ardor, it can only wane. Twice I have been wrong, and twice Death will have come to snatch away my happiness with its fleshless hand. It stole from me the most noble and devoted of men; today, it steals me from the most handsome, most charming, most poetic husband in the world. On the other hand, I will have known by turns the *beau idéal* of the soul and the body. Felipe's soul tamed his body and changed it; in Gaston, heart, mind, and beauty are all equal rivals. I die a woman adored, what more could I want?...To make my peace with God, whom I have perhaps neglected and toward whom I will soar full of love, asking Him to give me back those two angels in heaven. I would find paradise empty without them. I set a dreadful example: I am an exception. Here, given the impossibility of meeting a Felipe or a Gaston in this world, the law of society joins up with the law of nature. Yes, woman is a weak creature who must, through marriage, sacrifice all her will to man, who in return owes her the sacrifice of his egoism. The complaints and rebellions our sex has injected into these modern times are pure foolishness, earning us the rank of children so many philosophers have ascribed to us."

She went on in this way, with the gentle voice you know so well, saying the most sensible things in the most elegant manner, until Gaston came in, bringing his sister-in-law from Paris, along with the two children and the English maid, as Louise had asked.

"There are my pretty executioners," she said, seeing her two nephews. "Is my mistake not perfectly understandable? How they resemble their uncle!"

She was charming with the elder Madame Gaston, urging her to think of the chalet as her own home, and she welcomed her to it with the true Chaulieu politesse, which she possesses to the highest degree. I immediately wrote the Duchess and Duke de Chaulieu, and the Duke de Rhétoré and the Duke de Lenoncourt-Chaulieu, and Madeleine too. I did well. The next day, exhausted from these exertions, Louise could not go out walking; indeed, she only rose from her bed to put in an appearance at dinner. Madeleine de Lenoncourt arrived that evening, along with her two brothers and her mother. Gone was the chill Louise's marriage had created between her and her family. Since that evening, Louise's father and two brothers have ridden out each morning, and the two duchesses spend every evening at the chalet. Death unites people no less than it parts them, it puts all petty passions to rest. Louise is sublimely gracious, reasonable, charming, witty, and sensitive. Until the end, she is showing the elegance she is known for, offering us all the treasures of the wit that made her a queen of Paris.

"I want to be pretty even in my coffin," she told me, with the smile that is hers alone, as she lay down in the bed where she has been languishing these past fifteen days.

There is no sign of illness in her room: the syrups, the gums, all the trappings of modern medicine are carefully hidden away.

"Am I not having a beautiful death?" she said yesterday to the curé of Sèvres, to whom she has told everything.

We are all enjoying her greedily. Forewarned of her death by so many fears and terrible realizations, Gaston does not lack courage, but he is stricken; I would not be surprised to see him naturally follow his wife. Yesterday, as we were out walking around the little pond, he said to me, "I must be a father to those two children," and he nodded toward his sister-in-law, who was there with her nephews. "But, although I will do nothing to take my leave of this world, promise that you will be a second mother to them, and that you will allow your husband to accept the unofficial guardianship I will entrust to him, along with my sister-in-law." He said this without the slightest pomp, in the manner of a man who knows he is lost. His beaming face returns Louise's bright smiles; I alone am under no illusion. He has summoned a courage equal to hers. Louise wanted to see her godson, but I am not sorry that he is in Provence: she might have shown him a generosity that would have discomfited me.

Farewell, my friend.

August 25 (her name day)

Yesterday evening Louise was delirious for a few moments, but it was a truly elegant delirium, proving that people of good mind do not go mad in the manner of commoners or fools. In a muted voice she sang a few Italian arias, from *I Puritani*, *La Sonnambula*, and *Mosè in Egitto*. We all sat in silence around the bed, with tears in our eyes, even her brother Rhétoré, so plain was it that her soul was escaping her. She could no longer see us! All her grace was still there in the charms of that quiet, divinely sweet song. Her final agony began in the night. Just now, at eleven o'clock in the morning, I awakened her myself; she was feeling a bit stronger, she wanted to sit in her window, she asked for Gaston's hand. . . . Then, my friend, the most charming angel we will ever see on this earth left us only her body. Given extreme unction last night, unbeknownst to Gaston, who managed to sleep a little during that terrible ceremony, she wanted me to read the De profundis to her in French, while she sat and gazed on the beautiful nature she had created for herself. She silently said the words along with me, pressing her husband's hand as he knelt on the other side of the armchair.

August 26

My heart is broken. I have just gone for a last look at her, in her shroud. She has gone pale, tinged here and there with violet. Oh! I want to see my children! My children! Bring me my children!

TRANSLATOR'S NOTES

PART ONE

1. Logically, the year should be 1825 (Louise entered the convent in 1816 and was there for nine years), but the date of the seventh letter tells us that this one must have been written in 1823. Balzac's novels teem with minor inconsistencies of this sort; this is the last one that will be noted here.

2. As very young children, the Siamese twins Helen and Judith, sometimes known simply as the "Hungarian sisters," were exhibited as objects of fascination and curiosity throughout early eighteenth-century Europe, but at the age of six Judith was paralyzed by a stroke, and they entered a convent to live out their days. They died within minutes of each other at age twenty-two.

3. Louise-Françoise de la Vallière was a longtime mistress of Louis XIV; in 1674, seeing that she had been supplanted by a new favorite—Madame de Montespan, who will be alluded to a few paragraphs further on—she became a Carmelite nun under the name Louise de la Miséricorde.

4. A magical animal, part horse and part griffin, best known as Astolfo's mount in *Orlando Furioso*.

5. Some fifteen miles east of Marseille.

6. Founded by Abelard in 1122, the Order of the Paraclete became home to a community of nuns headed by Héloïse. It was there that she wrote the letters for which she is famous.

7. A silly little pun on Louise's part: *griffe* is the French word for "claw."

8. Which is to say three hundred thousand francs; the livre fell out of use long before Louise's birth, but the term was still used, interchangeably with franc, where matters of high finance were concerned.

9. A powerful family of bankers and merchants in Genoa from the twelfth century on, the Lomellinis would die out by the end of the eighteenth century for lack of a male heir.

10. Benjamin Constant's *Adolphe* (1815) and Germaine de Staël's *Corinne ou l'Italie* (1807) are two fundamental works of French romanticism.

11. Today's Place de la Concorde.

12. That is, one whose elevation to the nobility came after the Revolution and is owed to Napoleon.

13. The civil code requires that parental legacies be divided equally among offspring. In order to set the firstborn son up for life, families like Renée's claim payment of a dowry that is never actually paid; that sum, being deducted from the daughter's inheritance, can then be given to the son.

14. A fairly modest Provençal farmhouse of generally two or three floors; not grand but by no means a hovel.

15. The absolutist tendencies of the Bourbon Ferdinand VII of Spain were continually contested throughout his reign. The Liberal insurrection of 1820 to 1823—in which the fictive Don Felipe Hénarez was an important figure, along with the real Valdez and Riego—ended with the intervention of French troops led by the Duke d'Angoulême, but not before Ferdinand assured the Liberals, falsely, that they need fear no reprisals once he was back on the throne. While Hénarez and Valdez were able to flee, Riego was hanged.

16. That is, of course, to King Ferdinand, the "absolute king," as Felipe calls him.

17. Galignani remains an important English-language bookstore in Paris to this day.

18. Today the rue de Bellechasse, a few blocks east of Les Invalides.

19. Overthrown in 344 BC, Dionysius the Younger, King of Syracuse, fled to Corinth and became a teacher.

20. The mother of a sultan.

21. A representative in the National Assembly, a legislative body more or less like our House of Representatives.

22. The story goes that François I staged a lion fight for the amusement of the court; the anonymous lover of the Count de Lorge, seeking to prove her beloved's courage, tossed her glove into the ring and begged the count to bring it back to her. He did, but he ended his liaison with the lady then and there, on the grounds that she had exposed him to an unnecessary danger purely out of vanity.

23. A celebrated Spanish general, one of the architects of the retaking of Grenada from the Moors in the late fifteenth century.

24. Grand Inquisitor of Toledo (1436–1517).

25. The reference is to a struggle for power in first century BC Rome: Sulla was backed by the aristocracy, Marius by the people.

26. Louis XVIII would indeed die in 1824, to be succeeded by his brother, Charles X. The absolutist excesses of Charles's reign would lead to the revolution of 1830.

27. A *majorat* is a guarantee of a certain part of the family fortune for the eldest son, who would also be able to take his share of the remaining assets; Louise is thus to suffer the same despoliation as Renée.

28. Ferdinand VII spent the early years of his reign—from 1808 to 1814— as a ruler in exile, essentially under house arrest, on Napoleon's orders, at the Château de Valençay.

29. Louise is paraphrasing a line from Pierre Corneille's tragedy *Cinna*.

30. In addition to castles, presumably.

31. Lovelace is a character in Samuel Richardson's *Clarissa*, and Saint-Preux in Jean-Jacques Rousseau's *La nouvelle Héloïse*.

32. Madeleine de Scudéry's *Artamène, ou le Grand Cyrus* and Honoré d'Urfé's *L'Astrée* are two examples of the seventeenth-century "précieux" mode, full of long, abstruse discussions of subtle amorous emotions. The Courts of Love were perhaps fictive assemblies of noble men and ladies in eleventh-century Provence, charged with deciding tricky questions of love and gallantry.

33. Louis de Bonald (1754–1840) was a conservative politician and political philosopher, a foe of the Revolution, and an ardent believer in the divine right of kings. He argued that the family is the model for all well-ordered

societies; the authority of the father is reproduced in the authority of the king, and indeed in the authority of God.

34. That is, the Cortes Generales: the Spanish legislature.

35. From the *Paradiso*: "Imperishable wealth, without fear!"

36. "*Vive le roi quand même!*" ("Long live the king, all the same!") were the final words of a pamphlet written by Chateaubriand in 1816, in which he denounced Louis XVIII as insufficiently faithful to the Royalist cause. Louise could of course not have known—but Balzac did—that it was also the cry of the Legitimists in 1830, expressing their disdain for the newly crowned Louis-Philippe.

37. Balzac has *cirage* rather than *cigare*, making Felipe the color of "a Havana shoe wax"; I read this as a slip of the pen.

38. Rabelais's supposed last words: "I go to seek a great perhaps."

39. An epistolary novel by Étienne Pivert de Senancour, a classic of early romanticism in which a tortured young man living in the backwater of the Jura writes a distant friend of his loneliness, his ennui, his inertia.

40. The Roman goddess of childbirth.

41. "We always show our faces."

42. That is, in the fifteenth century.

43. That is, than any masterpiece or any fine painting.

44. A journalist and epigrammatist of staunchly Royalist sympathies, Antoine de Rivarol was the author of a scathing mockery of late eighteenth-century sentimental or pastoral writers such as Salomon Gessner and Jean-Pierre Claris de Florian.

45. The nymph Egeria offered wise counsel to the early Roman king Numa Pompilius.

46. The pun is of course intended: a *soeur d'élection* is a chosen sister; in this case, their sisterhood is not entirely untouched by electoral questions.

47. Either Renée or Balzac is evidently unaware that in English adjectives do not agree in gender and number with the noun that they modify.

PART TWO

1. Louise is citing a line from Racine's *Andromaque*.

2. To an English speaker, Marie is unambiguously a woman's name, but in French it can be a man's as well.

3. Lady Brandon's decline and death is recounted in the short story "La Grenadière," but in that tale Balzac does not suggest that her demise was caused by Lady Dudley, a recurring character in the Human Comedy and the archetype of the vengeful lover.

4. In her notes to the Garnier-Flammarion edition of this novel, Arlette Michel suggests that Louise is alluding to Princess Belgiojoso, who moved to Switzerland after separating from her husband.

5. A garden in the English style, so named because it was laid out on the orders of Louis XVIII in 1816.

6. Louise lives close by the royal domain of Saint-Cloud, whose maintenance was paid for from the Civil List (an annual allowance for necessary expenses) of Louis-Philippe. The slightly mocking tone of Louise's remark comes from her dislike, as a dyed-in-the-wool aristocrat, of the new, non-Bourbon king.

7. Horns being the emblem of the cuckold.

8. The Roman consul Publius Decius Mus died in combat in 340 BC, after a dream in which it was foretold that the battle to come would be won by the army whose general voluntarily sacrificed his life.

9. Cornelia Africana was seen as a model of feminine virtue in ancient Rome, not least for her devotion to her children and her skill at guiding their political careers. Asked why her appearance was so modest in spite of her wealth, she pointed at her children and replied, "These are my jewels."

10. A sort of goatee, covering the chin and the space beneath the lower lip.

11. Opposed to the absolutist tendencies of Charles X, the Marquis de Lafayette became the unofficial leader of the revolution of 1830, which broke out in response to the king's edict stripping the middle class of their voting rights. Charles rescinded that edict, but by that time Lafayette had already named Louis-Philippe as his successor, and so the king's change of heart came too late.

OTHER NEW YORK REVIEW CLASSICS

For a complete list of titles, visit www.nyrb.com or write to:
Catalog Requests, NYRB, 435 Hudson Street, New York, NY 10014

J.R. ACKERLEY My Dog Tulip*
J.R. ACKERLEY My Father and Myself*
J.R. ACKERLEY We Think the World of You*
HENRY ADAMS The Jeffersonian Transformation
RENATA ADLER Pitch Dark*
RENATA ADLER Speedboat*
AESCHYLUS Prometheus Bound; translated by Joel Agee*
LEOPOLDO ALAS His Only Son *with* Doña Berta*
CÉLESTE ALBARET Monsieur Proust
DANTE ALIGHIERI The Inferno
KINGSLEY AMIS The Alteration*
KINGSLEY AMIS Dear Illusion: Collected Stories*
KINGSLEY AMIS Girl, 20*
KINGSLEY AMIS The Green Man*
KINGSLEY AMIS Lucky Jim*
KINGSLEY AMIS The Old Devils*
KINGSLEY AMIS One Fat Englishman*
KINGSLEY AMIS Take a Girl Like You*
ROBERTO ARLT The Seven Madmen*
U.R. ANANTHAMURTHY Samskara: A Rite for a Dead Man*
WILLIAM ATTAWAY Blood on the Forge
W.H. AUDEN (EDITOR) The Living Thoughts of Kierkegaard
W.H. AUDEN W.H. Auden's Book of Light Verse
ERICH AUERBACH Dante: Poet of the Secular World
EVE BABITZ Eve's Hollywood*
EVE BABITZ Slow Days, Fast Company: The World, the Flesh, and L.A.*
DOROTHY BAKER Cassandra at the Wedding*
DOROTHY BAKER Young Man with a Horn*
J.A. BAKER The Peregrine
S. JOSEPHINE BAKER Fighting for Life*
HONORÉ DE BALZAC The Human Comedy: Selected Stories*
HONORÉ DE BALZAC The Unknown Masterpiece *and* Gambara*
VICKI BAUM Grand Hotel*
SYBILLE BEDFORD A Favorite of the Gods *and* A Compass Error*
SYBILLE BEDFORD A Legacy*
SYBILLE BEDFORD A Visit to Don Otavio: A Mexican Journey*
MAX BEERBOHM The Prince of Minor Writers: The Selected Essays of Max Beerbohm*
MAX BEERBOHM Seven Men
STEPHEN BENATAR Wish Her Safe at Home*
FRANS G. BENGTSSON The Long Ships*
ALEXANDER BERKMAN Prison Memoirs of an Anarchist
GEORGES BERNANOS Mouchette
MIRON BIAŁOSZEWSKI A Memoir of the Warsaw Uprising*
ADOLFO BIOY CASARES Asleep in the Sun
ADOLFO BIOY CASARES The Invention of Morel
PAUL BLACKBURN (TRANSLATOR) Proensa*
CAROLINE BLACKWOOD Great Granny Webster*

* Also available as an electronic book.

RONALD BLYTHE Akenfield: Portrait of an English Village*
NICOLAS BOUVIER The Way of the World
EMMANUEL BOVE Henri Duchemin and His Shadows*
MALCOLM BRALY On the Yard*
MILLEN BRAND The Outward Room*
ROBERT BRESSON Notes on the Cinematograph*
SIR THOMAS BROWNE Religio Medici and Urne-Buriall*
JOHN HORNE BURNS The Gallery
ROBERT BURTON The Anatomy of Melancholy
CAMARA LAYE The Radiance of the King
GIROLAMO CARDANO The Book of My Life
DON CARPENTER Hard Rain Falling*
J.L. CARR A Month in the Country*
LEONORA CARRINGTON Down Below*
BLAISE CENDRARS Moravagine
EILEEN CHANG Love in a Fallen City
EILEEN CHANG Naked Earth*
JOAN CHASE During the Reign of the Queen of Persia*
ELLIOTT CHAZE Black Wings Has My Angel*
UPAMANYU CHATTERJEE English, August: An Indian Story
NIRAD C. CHAUDHURI The Autobiography of an Unknown Indian
ANTON CHEKHOV Peasants and Other Stories
ANTON CHEKHOV The Prank: The Best of Young Chekhov*
GABRIEL CHEVALLIER Fear: A Novel of World War I*
JEAN-PAUL CLÉBERT Paris Vagabond*
RICHARD COBB Paris and Elsewhere
COLETTE The Pure and the Impure
JOHN COLLIER Fancies and Goodnights
CARLO COLLODI The Adventures of Pinocchio*
D.G. COMPTON The Continuous Katherine Mortenhoe
IVY COMPTON-BURNETT A House and Its Head
IVY COMPTON-BURNETT Manservant and Maidservant
BARBARA COMYNS The Vet's Daughter
BARBARA COMYNS Our Spoons Came from Woolworths*
ALBERT COSSERY The Jokers*
ALBERT COSSERY Proud Beggars*
HAROLD CRUSE The Crisis of the Negro Intellectual
ASTOLPHE DE CUSTINE Letters from Russia*
LORENZO DA PONTE Memoirs
ELIZABETH DAVID A Book of Mediterranean Food
ELIZABETH DAVID Summer Cooking
L.J. DAVIS A Meaningful Life*
AGNES DE MILLE Dance to the Piper*
VIVANT DENON No Tomorrow/Point de lendemain
MARIA DERMOÛT The Ten Thousand Things
DER NISTER The Family Mashber
TIBOR DÉRY Niki: The Story of a Dog
ANTONIO DI BENEDETTO Zama*
ALFRED DÖBLIN Bright Magic: Stories*
JEAN D'ORMESSON The Glory of the Empire: A Novel, A History*
ARTHUR CONAN DOYLE The Exploits and Adventures of Brigadier Gerard
CHARLES DUFF A Handbook on Hanging
BRUCE DUFFY The World As I Found It*

DAPHNE DU MAURIER Don't Look Now: Stories

ELAINE DUNDY The Dud Avocado*

ELAINE DUNDY The Old Man and Me*

G.B. EDWARDS The Book of Ebenezer Le Page*

JOHN EHLE The Land Breakers*

MARCELLUS EMANTS A Posthumous Confession

EURIPIDES Grief Lessons: Four Plays; translated by Anne Carson

J.G. FARRELL Troubles*

J.G. FARRELL The Siege of Krishnapur*

J.G. FARRELL The Singapore Grip*

ELIZA FAY Original Letters from India

KENNETH FEARING The Big Clock

KENNETH FEARING Clark Gifford's Body

FÉLIX FÉNÉON Novels in Three Lines*

M.I. FINLEY The World of Odysseus

THOMAS FLANAGAN The Year of the French*

BENJAMIN FONDANE Existential Monday: Philosophical Essays*

SANFORD FRIEDMAN Conversations with Beethoven*

SANFORD FRIEDMAN Totempole*

MARC FUMAROLI When the World Spoke French

CARLO EMILIO GADDA That Awful Mess on the Via Merulana

BENITO PÉREZ GÁLDOS Tristana*

MAVIS GALLANT The Cost of Living: Early and Uncollected Stories*

MAVIS GALLANT Paris Stories*

MAVIS GALLANT A Fairly Good Time *with* Green Water, Green Sky*

MAVIS GALLANT Varieties of Exile*

GABRIEL GARCÍA MÁRQUEZ Clandestine in Chile: The Adventures of Miguel Littín

LEONARD GARDNER Fat City*

WILLIAM H. GASS In the Heart of the Heart of the Country: And Other Stories*

WILLIAM H. GASS On Being Blue: A Philosophical Inquiry*

THÉOPHILE GAUTIER My Fantoms

GE FEI The Invisibility Cloak

JEAN GENET Prisoner of Love

ÉLISABETH GILLE The Mirador: Dreamed Memories of Irène Némirovsky by Her Daughter*

NATALIA GINZBURG Family Lexicon*

JEAN GIONO Hill*

JEAN GIONO Melville: A Novel*

JOHN GLASSCO Memoirs of Montparnasse*

P.V. GLOB The Bog People: Iron-Age Man Preserved

EDMOND AND JULES DE GONCOURT Pages from the Goncourt Journals

ALICE GOODMAN History Is Our Mother: Three Libretti*

PAUL GOODMAN Growing Up Absurd: Problems of Youth in the Organized Society*

EDWARD GOREY (EDITOR) The Haunted Looking Glass

JEREMIAS GOTTHELF The Black Spider*

A.C. GRAHAM Poems of the Late T'ang

JULIEN GRACQ Balcony in the Forest*

HENRY GREEN Back*

HENRY GREEN Blindness*

HENRY GREEN Caught*

HENRY GREEN Doting*

HENRY GREEN Living*

HENRY GREEN Loving*

HENRY GREEN Nothing*

HENRY GREEN Party Going*
WILLIAM LINDSAY GRESHAM Nightmare Alley*
HANS HERBERT GRIMM Schlump*
VASILY GROSSMAN An Armenian Sketchbook*
VASILY GROSSMAN Everything Flows*
VASILY GROSSMAN Life and Fate*
VASILY GROSSMAN The Road*
LOUIS GUILLOUX Blood Dark*
OAKLEY HALL Warlock
PATRICK HAMILTON The Slaves of Solitude*
PATRICK HAMILTON Twenty Thousand Streets Under the Sky*
PETER HANDKE Short Letter, Long Farewell
PETER HANDKE Slow Homecoming
THORKILD HANSEN Arabia Felix: The Danish Expedition of 1761–1767*
ELIZABETH HARDWICK The Collected Essays of Elizabeth Hardwick*
ELIZABETH HARDWICK The New York Stories of Elizabeth Hardwick*
ELIZABETH HARDWICK Seduction and Betrayal*
ELIZABETH HARDWICK Sleepless Nights*
L.P. HARTLEY The Go-Between*
NATHANIEL HAWTHORNE Twenty Days with Julian & Little Bunny by Papa
ALFRED HAYES In Love*
ALFRED HAYES My Face for the World to See*
PAUL HAZARD The Crisis of the European Mind: 1680–1715*
ALICE HERDAN-ZUCKMAYER The Farm in the Green Mountains*
GILBERT HIGHET Poets in a Landscape
RUSSELL HOBAN Turtle Diary*
JANET HOBHOUSE The Furies
YOEL HOFFMANN The Sound of the One Hand: 281 Zen Koans with Answers*
HUGO VON HOFMANNSTHAL The Lord Chandos Letter*
RICHARD HOLMES Shelley: The Pursuit*
ALISTAIR HORNE A Savage War of Peace: Algeria 1954–1962*
GEOFFREY HOUSEHOLD Rogue Male*
WILLIAM DEAN HOWELLS Indian Summer
BOHUMIL HRABAL Dancing Lessons for the Advanced in Age*
BOHUMIL HRABAL The Little Town Where Time Stood Still*
DOROTHY B. HUGHES The Expendable Man*
DOROTHY B. HUGHES In a Lonely Place*
RICHARD HUGHES A High Wind in Jamaica*
RICHARD HUGHES In Hazard*
INTIZAR HUSAIN Basti*
MAUDE HUTCHINS Victorine
YASUSHI INOUE Tun-huang*
HENRY JAMES The New York Stories of Henry James*
HENRY JAMES The Outcry
TOVE JANSSON The Summer Book*
TOVE JANSSON The True Deceiver*
TOVE JANSSON The Woman Who Borrowed Memories: Selected Stories*
RANDALL JARRELL (EDITOR) Randall Jarrell's Book of Stories
DAVID JONES In Parenthesis
JOSEPH JOUBERT The Notebooks of Joseph Joubert; translated by Paul Auster
KABIR Songs of Kabir; translated by Arvind Krishna Mehrotra*
FRIGYES KARINTHY A Journey Round My Skull
ERICH KÄSTNER Going to the Dogs: The Story of a Moralist*

YASHAR KEMAL Memed, My Hawk

YASHAR KEMAL They Burn the Thistles

MURRAY KEMPTON Part of Our Time: Some Ruins and Monuments of the Thirties*

RAYMOND KENNEDY Ride a Cockhorse*

DAVID KIDD Peking Story*

ROBERT KIRK The Secret Commonwealth of Elves, Fauns, and Fairies

ARUN KOLATKAR Jejuri

DEZSŐ KOSZTOLÁNYI Skylark*

TÉTÉ-MICHEL KPOMASSIE An African in Greenland

GYULA KRÚDY The Adventures of Sindbad*

GYULA KRÚDY Sunflower*

SIGIZMUND KRZHIZHANOVSKY The Letter Killers Club*

SIGIZMUND KRZHIZHANOVSKY Memories of the Future

SIGIZMUND KRZHIZHANOVSKY The Return of Munchausen*

K'UNG SHANG-JEN The Peach Blossom Fan*

GIUSEPPE TOMASI DI LAMPEDUSA The Professor and the Siren

GERT LEDIG The Stalin Front*

MARGARET LEECH Reveille in Washington: 1860–1865*

PATRICK LEIGH FERMOR Between the Woods and the Water*

PATRICK LEIGH FERMOR The Broken Road*

PATRICK LEIGH FERMOR A Time of Gifts*

PATRICK LEIGH FERMOR A Time to Keep Silence*

PATRICK LEIGH FERMOR The Traveller's Tree*

PATRICK LEIGH FERMOR The Violins of Saint-Jacques*

D.B. WYNDHAM LEWIS AND CHARLES LEE (EDITORS) The Stuffed Owl

SIMON LEYS The Death of Napoleon*

SIMON LEYS The Hall of Uselessness: Collected Essays*

GEORG CHRISTOPH LICHTENBERG The Waste Books

JAKOV LIND Soul of Wood and Other Stories

H.P. LOVECRAFT AND OTHERS Shadows of Carcosa: Tales of Cosmic Horror*

DWIGHT MACDONALD Masscult and Midcult: Essays Against the American Grain*

CURZIO MALAPARTE Kaputt

CURZIO MALAPARTE The Skin

JANET MALCOLM In the Freud Archives

JEAN-PATRICK MANCHETTE Fatale*

JEAN-PATRICK MANCHETTE The Mad and the Bad*

OSIP MANDELSTAM The Selected Poems of Osip Mandelstam

OLIVIA MANNING Fortunes of War: The Balkan Trilogy*

OLIVIA MANNING Fortunes of War: The Levant Trilogy*

JAMES VANCE MARSHALL Walkabout*

GUY DE MAUPASSANT Afloat

GUY DE MAUPASSANT Alien Hearts*

GUY DE MAUPASSANT Like Death*

JAMES McCOURT Mawrdew Czgowchwz*

WILLIAM McPHERSON Testing the Current*

MEZZ MEZZROW AND BERNARD WOLFE Really the Blues*

HENRI MICHAUX Miserable Miracle

JESSICA MITFORD Hons and Rebels

JESSICA MITFORD Poison Penmanship*

NANCY MITFORD Frederick the Great*

NANCY MITFORD Madame de Pompadour*

NANCY MITFORD The Sun King*

NANCY MITFORD Voltaire in Love*

PATRICK MODIANO In the Café of Lost Youth*
PATRICK MODIANO Young Once*
MICHEL DE MONTAIGNE Shakespeare's Montaigne; translated by John Florio*
HENRY DE MONTHERLANT Chaos and Night
BRIAN MOORE The Lonely Passion of Judith Hearne*
BRIAN MOORE The Mangan Inheritance*
ALBERTO MORAVIA Agostino*
ALBERTO MORAVIA Contempt*
JAN MORRIS Conundrum*
JAN MORRIS Hav*
PENELOPE MORTIMER The Pumpkin Eater*
GUIDO MORSELLI The Communist*
ÁLVARO MUTIS The Adventures and Misadventures of Maqroll
NESCIO Amsterdam Stories*
DARCY O'BRIEN A Way of Life, Like Any Other
SILVINA OCAMPO Thus Were Their Faces*
YURI OLESHA Envy*
IONA AND PETER OPIE The Lore and Language of Schoolchildren
IRIS OWENS After Claude*
ALEXANDROS PAPADIAMANTIS The Murderess
BORIS PASTERNAK, MARINA TSVETAYEVA, AND RAINER MARIA RILKE Letters, Summer 1926
CESARE PAVESE The Moon and the Bonfires
CESARE PAVESE The Selected Works of Cesare Pavese
BORISLAV PEKIĆ Houses*
ELEANOR PERÉNYI More Was Lost: A Memoir*
LUIGI PIRANDELLO The Late Mattia Pascal
JOSEP PLA The Gray Notebook
DAVID PLANTE Difficult Women: A Memoir of Three*
ANDREY PLATONOV The Foundation Pit
ANDREY PLATONOV Happy Moscow
ANDREY PLATONOV Soul and Other Stories
NORMAN PODHORETZ Making It*
J.F. POWERS Morte d'Urban*
J.F. POWERS The Stories of J.F. Powers*
CHRISTOPHER PRIEST Inverted World*
BOLESŁAW PRUS The Doll*
GEORGE PSYCHOUNDAKIS The Cretan Runner: His Story of the German Occupation*
ALEXANDER PUSHKIN The Captain's Daughter*
QIU MIAOJIN Last Words from Montmartre*
QIU MIAOJIN Notes of a Crocodile*
RAYMOND QUENEAU We Always Treat Women Too Well
RAYMOND QUENEAU Witch Grass
RAYMOND RADIGUET Count d'Orgel's Ball
PAUL RADIN Primitive Man as Philosopher*
FRIEDRICH RECK Diary of a Man in Despair*
JULES RENARD Nature Stories*
JEAN RENOIR Renoir, My Father
GREGOR VON REZZORI An Ermine in Czernopol*
GREGOR VON REZZORI Memoirs of an Anti-Semite*
GREGOR VON REZZORI The Snows of Yesteryear: Portraits for an Autobiography*
TIM ROBINSON Stones of Aran: Labyrinth
TIM ROBINSON Stones of Aran: Pilgrimage
MILTON ROKEACH The Three Christs of Ypsilanti*

FR. ROLFE Hadrian the Seventh

GILLIAN ROSE Love's Work

LINDA ROSENKRANTZ Talk*

WILLIAM ROUGHEAD Classic Crimes

CONSTANCE ROURKE American Humor: A Study of the National Character

SAKI The Unrest-Cure and Other Stories; illustrated by Edward Gorey

UMBERTO SABA Ernesto*

JOAN SALES Uncertain Glory*

TAYEB SALIH Season of Migration to the North

JEAN-PAUL SARTRE We Have Only This Life to Live: Selected Essays. 1939–1975

ARTHUR SCHNITZLER Late Fame*

GERSHOM SCHOLEM Walter Benjamin: The Story of a Friendship*

DANIEL PAUL SCHREBER Memoirs of My Nervous Illness

JAMES SCHUYLER Alfred and Guinevere

SIMONE SCHWARZ-BART The Bridge of Beyond*

LEONARDO SCIASCIA Equal Danger

LEONARDO SCIASCIA To Each His Own

LEONARDO SCIASCIA The Wine-Dark Sea

VICTOR SEGALEN René Leys*

ANNA SEGHERS Transit*

PHILIPE-PAUL DE SÉGUR Defeat: Napoleon's Russian Campaign

GILBERT SELDES The Stammering Century*

VICTOR SERGE The Case of Comrade Tulayev*

VICTOR SERGE Conquered City*

VICTOR SERGE Memoirs of a Revolutionary

VICTOR SERGE Midnight in the Century*

VICTOR SERGE Unforgiving Years

SHCHEDRIN The Golovlyov Family

ROBERT SHECKLEY The Store of the Worlds: The Stories of Robert Sheckley*

GEORGES SIMENON Act of Passion*

GEORGES SIMENON Monsieur Monde Vanishes*

GEORGES SIMENON Pedigree*

CHARLES SIMIC Dime-Store Alchemy: The Art of Joseph Cornell

WILLIAM SLOANE The Rim of Morning: Two Tales of Cosmic Horror*

SASHA SOKOLOV A School for Fools*

VLADIMIR SOROKIN Ice Trilogy*

VLADIMIR SOROKIN The Queue

NATSUME SŌSEKI The Gate*

DAVID STACTON The Judges of the Secret Court*

JEAN STAFFORD The Mountain Lion

RICHARD STERN Other Men's Daughters

GEORGE R. STEWART Names on the Land

STENDHAL The Life of Henry Brulard

ADALBERT STIFTER Rock Crystal*

THEODOR STORM The Rider on the White Horse

JEAN STROUSE Alice James: A Biography*

HOWARD STURGIS Belchamber

ITALO SVEVO As a Man Grows Older

HARVEY SWADOS Nights in the Gardens of Brooklyn

A.J.A. SYMONS The Quest for Corvo

MAGDA SZABÓ The Door*

MAGDA SZABÓ Iza's Ballad*

MAGDA SZABÓ Katalin Street*

ANTAL SZERB Journey by Moonlight*

ELIZABETH TAYLOR Angel*

ELIZABETH TAYLOR A View of the Harbour*

ELIZABETH TAYLOR You'll Enjoy It When You Get There: The Stories of Elizabeth Taylor*

TEFFI Memories: From Moscow to the Black Sea*

TEFFI Tolstoy, Rasputin, Others, and Me: The Best of Teffi*

HENRY DAVID THOREAU The Journal: 1837–1861*

ALEKSANDAR TIŠMA The Book of Blam*

ALEKSANDAR TIŠMA The Use of Man*

TATYANA TOLSTAYA The Slynx

TATYANA TOLSTAYA White Walls: Collected Stories

EDWARD JOHN TRELAWNY Records of Shelley, Byron, and the Author

LIONEL TRILLING The Liberal Imagination*

THOMAS TRYON The Other*

MARINA TSVETAEVA Earthly Signs: Moscow Diaries, 1917–1922*

IVAN TURGENEV Virgin Soil

JULES VALLÈS The Child

RAMÓN DEL VALLE-INCLÁN Tyrant Banderas*

MARK VAN DOREN Shakespeare

CARL VAN VECHTEN The Tiger in the House

ELIZABETH VON ARNIM The Enchanted April*

EDWARD LEWIS WALLANT The Tenants of Moonbloom

ROBERT WALSER Berlin Stories*

ROBERT WALSER Girlfriends, Ghosts, and Other Stories*

ROBERT WALSER Jakob von Gunten

ROBERT WALSER A Schoolboy's Diary and Other Stories*

REX WARNER Men and Gods

SYLVIA TOWNSEND WARNER Lolly Willowes*

SYLVIA TOWNSEND WARNER Mr. Fortune*

JAKOB WASSERMANN My Marriage*

ALEKSANDER WAT My Century*

C.V. WEDGWOOD The Thirty Years War

SIMONE WEIL On the Abolition of All Political Parties*

SIMONE WEIL AND RACHEL BESPALOFF War and the Iliad

GLENWAY WESCOTT The Pilgrim Hawk*

REBECCA WEST The Fountain Overflows

EDITH WHARTON The New York Stories of Edith Wharton*

KATHARINE S. WHITE Onward and Upward in the Garden*

T. H. WHITE The Goshawk*

JOHN WILLIAMS Augustus*

JOHN WILLIAMS Butcher's Crossing*

JOHN WILLIAMS Stoner*

EDMUND WILSON Memoirs of Hecate County

RUDOLF AND MARGARET WITTKOWER Born Under Saturn

GEOFFREY WOLFF Black Sun*

FRANCIS WYNDHAM The Complete Fiction

JOHN WYNDHAM The Chrysalids

BÉLA ZOMBORY-MOLDOVÁN The Burning of the World: A Memoir of 1914*

STEFAN ZWEIG Beware of Pity*

STEFAN ZWEIG Chess Story*

STEFAN ZWEIG Journey Into the Past*

STEFAN ZWEIG The Post-Office Girl*